LITTLE
LIAR

Also by Julia Gray

The Otherlife

'Gripping, bold and completely original'
Katherine Rundell

'A bold, original and engrossing collision
between the Norse gods and our
high-pressured school system. I love books
about gods in modern times and this one had
me gripped. An auspicious debut'
Francesca Simon

'A big, mysterious book full of dangerous
characters and half glimpsed truths. An
absorbing and unusual read. I loved it'
Melvin Burgess

'Stunning . . . a searing satire on the pressures
that privileged children are put under
by pushy parents'
Amanda Craig, *New Statesman*

'Grand and gripping'
Literary Review

'Truly marvellous'
INIS

'Intelligent and insightful . . . Perfect for fans
of Sarah Govett and Neil Gaiman'
Anna McKerrow, *BookTrust*

JULIA GRAY

ANDERSEN PRESS • LONDON

First published in Great Britain in 2018 by
Andersen Press Limited
20 Vauxhall Bridge Road
London SW1V 2SA
www.andersenpress.co.uk

2 4 6 8 10 9 7 5 3 1

British Library Cataloguing in Publication Data available.

ISBN 978 1 78344 691 9

Typeset in Adobe Caslon Pro by
Palimpsest Book Production Ltd, Falkirk, Stirlingshire

Printed and bound in Great Britain by
Clays Limited, Bungay, Suffolk, NR35 1ED

For my
grandmother,
Lois Sieff

My name is Nora Tobias. I am seventeen years old. I've noticed that this is how stories often begin: a name, an age. The formula seems safe enough. I am a quarter English, a quarter Scottish and half French. I'm on the short side. I have a birthmark that covers the upper left portion of my face. My father used to say that it looked like a map of France, and my mother that it was a squished starfish.

I live with my mother, whose name is Evie, on the eighth floor of a tower block on a housing estate in South London. We have lived there for nearly ten years. My mother works freelance for the costume departments of different television companies. She is a reformed Goth: her hair is no longer bottle-black-and-blue, but her ears are still pierced in eleven places. There is nothing she doesn't know about corsets.

My father's name was Felix. He came from a small village in Normandy, and he died when I was six. I remember certain things about him very well. Other things, not so well at all. He had dark hair. Green eyes. He was of medium height. His thoughtful voice barely broke the surface of a whisper; everything he said was accentuated with hand gestures, soft but precise. An artist and illustrator, who worked mostly with watercolour and pencil, he did commissions for books and magazines. Everything he drew was careful, meticulous, never coloured outside the edges he marked with such certainty. My mother seemed loud and chaotic by comparison, I recall, although she does not seem that way to me any longer.

I wonder what else would be appropriate to mention.

My early childhood was spent in Paris. After my father's death, Evie and I came to England. We lived in London, but went often to Glasgow, to visit my newly-widowed grandmother. But if ever a home appears in my dreams, it's not our Paris apartment, or the one where Evie and I live now, or Nana's old rose-covered bungalow, before she moved a year or so ago into sheltered housing. I see the little cottage near a Normandy beach, where I spent many childhood summers. This is the place I associate most with my father.

At present, I am staying with my Aunt Petra, who is not my aunt at all, but a lifelong friend of Evie's. The name 'Petra', she tells me, means *rock*, but there is nothing rock-like about my non-aunt, who is as curved and soft as candyfloss. She runs a guesthouse here, in the Scottish Highlands, with her husband Bill. People come to relax, and meditate and heal. They walk beside the lochs that lie on either side of the peninsula; they learn about Thai food and how to build walls. I've been here a fortnight or so, but I've learned none of those things. There are six other guests, and mostly we keep ourselves to ourselves. Two people are doing a silent retreat, which makes for minimal interaction. Another guest, with whom I'm now on quite friendly terms, is recuperating after an accident. The rest are yoga devotees.

It's July, not that you can tell; every day dawns uniformly grey, and the rain cycles from a spatter to a thundery relentlessness. When the sun does come out, it does so apologetically, like a ballerina who is unsure of her entrance on stage. I do not mind the weather. The climate suits me.

Aunt Petra is keen for me to take part in classes and workshops: T'ai Chi, for example, or Spiritual Healing (this one, she feels, might be especially appropriate). Each morning, over porridge resembling wet sand in colour and texture, she tries to sign me up. Each morning, I decline. I came to Scotland for peace and silence, not to participate in her Organised Wellness. However, I do quite often agree to take her dog, Oscar, for a walk. He purports to be a Jack Russell, but there's a touch of Rat somewhere in his heritage, I'm sure. As long as it isn't raining too hard, Oscar and I wander through fields thick with stubby nettles, beating pathways down to the loch; or else we follow one of the narrow tracks that crisscross through woodland to the top of the peninsula, passing isolated farms and small rivers, until we reach one of the nearby villages. And then it begins to rain harder, and we wait for a bus to take us back.

Sometimes, I wonder why Aunt Petra, with all her talk of Zen and just-being and mindfulness, isn't more content to let me do nothing. Perhaps it's because the state of doing nothing, of thinking and feeling nothing, is allegedly hard to attain but I already excel at it. I don't really know what she's thinking when she enquires, like clockwork, about my plans for the day. Perhaps it is simply part of her repertoire, essentially without meaning.

This morning, I made an announcement. I don't know who was more surprised, Aunt Petra or me.

'I'm going to write,' I said.

Aunt Petra paused at the breadboard. 'To . . . to what, love? To light?'

'Write,' I said.

'Poems? Fairy tales?'

'Something like that.'

She couldn't have been more pleased. Before I knew it, Bill was bringing in an old sewing table with a missing foot, like a lame calf, and setting up a computer with a yellowed keyboard and arthritic mouse.

'What about your wounded arm?' Petra said, looking down at the bandage that hid the savage purple scar on which all her lotions and potions had had little effect. I said I'd go slowly, which was very much my intention, and see how it felt. She should have guessed that I didn't mind pain.

So here I am, with time, as well as potions, on my hands.

I have never tried to write anything before. I'm more of a reader; I don't like to commit myself to the page. I'd rather judge others for what they have chosen to commit. There's a daunting finality to writing. Even though I am working on a computer, and hardly carving quill-ink letters onto leathery parchment, even though I can delete and redo to my heart's content, the words still glower darkly from the screen. *We are finished articles*, they say. *We are evidence. We can be used against you.* In their straight-line sentences, they form a solemn procession, like ants plodding towards a cliff edge. They look 'right': that's one of the problems with typed words. I think I am scared of that, and of what may be used against me.

Because this is no fairy tale.

It is almost, for want of a better word, a confession. I'd say 'memoir', only that conjures something more grown-up than this, something less messy. I quite like the word *chronicle*. What I mean to set out is a series of events – perhaps not always strictly in chronological order, because my memories aren't arranged in such a linear way – at which I was present.

I want to explain what I did, and with whom. And where, and when and why. What happened, and what happened next.

The Chronicles of Nora, if you like.

And it will be a true story.

What will become quickly apparent is that I have not always told the truth before. To put it another way: I have told a number of lies. Some of them have been small, and some of them have been significant. I am writing this now because the lies I have told have resulted in some bad things. Whether I think I shall lessen my guilt through the act of setting things down, or whether I think I will be able to make sense of what has happened by so doing, I am not quite sure.

Aunt Petra is delighted with this pursuit. Already, a *Do Not Disturb* sign hangs outside my door. Only Oscar comes in from time to time, to rub his rodenty fur against my ankle.

I am growing familiar with these ancient keys, and it is appropriate that they are keys, I keep thinking, because something is being unlocked. And although sometimes I think this will drive me mad – the endless, oppressive silence, the rain, the view of the loch through my window – a small part of me knows that what will really drive me mad is if I let this go unwritten.

So here are my hands, at a keyboard. Here is an open document. And here, at my elbow, is an envelope on which I have scribbled, in pencil, a kind of shape.

A timeline, with loops and bends.

A map for me to follow.

I would like to start in January.

PART ONE

THE TRACE INCIDENT

1

Evie and I spent Christmas as we always did, watching movies of the lushly-orchestrated, black-and-white variety, and dozing, she on the sofa, me on the rug, by the twinkling lights of the tree. We snacked on things: banana chips, peanut butter from the jar. On Christmas Day, we ate macaroni cheese with mushrooms and peas, spooned directly out of the dish. Evie talked about mending the leaking tap in the bathroom, replacing the shower curtain; such talk was strictly traditional. We visited the neighbours. After living on the same estate for a decade, we had forged a cluster of good friendships with the people nearby, like elderly Mrs DeAndrade.

My mother, a genuine workaholic, makes a real effort around the festive season to indulge in the kind of prolonged, companionable mother-daughterness that might evade us at other times. This Christmas was no exception. We played Scrabble, which I won consistently, and Gin Rummy, which she won intermittently. We went for manicures at the local nail bar; we both had a great love for things being done to our hands. On New Year's Eve, we sat on our balcony and watched the fireworks blooming over the river, each of us with a mug of hot chocolate. Once, Evie would have had red wine in a tumbler, or an inch of Amaro – a bitter liqueur – in a glassful of ice, but not any longer.

I suppose it must have been January the second or third. It was a Monday. The spring term was not due to start until the middle of the week. Evie was just beginning to clear the crumpled wrapping paper from the corners of the living room, to tweak open the curtains; she was talking about her upcoming projects; she was sketching with her left hand while she watched TV. Clear signs that the holiday was coming to a close. One of the main differences between me and my mother is that she has the ability to look forward to things; I don't. There was nothing to look forward to at school. Being there, in those cramped, corridored buildings made me feel like I was acting in a play but didn't know the script.

My school, the Agatha Seaford Academy, named after Lady Agatha Seaford, who had endowed it, was for girls only. It was known colloquially as Lady Agatha's and was one of the best state schools in the borough. To get in you had to be religious; we weren't, but we jumped through the holy hoops all right (church on Sundays for a year, Evie hiding her pierced tongue) and I did well in the entrance exams, so they let me in. The grounds, not far from Pimlico, were packed with once-shiny facilities, and a chapel to which we went daily. The teachers – called, unusually, by both first name and surname – were an approachable, professional bunch. There were well-run, though uninspired, after-school clubs and societies with which I could have liberally filled my free time, if I'd wanted to; as it was, I went to only one, and that turned out not to have been a good idea.

My chosen A-level subjects were Art and Design, English Literature and French. The obvious ones; the ones I didn't have to try in. I had always been pretty fluent in my father's language, though lack of practice made me careless with my pronouns, while English and Art came easily to me. But just because I found my choices easy doesn't mean to say I was enjoying myself.

While my mother began stripping the tree of its shiny ornamentation (this year we had gone for a footwear theme, and from the thorny branches hung tiny stilettos, clumpy boots, hot-pink ballerina slippers), I felt my usual rush of envy for the passion she had for her work. Evie lived inside her passion: our flat was papered with clippings and costume ideas. In the shifting histories of fabrics and patterns, my mother had found a kind of temple of grace. Without it, in so many ways, she would have been lost. I had no such temple.

'When do you start back at work?' I asked her.

'Friday. Costume drama,' she said in her patchwork accent (part Essex, part Glasgow), and full-mouthed. I looked over; she had a piece of Sellotape between her teeth. I rolled myself up from the floor and went over to help her. We unhooked the shoes, bundled them in tissue paper and

11

packed them, appropriately enough, into shoe boxes, even though by the following year my mother would have come up with a different theme, and we would have no more use for the shoes.

'What period?'

'Tudor. They think people don't know about anything but the Twenties and the Tudors.' This came out with her usual soft disdain: Evie longed for lesser-known eras to be brought to life on the screen.

'These are nice,' I said, holding up some red-and-white trainers made of papier-mâché. 'I'd wear these.'

Evie grinned. Although – as I have said before – she is a reformed, rather than committed Goth, she still likes to dress in monochrome; that morning she had on a lace camisole, a cream silk shirt with an ink stain blossoming over one breast, a man's grey cardigan with several buttons missing and a long black skirt with a side split. She still had that vampiric whiteness you expect in Goths; her skin was so icily pale it was almost blue in places. Lady Agatha's had no uniform in the Sixth form so I modelled my own clothing for school on Evie's monochrome style, often borrowing things that fitted me, although I preferred camouflage to costume. In point of fact, I would not have worn red-and-white trainers. It was a lie, albeit a small one, designed to please Evie.

I could pause this frame so happily. Although not a particularly emotional person, I catch a glimpse of Evie at odd moments like this one, when we are both on the pine-needled carpet with our hands full of hooks and tissues, absorbed in the process of dismantling Christmas, and I am replete with simple gratitude. I am grateful, you see, that my mother is still alive. She might so easily not have been.

But I cannot pause the frame. Because the phone is about to ring, and the sound of it will shatter the cocktail of tree, hooks, carpet and gratitude that I have assembled so temptingly for myself. And there is nothing I can do about it. I cannot stop the phone from ringing.

2

Evie picked up the phone in her room, only because she had gone there to fetch more shoe boxes a fraction of a second beforehand. If she had picked it up in the living room (the only other place where there was a handset), I'd have absorbed, at least on our side, part of the conversation. As it was, I had no idea what was taking place. I carried on undecorating the Christmas tree, pump by sandal, wondering what to have for lunch, ruling out various options as they occurred to me. Sushi: too cold; a sandwich: too dull.

'Aliénor.'

Just as I seldom call Evie 'Mum', she rarely calls me the name she and my father chose for me. Laid-back and accepting to a fault, she unquestioningly embraced my acquisition of Nora. Everyone, said Evie, has the right to rechristen themselves, to pick a name that resonates truly. She herself has always hankered after 'Elvira'. She stood in the doorway to the living room, holding the BT handset; for a moment, I thought someone had called for me.

'That was your headmistress on the phone,' said Evie. 'Mrs Bane.'

'Braine.'

'Braine. She wants us to come in. Both of us. Tomorrow. Before term starts.'

'Oh yes,' I said. 'What about?'

'She didn't say. It concerns a member of staff, apparently. What's she mean? What's happened?'

I sat back on my heels. It wasn't a surprise. The indomitable Caroline Braine was now involved in the situation; it had, I realised, only been a matter of time before the other shoe dropped. So to speak.

Which meant that before we went in, I'd have to explain matters to my mother.

Evie never came in to school; she wasn't hands-on in that way. She herself had had a chequered education; it was only after my father died that she went to college to study textiles and costume design. Her own memories of school seemed to be a catalogue of boys and cigarettes and punk rock; teachers were idiots or enemies, and the system only existed to be undermined. In her hooded cloak and lace-up boots, she looked almost beautifully out-of-place as we approached the main gates.

'You're very quiet, Norie-girl,' she said.

The winds were up; the sky had an ice-clear January chill about it, like a Snow Queen's mirror.

'Just tell them exactly what you told me, and everything will be fine.'

15

'I already have,' I said. 'I told my form tutor the whole story.'

My mother reminded me of the White Witch on the verge of battle. The gates loomed above us, and she prodded the bell. 'I'm livid, by the way,' she said. 'But don't worry. I'll behave. Otherwise I'd have brought my pattern-cutting scissors for his balls.' As we waited for the gates to open, she added, 'But I'm always livid. Right? Livid means white.'

True: she is always of a tomblike paleness. But I explained to her that *livid*, as in a livid bruise, is purplish blue, not white. I'm better with words than Evie. She reached for my hand; I counted the bones in hers, and we went up the steps together, one at a time, with synchronised feet.

We were met by the school secretary at the big oak door, who greeted us quite formally. She showed us into the Head's office, a place I'd only been to once, a long time ago, for an interview before I became a pupil. Without the sound of six hundred stampeding girls, chattering in their birdcall voices, clattering in their thick-soled shoes, the building felt larger, colder, unfamiliar. I felt like I was going for my interview, aged ten, all over again. And, of course, this *was* an interview.

Inside the office was arranged a panel of people, as much like the row of judges on a TV talent show as anything else. There was Caroline Braine, the Head, and my form tutor, Sarah Cousins, and a tall grey man who introduced himself as Director of the Board of Governors. They were seated around Mrs Braine's desk in a kind of semicircle. Evie and I were invited to sit opposite them. It was clearly not supposed to look too confrontational, but it felt confrontational nonetheless. The panel's faces were stone-set and unmoving, and I wondered what was about to happen. I do not like situations that I cannot control.

We were offered tea, coffee, water; we declined, and then Evie changed her mind and asked for a glass of water. She is a reformed drinker, as well as a reformed Goth, and she has a theory that if you're in recovery you always need to be drinking something. Her tipple of choice is cranberry juice.

I wished my mother's heels weren't quite so high.

I thought: what if they don't believe me?

I could have frozen that frame too. The stone-set faces, the clouded window, the Aboriginal art, the plant in the corner with its plump, spiked leaves.

Then Caroline Braine leaned forwards and began to speak.

'Firstly, I should tell you that Mr Trace will not be attending this meeting. We did not think it necessary for him to be here today. We have, of course, heard Nora's side of the story. Nora, we will not be asking you to tell it again.'

A tossed coin flipped and flickered in the air above her head. The coin that nobody could see but me.

'We have asked you here to let you both know formally that Jonah Trace will not be returning to work at the Agatha Seaford Academy. His contract has been terminated, with immediate effect.'

My mother reached for my hand again. She was still wearing her long black cloak; her sleeve made a scratchy sound against the arm of my chair. 'Thank you,' she said. This was the right thing to say.

'His version of events did not tally precisely with Nora's,' said Caroline Braine, her voice straining under the weight of her necklace.

'So the bastard denied it,' said Evie. This was not the right thing to say. *Don't swear, please*, I willed her, inside my head. But no one, not even the tall grey man, looked offended. Perhaps a burst of pure emotion was not unacceptable in these circumstances. What, exactly, had Jonah Trace's version of events entailed? They didn't say.

Mrs Braine went on: 'Needing, of course, to look into the matter further, we made contact with his last two placements, a school in Bath and another on the Isle of Wight. Although both had provided good references for Mr Trace before he came to us, we were told anecdotally that they had received complaints in several instances, from the girls in question or from their parents. Nothing was ever proven, but the pattern seems to be clear. In short, he may have done this kind of thing before.'

'Please be assured,' said the tall grey man, 'that this will prompt a thorough review of our recruitment policy.'

They retreated, all of them, into a kind of blizzard of professional jargon; I realised they were concerned we might sue them, or talk to journalists, or call the police. They wanted us to know that they were sorry. This has never happened before at our school, they said. I watched Caroline Braine's necklace – geometric, sharp-edged, bronze – catch the light at different angles as she spoke with more and more conviction and urgency: professional misconduct; not a matter for police investigation; primary duty of care. The grey man looked as solemn and sad as a chaplain at a funeral. Only my form tutor, Sarah Cousins, remained somehow unengaged, thoughtful.

Sarah Cousins taught biology, so I had no lessons with her. She was tall and thin and wore long scarves and knee-length skirts that displayed shapely calves. She was known as one of the 'nice' teachers. But she was not without a kind of internal steel. Anyone who had seen her dissect a sheep's heart could bear witness to this. The only time we really exchanged words was when she took the register. She offered a weekly walk-in counselling service for the girls in her form, so that you could go and describe your difficulties with food or friendships or contraception or whatever. I never went, so we didn't have the kind of chummy relationship that it was possible to have with your form tutor.

Not long before the end of the Christmas term, she'd asked me to come and see her after school. It was important, she said. There was something we needed to discuss. When I showed up, she greeted me with crows'-feet of concern on her face. She had a pad of paper on her knee, and a pen resting in her hand.

It was a moment I'd been expecting.

'This is difficult, Nora. Sorry,' Sarah Cousins began. 'Someone came to me recently with a rather disturbing report. I'm keen to get to the bottom of it. Apparently, you were seen this weekend, in Borough Market. The choir was singing carols there. I don't know if you were aware of that?'

I shook my head.

'They saw you with Mr Trace. It seemed like you were having an altercation of some kind . . .' She hesitated. 'I'd . . . would you be able to tell me what happened? In your own words.'

I am superlatively good at owning words.

I told her.

While Caroline Braine talked, and Evie listened, thankfully contributing no further swear words, I watched Sarah Cousins' face. I remembered our conversation from a few weeks previously. My form tutor was very quiet. She added little to the web of platitudes being spun between the chairs, and sat with her hands folded in her lap, like a Victorian schoolchild.

After a while there were no more platitudes left. Evie and I were shown back out through the doors. My mother swept down the steps, humming the opening of *The Wall* by Pink Floyd. Although the sun had tiptoed out again into full view, she tugged her hood over her head in a magnificent gesture of autonomy and pulled me away with her sleeves flapping like long dark wings.

'Nora, I think you were bloody brave,' she said, on the bus home. The crisis had made her more communicative: she was given to bouts of endless silence, especially when in transit.

I traced lacy patterns in the fogged-up window of the upper deck. 'Are you still livid?' I asked her.

'Of course I'm livid. White, purple, whatever with lividity. I see this stuff on film sets all the time,' she went on. 'Comments, inappropriate gestures, jokey propositions . . . Maybe it's a female technician getting unnecessary hassle, maybe an actress. Most of the time it all just gets kind of swept under the rug. They're afraid to speak out.'

I nodded.

'The fact is, he was your teacher. That makes it worse. Seriously, Noric. What you did . . . that must have been hard. I wish there were more people like you.'

She stopped abruptly, and fished out a paperback book from her bag. I closed my eyes, replaying the interview again in my head. Throughout the entire thing I had said nothing at all; nothing was safest and best, I thought. But inside me, a tiny nugget, hot as desert stone, glowed gold with hidden victory.

3

I had no fewer than three alternative stories about my father's death, if anyone really wanted to know (and not many people did). I viewed this as something akin to my old Choose Your Own Adventure books, where different page numbers held diverging plot strands, dependent on the reader's choices. *'Do you want to go deeper into the jungle? Turn to page 67! Do you want to turn back? Turn to page 68!'* Sometimes the story would end happily, and other times it wouldn't.

None of my stories had happy endings.

My selection depended on the temperament of my listener as well as on my mood. Since they were asking for their own satisfaction, and not for mine, I would either thrill them with a story dovetailed to their own particular interests, or else – if I was feeling a little less sympathetic – I'd choose the one that would make them cringe the most, the one that would make them wish they hadn't asked.

Loosely, my three stories could be classified thus:

1. Obscure Illness.
2. Mysterious Disappearance.
3. Unfortunate Tragedy.

This is not the order in which they were first told, incidentally. It's just how they seem to be listed in my head. The first one I created, I'm pretty sure, was Mysterious Disappearance. This took its inspiration from my memories of taking the ferry as a small child between Dover and Calais; I believe that the most successful inventions, even if they contain elements of the fantastical and far-fetched, must have strong authentic origins.

This is how it goes.

'We took the ferry to England from France, and back again, a couple of times a year,' I would begin. 'P&O, always. Massive, with great big funnels. As soon as we parked the car, I would go straight to the slot machines – on some ferries there would be a whole room, just for slot machines. I never played; I just had this weird fascination for watching other people play. The fruit machines especially. I'd stand next to the player and whisper advice. "Press HOLD now," I'd say. "You've already got two cherries." And pretty often, they'd do what I told them, maybe because they thought I was psychic. I probably looked a bit weird and other-worldly, with my birthmark, and because I was so small, and because my mother always put me in these fancy, embroidered dresses. And sometimes I got it right, and the kid would win. I was addicted to the sound of the money cascading, all chunky and satisfying, into the slot. Sometimes they'd give me twenty pence or a pound, and I'd go and buy an ice cream.'

All this, so far, by the way, was true.

'My parents liked to set up camp on the middle deck. They wanted to see the sea, and to be as far away from other people as possible. My father would drink black coffee and then complain about its poor quality. My mother would have a gin and tonic, just one, if it was after twelve. If not, she'd have tea. Then she would knit, and my father would draw, or they both would read. We played card games: Happy Families, Go Fish. Sometimes my father would take me outside, if it wasn't too rainy or windy, and we'd look out across the Channel, and he'd sing me a song about the White Cliffs of Dover, or a French one called *La Mer*. He would take me up to the rails, holding my hand. "Look down, Aliénor," he'd say. "You see the white horses? Look – they are white horses, charging through the waves, keeping pace with the boat." He always referred to the ferry as a "boat". And I'd look down, and gradually I began to see the horses, in the white-tipped froth that surged around the keel as the ferry cut a path through the sea.'

All this: also true.

'One evening, when I was six years old, as we were crossing towards Dover, there was a storm. I used to love storms in Paris, where – watching them from the windows of our high-up apartment – they seemed so safe. But at sea, even on those big ferries, storms were different. When this one hit, I was in the windowless games room, watching somebody shoot a miniature basketball. There was so much noise coming from the machines that for a while I wasn't aware that a storm had begun. But when I came out into the stairwell, making my way back to where my parents were, I realised how dark the sky had grown, how the ferry had somehow become wrapped in the rustling sound of the rain. The sound was everywhere: battering the windows, the glass doors that had been closed for safety. Then the thunder started, and I scrambled up the stairs, as fast as I could, to find my mother and father.

'I was halfway up as my mother came down, calling for me.

'"Where's your father, lovie?" she said.

'I told her I didn't know.

'"He went to look for you," she said, "when the storm began. But that was a while ago now."

'Keeping hold of my hand, she led me on a search of the ship. We looked everywhere: the cafeteria, the toilets, the games room, the shop. We went down to the parked cars and threaded our way in and out of them, as though we were playing a game, and as we went we called for him. Every staircase. Every doorway.

'And then: "We must find a steward," my mother said. "We must tell them that someone is missing."'

I had several minor variations on what happened next. In the first tellings, I described how my mother and I managed to break open the locked doors onto the deck and pulled ourselves along the wall by the rope, hair slicked horizontal by the wind. Our screams wrestled with the sounds of the storm. Sometimes, I said that we saw – far off, almost impossible to make out – what looked like a human head in the water. Other times I said that we saw another shape with him, something dark and looping and tangled: a sea snake, a monster. But that would have been more appropriate for Greek waters, I decided later; I did not like to test the credulity of my audience. Once, I said that we saw my father fall from the railings of the deck. Generally, however, I enlarged upon the agonies of our quest, how the stairwells echoed with our calling, and how various Good Samaritans joined in the search.

The ship docked at Dover, and the police came, and each passenger was asked their name on departure, and a thorough search was conducted.

And there was no sign of Felix Tobias, forty-seven years old, of French nationality.

There was no sign at all.

4

I have a certain talent for negativity. It's subtle enough not to be that noticeable the first time you meet me. My face, although imprinted with a starfish-or-France-shaped birthmark, does not have the downturned eyes and mouth of a habitually sad person. But sad people, negative people, should not be defined by such basic landmarks. A tone of voice can be misleading. Or the way a curtain of hair falls to the shoulders, the way it moves when a person shakes or nods their head. Perhaps I will go so far as to say that I believe that it is almost impossible to spot a real interior sadness, unless you are gifted with unusual empathy, or have been a witness to something in that person's life. With my father, and my mother too, I have been a witness.

But who is my witness? Partly, maybe, that is why I am writing this now. You, the reader, are invited ringside, or to the one-way glass of my cell. To my sadness. And because I have assured you that what I am writing is the truth, you are invited to believe me. One clue, by the way, is in my name. Long ago, I parted with my birth name, Aliénor. Teachers at all points in my English education made me sound like athlete's foot cream or air freshener. Disliking variations on the theme of Allie, I settled for Nora because it had an undertone of denial that pleased me. It sounded like both *nor*, as in *neither/nor*, and *ignore*. It suggested negative space: a yawn of air between rigid shapes.

Nora is not-being. Nothingness. Thank you, but no.

And so: one aspect of my Nora-nature is my tendency to define myself in negative terms. 'That's not my favourite genre,' I will say, to the friend who eagerly proposes a rom-com or a musical. 'I'm not very good at making this,' will preface whatever I'm about to cook and serve to a guest. I know a lot about what I don't want, what I don't like, what I am not.

I do like to read, by the way. And I like to swim. I am not without occasional sparks of positive interest. Another thing I do – and maybe 'like' is the wrong word for it, and maybe it isn't – is tell lies. I certainly have a talent for it. People tend to believe me. There are plenty of small histories I can relate, in which I am believed. The day that Evie and I were called in to Caroline Braine's office was, as I have explained, a victory. They believed me. Mr Trace did not have a leg to stand on, not unlike the computer table upon which I am writing this now.

But perhaps you would like to know what actually happened.

I shall explain.

Flip the calendar back to September. A fortnight in, and the school term is already slipping into a familiar routine:

wood polish and steamed carrots and fire drills. Picture me here. Oh: you do not know what I look like, apart from my birthmark. Sorry. I am small, with a ringletty mass of leonine curls, and in fact a rather leonine face; I would look good with whiskers. I am coming down the stairs with my three obligatory friends: Perfect Melody Wilson, Frederika Olsson and Sangeeta Lakhani, and we do not need to dwell upon my three obligatory friends at this point, because they are just about to go home.

Thursday. It is definitely a Thursday.

It must have been a quarter past four, because the school day was over. Perfect, who spent much of her life trying to find things to be perfect at, was going to run home along the Thames towpath. Sangeeta and Fred would take the tube. Ordinarily I'd have gone with them, stopping for chocolate and maybe a magazine or a coffee along the way. But on this particular Thursday, Life Class was due to be held for the first time that term. The head of art, Graham Gibbons – an adenoidal man with sparse red hair combed thinly over his head, like inadequate jam on bread – had explained to me that although it was listed as an optional club, regular attendance at Life Class was essentially compulsory.

'It will mark the difference between an A and a B,' he intoned, with unnecessary pomposity.

I allowed this to persuade me. Although I didn't care particularly about getting straight As – I hadn't made any plans yet for university courses or further study – I didn't *not* care, either. Really, I'm not a joiner. If he'd called it Life Drawing *Club*, I would never have agreed to go.

The Art and Design Centre was in the basement of a large modern building at the edge of the school complex, beneath the gym. Whoever had designed the layout had not given much thought to the possibility that developing artists might like, in their efforts to observe and put the world in perspective, a bit of a view. It was more like the second act of a horror film down in the Art and Design Centre: damp, gloomy, littered with old props from stage plays. Flickering fluorescent bars lit the room where Life Class was to be held. There were maybe fourteen or sixteen students, and then there was the art assistant, a man called Jonah Trace, who would be directing the class. He couldn't have been more than mid-twenties. Probably he was fresh out of art or teaching college.

Male teachers at an all-girls school were enough of a rarity to draw our immediate attention, and I had not seen much of Jonah Trace before, though I dimly remembered seeing him around the studios, pinning up sketches and scouring palettes. He was tall and narrow-shouldered, round-faced: what Evie would call 'boyish', and by which I think she would mean young-at-heart-looking. There were teachers who would try to be your mentor, and there were teachers who would try to be your friend, and Mr Trace was one of the second type. His warm brown hair was ruffled up with gel, and he had a soft Bristolian accent, easy to imitate. He talked a lot, I heard, about his girlfriend, although no one had ever seen her. Already, I heard, he had a fan club among the younger girls. Like I said: male teachers, especially those under forty-five, were a rarity. We weren't fussy.

He went around the room distributing paper and sticks of charcoal. The heating was well up; it gave the air in the basement a sticky, dusty feel, as though particles of old paint were collecting on our skins.

I watched Jonah Trace, all elbows and awkwardness, open the studio door to welcome the model, and from the way he hurried forwards to kiss her on one cheek I decided that he must know her from somewhere. He showed her into the office, where she could get changed. When she emerged, I had to suppress a kind of judgemental surprise: surely you'd only take your clothes off in front of opinionated teenagers if you were long of leg and whittled of waist? This woman was not. She was thick from neck to ankle, like a badly made jar; her small breasts piled on top of each other like sandbags as she lay down, her dressing gown unwrapped, on a quasi-ceremonial plinth in the centre of the room. But, remembering that my father always said that we can take delight in drawing anything and anyone, of whatever description, I felt bad about my judgemental surprise.

Jonah Trace fussed with the folds of material around her stomach, pulling them ineffectually into other wrinkles. Then he began directing us.

'Look carefully now at the angle of the neck, the relationship of the head to the shoulder. Draw what you see. Draw what you see, girls.'

He was nervous. Everything about him was nervous, from the glitches in his voice to the unsteady way that he held out his hand in front of the model to point out some miraculous curve or opportunity for shading. I thought: why so twitchy, Jonah Trace? Is this not the job of your dreams? Perhaps the heat was making him uncomfortable. Perhaps he had never led a Life Class before. Perhaps he fancied his friend, the model. But *she* was the picture of relaxation, her limbs unmoving, her face expressionless. Her professionalism delighted me. It made me want to draw her. I realised, as I looked down at my A3 sheet, that everyone else was much further along than me.

But before I had done much drawing, I began again, in that hot room on that Thursday in September, to think more about my father, the artist. His illustrations were so small they were practically miniatures. I remember his brushes, which he kept in a collection of old jars in his study; some had only a few teased hairs apiece, like insects' brooms. Back in Paris, Evie had worked at a bar in Pigalle; I went to a local Montessori, and then to a funny international school where all we seemed to do was tell the time in four languages, and my father drew for work in the daytime, and pleasure in the evening. I loved to watch him at his high architect's desk, a small *tasse* of black coffee on the floor beside his feet.

Often, he would give me a square of paper and a set of pencils and invite me to create something. 'Draw me a monster,' my father would say, in French. 'Do not use green. He must have six eyes and a suspicious smile.'

I would puzzle this out, trying my best to capture whatever it was that my father had asked for, my fingers heavy with intent. A little chuckle of pleasure at the sight of my illustrations was what I lived for; his praise was worth more to me than pocket money.

'Asleep, are we?' said Jonah Trace.

I looked up; he was standing beside me, a look of disapproval drawing down his brows. I do not like to be interrupted when I am thinking about my father. I do not like being called *we*.

'I'm just thinking,' I said, which was true.

The art assistant seemed unimpressed. 'I'm keen to move on to a smaller sketch in a minute,' he said. 'Best hurry up.'

And for the next forty minutes, he continued to glance irritably in my direction, or to come and stand behind my head, casting a long shadow over my paper, as though he had identified the potential Problem Girl in the room. Gradually, it began to have an effect on me; his nerves became my nerves. Two or three times, I had to start my work again, having mangled the jar-like body and sandbag breasts beyond recognition. Towards the end of the class, I managed to knock over the water glass of the girl next to me onto her work. The glass did not break, but the soft clunk was audible in the industrious silence and a pool of dark water engulfed her page. Before I could react, before I could even say sorry, Jonah Trace had leaped across the room with a handful of paper towels, awkward as ever.

'Now you've done it,' he said, clicking his tongue, blending the charcoal lines into a single indistinct smudge as he mopped up the spillage. 'What a shame. What a real shame.'

I looked around, to see if anyone else could hear what I could hear. But I had no friends in this group of students; they were not all from my year, and I only knew some of them by name. No one had even looked up, except the girl next to me, who shook her head and smiled in a kind sort of way.

'It was only a rough sketch,' she said.

'Sorry,' I said.

'It's fine.' She seemed embarrassed by the fuss.

At the end of the class, as Mr Trace sprayed our pages with hairspray and switched off the portable heater, he had words of praise for everyone except me. When I left, he looked at my work and shrugged, with a little side-nod of his head, as if to say, 'I'd say you could do better, but you probably can't.'

I do not like to be disapproved of. I hate it. It curdles in my bones, like the beginnings of some degenerative disease. From that day onward, I developed an instantaneous kindling of loathing for Jonah Trace, newly recruited art assistant at the Agatha Seaford Academy.

5

All through September, as the trees grew tired of their leaf-colour and started to experiment with henna and Hovis brown, I continued to think about Jonah Trace. The first thing to do – the only fair thing, in the circumstances – was to ascertain whether that Life Class had been a one-off. It was a definite possibility: Mr Trace was new; he was stricken with the nerves of a recent teaching initiate; he understood that teachers needed favourites and unfavourites, so he chose me for the latter role. I was easy to pick out in a line-up, with my frayed-ribbon hair and my birthmark. If he struggled with names, as many new teachers did, he could identify us by the signposts of our skin, hair or jewellery, and give us crude labels. Megan Lattismore, for example, would be Large Breasts and Ponytail. I was Problem Girl with Birthmark. Fine. I could allow him this, if it were reversed once he had found his professional feet.

I would give him, temporarily, the benefit of the doubt.

I came early, but not too early, to Life Class the following week. I came early so that I could choose where to sit; it was important, I thought, that I should occupy a different space with, as my Aunt Petra would put it, a different energy

– Petra was all for cleansing negative spaces with jagged hunks of quartz, for clapping her chubby hands into clogged-up corners. I was not quite in that league, but I saw her general point. I had not seen Jonah Trace all week, other than once, across a crowded lunch hall, and a second time, parking his moped in the staff car park. Neither time had he seen me. That was good. I didn't want to misread his behaviour towards me. I wanted to be sure.

The room was nearly deserted when I entered. From the sounds of radio and kettle humming in the office, I deduced that our leader was in there, preparing for the session. Only one corner of the room was occupied. At first, I thought it was another student who had come early to Life Class, but it wasn't. It was a girl in the year above me, working on a piece of coursework.

Annabel, she was called. I didn't know her surname. I had an idea that she seldom came to school; whether through illness or lack of desire I didn't know. She hadn't been at Lady Agatha's very long – a couple of years at most. Perhaps her family moved about a lot. I felt that I'd seen her in something – a choir, perhaps, or a Chapel assembly, or a debate. I couldn't quite remember. It was said that she was the daughter of somebody famous, but this detail eluded me too. Annabel wore very unusual clothes: fairy wings, patched leather trousers, a headband woven from peacock-feathers. Evie would have enjoyed her outfits. Today was no exception: her russet skirts, properly voluminous, could compete with autumn itself, so much did they resemble a carpet of leaves, and in her feather-blonde hair was a thorny garland such as Jesus might have worn at his death.

Annabel was at work on a painting. She had not bothered with an overall, and was using her skirt to wipe her brush each time she dipped it into the jar of white spirit. The sleeves of her top were smudgy with oil paint.

As unobtrusively as I could, I found a table where I could see what it was that she was doing. I have always been interested in work-in-progress; years of watching my father had made me a lifelong admirer of those who have the commitment to finish pieces of art. Annabel's painting was of a man and a woman standing on a wooden bridge, facing away from the viewer, their hands not quite touching. It was well-composed and somehow unsettling. It made you want to know more about the couple – how they felt about each other, and why. Just then Annabel turned, and for a moment met my gaze. She seemed to be considering me, evaluating. Then the blue-green eyes looked away again. I was of no interest to her.

'Time you packed up, Bel,' said Jonah Trace, coming out of the office.

'Sure thing,' she replied, in an American accent. *Sure thang*. But she was surely not American. 'I'll never get the goddamn thing done in time for the deadline,' she added, and this time she said it in a kind of vowel-perfect Radio English.

I watched her clearing away her things. She did not tidy

up much: she swept her brushes and jars into the sink, leaving her canvas where it was and sheets of newspaper, damp with linseed oil, all over the floor. Jonah Trace, I saw, was watching her too – quite casually, while he sharpened pencils, over by the window. Here was a moment of interest. Would he exercise his teacherly authority and ask her to leave the art room as she had found it?

He did not.

Annabel pulled on a kimono with a silvery belt and a long rip at the back. She picked up a Mary Poppins-ish bag. 'Ta-ta,' she said to Jonah Trace.

'You dropped something,' he said, stooping to pick up two or three leaflets from the floor.

'Oh, my flyers. Thanks. Look – what d'you think of them? I helped with the design.'

'*Gimlet and the Grenadines*,' read Jonah Trace. 'A twenty-four-hour play. Sounds very cool. And you're in it?'

'Yeah,' she replied. 'It's not a big part. Just helping out a friend.'

'Does it really take twenty-four hours to perform?'

'Sure does.'

'How d'you stay awake that long?'

'Oh! *That's* not difficult.' She smiled at him generously. 'You should come down. Tomorrow night, from midnight.'

'Ah, that's annoying,' said Jonah Trace. 'I'm at the footie this weekend.'

He sounded genuinely sorry that he couldn't go. The look

of sorryness persisted as he watched Annabel leave, with a sweep of kimono and a slam of the studio door. And at the mention of a play, I realised where I remembered her from: she'd been in last year's Lower Sixth form production of *Cabaret*, the musical set in wartime Berlin. A glitzy, rather slick production it had been. Some of the props were still lying about in the art rooms. Annabel had played the part of Sally Bowles, made famous by Liza Minnelli in the film adaptation. Although her singing voice was not particularly strong, I remembered thinking at the time that her acting style sparkled with something genuinely brilliant, if a little uneven. There had been some kind of issue, though I forgot what exactly. She'd been very late for one of the performances, perhaps. Or some friends of hers had turned up drunk and disorderly. I wasn't sure. I wondered what it would be like to perform in a twenty-four-hour play. It would require a peculiar kind of determination.

Jonah turned and saw me, and looked put out. 'You're very early,' he said.

We had a different model this week – sinewy, flame-haired, prone to giggling – and a different assignment.

'Draw a line down the middle of your page,' said Jonah Trace. He was dressed more smartly today; maybe he had an event to go to later. I pictured him at the opening of some installation at a Shoreditch gallery, glass of tepid wine in one hand, girlfriend tethered to the other. What was his girlfriend like? I wondered. If he even had one.

'I'd like you to draw Vanessa first with your dominant hand – right if you're right-handed, left if you're left-handed. I'd like you to spend about fifteen minutes on this,' he said.

I noticed that he said many things twice; his speech patterns were curiously limited, as though he were a robot, or English were not his first language. I wondered if he repeated himself because he doubted his own authority.

'Then – no cheating, please, girls – I'd like you to transfer your pencil to the opposite hand. Repeat the process. See what feels different.'

At this there were gasps and giggles, as he had probably predicted. Lady Agatha girls were known for their diligent, risk-averse attitude; Perfect was not the only student who openly yearned for perfection. The Life Class attendees would not like the imprecision of drawing with their undominant hand, the flaws in their artistry that this would expose.

I drew a line down the middle of my page. Jonah Trace put on Heart 106.2. For ten minutes, I drew Vanessa, who was making an effort to keep still, but who seemed unable not to smile when someone made eye contact with her by mistake. I used my left hand for this. I tried, as I did so, not to dwell on Jonah Trace and how he did not like me. He *would* like my work this week. That would be the way to his approval. My strokes with the 2B pencil were clear and definite; I captured the length of Vanessa's spine, the way it flattened into a small plain before the round of her buttocks. I drew her ear, which was almost pointed, like a pixie's, with just the right amount of hair falling over it. I got what for me is always a tricky bit, in faces: the exact relationship of the tip of the nose to the upper lip. By the time Jonah Trace murmured that it was time to move on to the other hand, I felt pretty intimately acquainted with Vanessa's anatomy.

I was sitting in the corner, in front of the bookshelves and not far from where Annabel had been working. Jonah Trace, alerted to the huffy sighs and protestations that it was *just too difficult*, was over on the other side of the room. Vanessa reposed between him and me; all I could see was his dried-mud hair as he leaned over sketchbooks, talking about the left and right sides of the brain, something appropriated from *New Scientist*, I assumed. Meanwhile, I redrew Vanessa with my right hand. I took real care with this drawing, spending the same amount of time on the same parts of her body. The pencil rested more loosely in my grip; the resultant lines were lighter and more tentative. Yes. Good. The hair a little too much over the ear; the ear too pointed this time, like an architrave. Jonah Trace was nearing the bookshelves. He was very democratic about his time, moving from artist to artist with the regularity of a speed-dater. Now he had reached Megan Lattismore. Today Megan was wearing a black bra underneath her white shirt, difficult to ignore since she was generously endowed in the breast area.

'Something we rarely think about when we write or draw

is that the muscles don't start in our hands, or even our arms,' Jonah Trace was saying to her. 'It actually starts all the way up here.'

To demonstrate, he touched her lightly, once, on the left shoulder, as she nodded and smiled and drew her lopsided sketch. Then – I tried to look as though I wasn't watching – he touched her again, a gentle pat, as he moved away. A 'keep it up, you're doing great' kind of pat, for sure. Harmless. And yet . . . a lidded, sleepy, guilty, transfiguring look flashed – just for a second – across his face. And he glanced straight down the open neck of her shirt. Just for a second.

He did.

So that was what was up with Jonah Trace, his mysterious quirks, his nerves. When I said I like to read, by the way, I didn't just mean books. I like to read people too.

By the time he got to me, I was nearly done. I was pleased with both my pictures, with the lengths I had gone to in order to present their discrepancies. Jonah Trace stood behind me and surveyed my work.

Then: 'This is a joke,' he said, so loudly that everyone – even Vanessa – looked up. 'This is a joke, right?'

'What do you mean?' I said.

'Which hand did you just use?'

'My right.'

'These pictures are practically identical,' he said, his voice thick with accusation. 'So you used your right for both, did you?'

'I used my left first, then my right,' I said. I was beginning to blush. I hated blushing. It clashed unhappily with my birthmark, like strawberry sorbet scooped next to salted caramel.

'Well, I'm sorry to contradict you, but you plainly didn't.'

'I'm sorry to contradict *you*,' I said, 'but I did. I'm ambidextrous.'

He breathed out heavily through his nostrils. 'Ambidextrous,' he repeated.

'Shall I show you?' I offered. I hate to be disbelieved. The blush was spreading, swift and feverlike, to the top of my neck.

'There isn't time. There isn't time,' said Jonah Trace, with disgust. He seemed to be blushing too.

I could not help but feel that had it been Annabel, drawing Vanessa with dominant and undominant hands, he'd never have dared to challenge her.

That night, while Evie watched *Casablanca*, I borrowed her laptop and spent a profitable hour on the Internet, making careful and creative searches. I wanted to know more about Jonah Trace: his interests, specifically; his background; whatever details of his life might be out there to find. Even the most basic use of search engines can yield fascinating results.

Then, writing in my smallest handwriting on a sheet of A4, I made a list of what to do next.

6

The nights grew colder. Evie finished working on one ITV murder-mystery drama and started on another. In the Lower Sixth, we settled into our A-level choices. In English, we were studying the poetry of T.S. Eliot. In French, there were short stories by Maupassant to read, not uninteresting. In Art, we were making lithographs of small birds in bright colours.

Meanwhile, Annabel finished her painting and moved on to a second. This one was on a long rectangular canvas; her preparatory sketches seemed to show a cream-coloured Georgian house set against dark green hills, with a blonde girl in a white dress in the foreground. I assumed it was Annabel herself. I imagined she was the kind of person who liked herself a good deal. It would never have occurred to me to do a self-portrait.

There had been two more life drawing classes on Thursday afternoons; one of them I'd missed, citing, more or less truthfully, a headache. In the other I'd kept my head down, responding to the art assistant only when necessary, and drawing (if you pardon the pun) little attention to myself.

I noticed on that Friday lunch time that Jonah Trace had

not brought his moped to school. Perhaps he had taken it for repairs, or maybe he was going somewhere for the night, or for the weekend. Perhaps he knew he was going to drink a lot. I knew about this from Evie, from Old Evie, at least: that if you are going to imbibe quantities of alcohol, you may have to plan your travel arrangements carefully.

I managed to avoid walking to the tube station with Fred and Sangeeta, telling them that I needed to fetch a few books from the library. I went to the toilets and brushed my hair. Left to its own devices, it hangs in a woody tangle down my back; brushed, it diffuses a kind of tiger's-eye light that both my parents always said made me look like an angel. Possibly a slightly fallen one, one with singed wings, but an angel nevertheless. I added also some war paint: a burnish of lip gloss, some mascara. Not too much, of course. Then I left by the side entrance, walked round the corner, to where the roads diverge at right angles – one to the tube, and the other to the bus stops. Either route would get me home.

I took out my phone.

I don't know what people did, when they wanted to look busy, in the days before mobile phones. They could have read books, of course – but I could not lounge against the wall with a book, just as Elizabeth Bennet could not talk of books in a ballroom. I needed to look like I was waiting for a call, or checking my messages, and I was prepared to linger as long as necessary. Four thirty came and went. Four forty-five . . . Was Jonah Trace running a club? But he only took Life Class, and that was on Thursdays.

By five to five, I was starting to think that he'd gone the other way. There was always a chance he could have done that, but I hadn't wanted to wait at the actual gates. It was too obvious, somehow. Our meeting needed to have the appearance of absolute chance.

Pretty soon the last dregs of Lady Agatha's came dribbling past: the girls from Choir, from Aikido Club, the staff. But no Jonah Trace. I shouldered my bag, stowed my phone and started to weigh up which – the bus or the tube – would be less unpleasant. I felt a twinge of something like regret: it was a Friday and I had nothing better to do than go home, to where Evie would be deep in some library book about hook-and-eye fastenings or the history of PVC. I would think about doing my homework, to get it out of the way, but I would not do it, of course, until Sunday night; I would eat Petit Filou yogurts from the fridge, although I did not especially like them.

'Nora?'

At my name, I turned, and with a slight but muscular movement that he'd almost certainly not have noticed as deliberate, I flicked my hair so that it swung round in front of me, like a matador's cape. Like I said, when it's brushed, my hair becomes a kind of dream-catcher of light, gauzy and burnt-umber and, in my opinion, one of my best attributes. The hair-flick may be a cheap trick, and an old one, but we must all choose our weapons wisely. I didn't take too long about it, though. Flick, turn, smile . . . and—

'Hey, Mr Trace.'

And there he was, approaching, and – a good sign, this – slowing down as he neared my corner. We were just close enough to the school grounds for him still to be wearing his (metaphorical) teacher's hat; some teachers never took them off, but I doubted he'd be one of them, with all his jovial chat about his girlfriend. He'd shared some details at the previous day's Life Class: her name was Helen; she was also a teacher, of Modern Languages; she was allergic to his parents' cat. I wondered whether, as a staff member, he was going to tell me to stop loitering.

We would see.

'Which way are you walking?' he said.

I hesitated. I realised I should have tracked his moped-less journey one time, just to see what his usual route was. Now there was only a fifty-fifty chance that I'd get it right. The flipped coin hung in the air.

'To the tube,' I said.

'So am I,' said Jonah Trace.

And fell into step beside me.

For a few minutes, neither of us spoke. The hostility he'd shown in class seemed not to be present at all, and I wondered why. Then I realised: he'd been told, or had decided, to be strict, especially at the start; he'd used me for target practice, and that was all. It did not make it any more forgivable, mind. Then, as we neared the shops, Jonah Trace began to talk. He asked me about my route home, which I explained. I told him where I lived, and he mentioned that he knew the estate: it was a fine example of Brutalism, he said. Had I heard of that? I had, yes.

I asked him if he had any nice plans for the weekend, and he told me about a mate's BBQ (two words I have never willingly used until now, 'mate' and 'BBQ') in Streatham. Everything about Jonah Trace was ordinary: his skin was ordinary, with its round rough patches on each cheek and glint of oiliness around the nose. His hair was ordinary, despite his efforts with gel, which made it look even more ordinary. His clothes (rust-red jumper, rumpled tie, white shirt, dark trousers) betrayed no personality at all, although I knew that teachers often tried to promote this on purpose. His language was ordinary. His voice, with its soft round vowels that made me think of honey poured from a honeycomb, was more interesting, but on the whole, as far as I could see, Jonah Trace was nothing if not deeply average.

'How about you?' he said, as we walked past the old piano factory. 'Have you got any plans?'

'Nothing much,' I said. 'My mum's working. I have a date tonight with the *Alien* box-set. The original quadrilogy, that is. I might not get through all of them, but there's always tomorrow.'

At this, he dropped his pace by a couple of beats per

minute and threw me a glance that I knew without looking contained surprise, interest, pleasure.

'They're my favourite films,' he said. 'It's interesting that . . . that you . . .'

'What, because I'm a girl?'

'No. Well, yeah.'

'Ellen Ripley's my heroine,' I said.

And I pressed START on my internal voice recorder, and began. I compared the relative strong points of *Alien* and *Aliens* – the first really a horror film, the second more action than horror – but how I liked both almost equally; I lamented the omission of Newt and Hicks from *Alien³*, and digressed into the on-set difficulties they'd had with that tricky third film. And yet, I said, it was the fourth, with its heart-tweaking final sequence, that I liked the least, that despite some standout scenes (one of the most prominent being Ripley's discovery of her many aborted, mutant selves) I found I couldn't enjoy it quite as much. Too much like a cartoon, I said.

'I agree with you there,' said Jonah Trace. 'As for the rest of the franchise, well . . . what do you make of those?'

I sighed dramatically. 'The less said about them the better,' I told him.

'Spot on,' said Jonah Trace, as I had known he would. 'Careful now.'

We had come to a pelican crossing. He put his hand out towards my arm as we crossed, just as he had done with

Megan Lattismore in Life Class. Would he touch it? I think he thought better of the gesture: we were not at school, and I was not a child. But I'd seen him raise his arm, nonetheless, just for a moment.

'You said your mother's working this weekend. What does she do?'

'She works in costume. Design, wardrobe mistressing, that kind of thing. Mostly TV, but theatre too sometimes.'

'Oh, right. Did you get your love of sci-fi from her, then? Or was it from your dad?'

I glanced at him. 'My father's dead,' I said.

'Sorry. I'm sorry.'

I realised that he repeated himself when he was uncomfortable.

'Look,' said Jonah Trace, when we got to the station. 'I think we got off on the wrong foot somehow, at school. I . . .'

I wasn't sure how he planned to finish the thought and, clearly, neither was he, because he let it trail off, like a fade-to-black ending to a film. To help him out, I gave him a smile. He smiled back, and it was a nice enough smile, at first. And then I saw it again: the slipping of a mask, as he looked me over. That sleepy, lidded look, that I'd seen on him before. And then it was gone.

'You're a promising young artist, Nora,' he said.

'See you,' I said. 'Have a lovely weekend.'

7

A week after that, we were paid a visit by my Aunt Petra.

Once upon a time, before Evie met my dad on the steps of the National Gallery (he thought she was a mime artist, apparently, and threw tulips at her boots), she had a stall in Greenwich Market where she sold handmade earrings and leather belts, and incense and Indian tablecloths, and flaky, tie-dyed candles. And she shared the running of this stall with a girl called Petra McBride. Though Petra was short and fat while my mother was beanpole tall; though Petra wore nothing but colour and my mother wore nothing but black, they essentially shared the same traits and values: compassion, freedom of expression, open-mindedness and so on. When my parents got married at a church in Rouen, Petra was Maid of Honour, resplendent in a maroon kaftan; when my father died, Petra was there at Dover to meet us. She had married a large, slow man called William Quick and moved to the Rosneath Peninsula, where they opened a kind of retreat called the Seat of Tranquillity, where, as you know, I am writing this now. Evie went there, once, after she gave up the booze, and said it was the silentest place you could ever imagine, where the only sounds were the rain and the noises in your imagination. 'It made me want a McDonald's so *bloody* much,' she said. 'But I felt pretty chilled out, by the end.'

It sounded terrible to me, but I was fond of Aunt Petra. My mother didn't have a lot of genuine friends, and on the occasions that she came to London, Petra always stayed with us. When I got home from Life Class, Evie was in a rare state of excitement, putting the best sheets on the sofa bed, and baking biscuits in Petra's honour.

'What's she coming down for?' I asked my mother.

'She's doing some course at the weekend,' said Evie vaguely; she was only interested in courses if they involved beading.

Late on Friday evening, Petra appeared at our door, with a large suitcase, two bunches of chrysanthemums and a small mixed-breed terrier on a lead. The terrier burst into the flat before his mistress, shedding a cloud of white-rat fur, and raked his little claws down the front of Evie's legs.

'You haven't met Oscar, have you?' said Aunt Petra.

'He's a welcome surprise,' said Evie, who preferred reptiles.

'Oh, did I not tell you I was bringing the dog? It's just that Bill's in Edinburgh this weekend. I knew you wouldn't mind.'

Over tea, she told us about her plans. Her course, she told us, was called 'Spiritual Awareness for Beginners', and would be held over two days at the world-renowned Institute of Psychic Development in East Finchley.

'After so many years of reading about the spirit world,' said Aunt Petra, dipping shortbread into her tea, 'I realised I'd never investigated my own, well, psychic potential.'

Aunt Petra, just so you know, is about as potentially psychic as a sanitary towel.

The two-day course would cover everything, she said, from the astral planes and the chakras to the basics of telemetry, flower readings and mediumship. And all for the moderate price of £175, which would include refreshments.

'Do you have a specific goal?' I asked Aunt Petra, thinking of the Learning Objectives so beloved by my school.

'Well, yes, I do. So many of the people that come to the retreat are seeking something; they seem so lost, so unable sometimes to find their own spiritual path, and I feel like I'd be able to help them better if I could point them in the right direction. Whether that's through the Tarot, or the Angels, or some other method, I'm not quite sure. I shall do this course as a starting point, to see what talent, if any, I possess.'

Absent-mindedly, my mother picked up Oscar the white-rat terrier and held him on her knees. I wondered what she was thinking about.

'Evelyn!' said Aunt Petra. 'Why don't you come too? There may still be places.'

'Do you know,' said Evie, 'I think I might. It might be interesting.' She looked at me sideways.

'No,' I said immediately. 'Thank you, but no.'

They were up at six the next morning, gossiping like school-girls and making French toast and fennel tea. It reminded me how seldom I had sleepovers with Perfect, in her pink-and-gold bedroom, or Fred, who shared a room with her sister, or Sangeeta, who hated mess. It occurred to me, as it had done before, that Evie would make a better teenager than I would.

'Now, Nora,' said Aunt Petra, 'I'm leaving you in charge of Oscar. Is that all right?'

I looked bleakly at Oscar's stuffed white face. He looked back at me with distrust. 'Sure,' I said.

What, I wondered, would she have done if I'd said no? Taken him with her, I supposed. While they clattered about, putting on coats and shoes, packing water bottles and books to read on the bus, I entertained a vision of a circle of earnest men and women, each ready to embark on his or her path towards Spiritual Awareness, and Oscar right at the centre, with his eyes closed in silent meditation.

Aunt Petra explained to me the schedule of Oscar's needs, from what and when I had to feed him to how long he preferred to spend walking in order to evacuate his bowels.

'We'll be fine,' I said, not really listening. 'Don't worry.'

They'd be back in time for dinner, they told me. My

mother – unusually – kissed me goodbye. Then they were gone, and I was left alone with a pink-eyed, ferret-faced dog, who hated me. As soon as the front door swung shut, he leaped proprietorially onto the chair I usually sat in and growled softly whenever I approached. I wasn't fussed; we did not need to be friends. I did a little more work on Evie's laptop. Then I went back to bed and slept for a couple of hours. It was the start of half term and I had no interest in being up early.

When I woke, Oscar was sitting on my bedroom floor, with the same distrusting expression; I interpreted it this time as hunger. I offered him a bowl of something that looked like hole-less Cheerios, which he ate with enormous enthusiasm. I cleared his bowl away. He was still looking at me with a distrusting expression.

'Let's go for a walk,' I said.

He immediately launched into a tribal dance, circling crazily on his hind legs like a wind-up circus toy. I clipped his lead to his collar, and he began to bark with a kind of urgent, high-pitched quack. A baby in the flat beneath us started to wail.

'Shut up, shut up,' I hissed, toeing him out of the door.

It was only as we were halfway down the fire escape that I realised that today was the ten-year anniversary of my father's death.

I took Oscar to the park for a short while, keeping an eye on the time, letting him go about his canine business.

Then we walked for the best part of an hour in a westerly direction, along the river. My father, who was easily lost wherever he went, used to say that you could always find your way if you followed the river. Oscar and I kept up a fairly brisk pace as we passed the spot where Evie had once tried to go for an ill-advised swim. It was sometimes a struggle to keep him out of the gutter, but in general he wasn't too tricky to handle.

I wondered how Evie and Aunt Petra were doing, and whether they had got onto Past Life Regression yet. I had a sneaky interest in Past Lives; I quite liked the idea of having lived through some place and time and circumstances that bore no relation to my own. Evie had probably been a vampire, I decided, while Petra . . . I saw her as a kindly old washerwoman. I told Oscar that he would have been a locust in Ancient Egypt, or maybe a germ of some kind.

Now that I knew what day it was, I kept seeing the date everywhere I looked. There it was on a rusted news-stand; there it was on a poster at a bus stop.

Had Evie forgotten?

No, I decided: she hadn't. We did not observe the anniversary of the death of my father, you see, other than with a silent hug or a quick, soulful catching of each other's eyes. Long ago we made the decision to celebrate his life, and not his death; we marked his summer birthday, not his autumn demise. It was better that way. That was why she had kissed me goodbye, I thought. She wanted me to know: she hadn't forgotten.

'Did you know,' I said to the rat, 'that my father died ten years ago today, exactly?'

Tell me about it, said Oscar, doing a quick 360-degree shuffle and crapping on the pavement. As soon as he was done, I hustled him on, before anyone could accost me. Dogsitting was enough of a task; I wasn't going to clean up after him as well, not unless Aunt Petra was planning on paying me.

'Well, young sir,' I said. 'It just so happened that my father, a very quiet man who hated crowds, was in a terrible hurry one day, and he needed to get across Paris *très rapidement* in order to meet with a magazine editor. So he did something which, for him, was most unusual. Instead of taking his bicycle, he decided to get on the Métro. It was a complicated journey my father had to take, changing not twice but three times. And he was a shy, anxious man, very easily discomposed. But we know, from where he was found, that he'd taken the right trains and changed at the right junctions, two times out of three. The third time, he missed his stop. So he was still on the train, Oscar, when the Unfortunate Tragedy took place. Perhaps there was a signal failure of some kind, or perhaps the driver fell asleep – we will never be sure. But the train was still travelling at high speed when it collided with another . . . and Oscar, there were no survivors from my father's carriage.'

Oscar, nose-deep in the gutter, failed to react with quite the shock and horror that I'd been anticipating.

'Heartless brute of a rat,' I said. 'You are not paying attention.'

He got hold of a chicken bone, green with decay, and I spent a while wrestling it from him. The kerfuffle resulted in some piteous howls, but I won and he lost, and on we walked. From a not-too-horrible-looking bakery I bought a few small cakes. Some I would save for Evie and Petra. Another I ate, crumb by crumb, dropping the occasional morsel for Oscar as I walked. Soon there was nothing left but a frill of damp paper. As I dropped it into a bin, I found myself wondering when I would stop telling those stories about the death of my father, and who I would be – what sort of person – if so.

Finally, the Rat and I diverged from the river path and made our way through the eye-candy streets of Fulham. I'd made a careful study of the route before we left, as I do not like to track my progress with my phone when I'm out and about. I find it distracts me too much. I checked the time. Just about perfect, I reckoned, if I'd done my research correctly.

By the time Oscar and I reached the Stamford Bridge football stadium, the cacophony of chanting told me that the match was about to end. I knew that Jonah Trace was a Chelsea supporter. When he'd told Annabel that he went to the footie, this, surely, was what he'd meant. It was another kind of temple, I realised.

'Now, where to wait?' I said aloud to Oscar.

This was new terrain. It wasn't Lady Agatha's, where I knew the geography well. In the end, I settled for a nonchalant lamppost, in sight of the main entrance. There was, I thought, a low-ish chance of this experiment working. But what else did I have to do with my Saturday, other than experiments of this kind? I fished out the package of cakes and shared another with Oscar. They were oversweet, lemony, quite delicious. Mentally I made a note: we would wait ten minutes, perhaps fifteen, and then take a bus back home.

But we did not have to wait even half that time.

A hand touched the back of my arm, and I'd been expecting it, but I jumped in surprise as anyone would if a strange hand touched them in the street, while they are midway through a cake of lemony sweetness.

'Oh!' I said.

'Sorry, so sorry,' said Jonah Trace. 'I didn't mean to startle you. Fancy seeing you here! You haven't just come out, have you?'

He was with a handful of people. Nodding at them in an I'll-catch-you-up way, he bent down to pet Oscar's head. Oscar, rather sluttishly, looked pleased by this attention.

'No,' I said. 'We just went for a walk. I'm dogsitting.'

This sounded noble.

'But you don't live round here, do you?'

'My aunt does,' I said.

'I love dogs,' said Jonah Trace. This, of course, I knew

already, along with most of his other likes and dislikes. His social media profile pages were all publicly viewable, and concealed little.

'So do I,' I said.

A blue tide of football enthusiasts washed us down the road.

'How was the game?' I said. I considered asking some questions that would indicate that I, too, was a Chelsea supporter, but I didn't. Firstly, I hadn't had time to properly revise. Secondly, I didn't think I could carry it off. I'm not a fan of the half-hearted lie. But I listened intelligently as he described a match of indescribable dullness, clinched by a single, victorious penalty just before the final whistle.

Then, as we came to a street corner, I said, 'My favourite café is just near here. Do you know the Troubadour?'

He beamed at me. 'Seen a couple of acoustic gigs there not too long ago. I dunno – I'm meant to head to a mate's house, but – d'you fancy a coffee there now? I feel . . . I owe you a coffee. To make up for the ambi— the two-handed thing. I was so totally shit scared, those first few weeks at school. I feel like I singled you out unnecessarily.'

I said I quite understood. We crossed the road. This time he touched my arm, as though to protect me from the waiting traffic. Oscar, forging across to the opposite pavement with a wag of tufty tail, seemed to be in an unusually cheerful mood, which would soon be enhanced by a gift of bacon from a waiter at the Troubadour.

Although I hadn't been for years, I did know the Troubadour. Evie had a penchant for their Full English breakfasts. Famous for its history of players (Bob Dylan and Jimi Hendrix had filled its basement with noise in the 1960s) and its window display full of variegated teapots, the Troubadour drew a mixed crowd of artistic locals and grungy tourists. My father would have liked it, for sure. That Jonah Trace liked it too, I did, of course, already know.

And I also knew this: he liked me. Already.

Quite a lot.

I smiled up at him through my eyelashes as he held open the café door.

8

After a day of Psychic Awareness, my mother looked wan, and Aunt Petra looked elated. 'Oh,' she said, as though I'd had a choice, 'it *was* good of you to look after Oscar.'

'He was no trouble,' I said. 'We went for a walk. Sat in a café.'

'Did he eat his kibble?'

'Yeah.'

I made no mention of the bacon gift. I had an idea that Oscar was also supposed to be a vegetarian. I watched as he wound himself around Petra's portly ankles, and listened to Evie and Petra describing their day, their accounts and impressions spilling over each other like competing radio stations.

'And what *about* the man in the khaki jumper!' Aunt Petra was saying.

Evie, who was now on the phone to our local Indian restaurant, rolled her eyes, saying: 'Graham! Ugh.'

'What about him?' I said.

'Peshwari naan or regular?'

'Regular,' I said, at the same time as Aunt Petra, ever sweet of tooth, said, 'Peshwari!'

'Make it two of each,' said Evie. 'Mutter paneer. Sag aloo – no, sag gobi. Mushroom rice for three. And that's everything, thanks.' She hung up the phone and exhaled. 'Really,' she said, 'I just don't know . . . how far I was really able to suspend my disbelief, if you see what I mean. You have to be essentially open-minded to begin with – if you're an absolute cynic, you're not going to pay good money to attend, are you? But then . . . there's always a moment where you look around, and everyone's holding hands and sniffing the air and imagining their sodding chakras opening up like roses and you just think: "Oh, Lord, I have to get out of here!" Don't you?'

'Evelyn, really?' said Aunt Petra. 'I thought you were enjoying yourself.'

'Oh, I was.' My mother caught my eye and smiled. 'They just wouldn't let me drink my coffee in there. Caffeine messes with the energy fields. Apparently.' She rolled her eyes again, very subtly.

I listened as Aunt Petra gave a detailed account of the day's activities, from a thorough review of the different 'planes' – physical, etheric, astral – to a session at the end of the day 'tuning in' to each other's energies. The group had spent a long time practising the opening and closing of the chakras. The chakras were seven energy points, each with a different associated colour and with a different location on the body.

'How did it feel?' I said.

'Oh, astonishing,' said Aunt Petra. 'Like opening a jewellery box inside oneself.'

'I dunno. I just felt hungry,' said my mother. 'My stomach kept rumbling. My problem was, I couldn't see what I was supposed to see: you were meant to think of these different coloured flowers opening up and the energy flowing through them, and I'm just not visual like that. You'd have been brilliant at it, Nora. With your imagination.'

'I don't think you tried hard enough,' said Aunt Petra to my mother, earnestly. 'Truly, it was the most empowering sensation.'

I have always been interested in the concept of tuning in to other people, and I found myself listening closely to Aunt Petra's tale. After the chakras were open, each took a turn at sitting in the middle of the circle, eyes firmly closed, mind open. The rest – eyes also closed – tried to pick up images, thoughts, and memories from the sitter's head. After five or six minutes of silent contemplation, all eyes would be opened, chakras paused or dimmed or whatever the correct expression should be, and the tuners-in would each report what it was that they had seen. The results, as described to me, sounded full of curious discoveries. The man in the khaki jumper, Graham – who apparently had been very quiet all day – was one of the last to sit in the middle of the circle.

'One of the first things I saw – absolutely clearly too – was a red tractor, outside a tractor shed, on a farm,' said

Aunt Petra. 'And when I said as much, Graham looked so surprised – I'm sure he wasn't faking this at all – and said that he'd been deliberately thinking of a tractor the entire time! There was one next to his house in Ireland when he was a child.'

So saying, she relaxed her frame into the sofa, as though the entire realm of the Occult had now been categorically proven to exist. On the TV screen behind, highlights of the Chelsea game were flickering. The match looked just as dull as Jonah Trace had made it sound.

'Was it red?' I asked.

'I'm sorry?'

'Was Graham's tractor red? The one he was thinking of?'

Aunt Petra was explaining tersely that the redness or otherwise of said tractor was hardly the point, when the buzzer sounded from the street; our takeaway had arrived.

Oscar, for some reason, insisted on sleeping on my bed that night. I didn't know our relationship had developed so much. It made it really impossible to get to sleep, particularly since I had just watched *Alien* for the second time, in case Jonah Trace and I ever discussed it in finer detail. Around midnight, I went to the kitchen for some water. I saw that Evie's light was on. Crossing the hallway, I knocked softly on her door.

I heard feet on floorboards; the door opened and Evie stood there in a Where's Wally nightdress and bright pink socks. She had obviously been crying.

'What's the matter?' I said.

'Don't wake Petra,' she said. 'Come in.'

I sat on the edge of her bed while she climbed back into it. 'What really happened today?' I asked her.

She took her time.

'There was just so much desire in the room,' she said eventually. 'You could feel it. I saw a black-and-white film, once, a long time ago, about a row of broken toys in Santa's workshop, and they all just wanted to be fixed so they could be packed onto the sledges by the elves and taken away. We were like those broken toys. The people in the group. Just wanting to be . . . I don't know, healed.'

'Even Aunt Petra?'

She shook her head, and said, 'I don't know. When it was her turn to sit in the middle, I switched off completely. I couldn't peer inside the head of my oldest friend. Not that I'd have been able to anyway, I suppose.'

'What about when you sat in the middle? Did you feel . . . peered into?' As I said this, I felt a little shiver of sympathy: I couldn't stand the thought of allowing myself to be scrutinised, like somebody's crystal ball.

'Oh, no. That bit was funny. This Russian girl said she saw "a really English childhood, with a castle in it". As if! Your grandad worked at a car dealership; we lived above a fishmonger's. It really wasn't my thing, any of it. I mean, let's face it. It's all a big lie, isn't it? So many lies we tell ourselves.'

I said nothing, waiting.

Evie's room had changed over the years. It was still over-stuffed with clothes, but now they were lovingly stored, ranged from light to dark (mostly dark) in her custom-built closets. The ashtrays and drink-rings were gone. Books were piled like bricks beneath the window. Her favourite pieces of clothing – a Vivienne Westwood basque, a Harlequin costume, a Pucci bikini – were hung on padded hangers around the walls, like museum exhibits. In the dim light of her bedside lamp, they floated like watchful ghosts.

My mother said: 'I thought I'd find out how to reach him. Somehow.'

'Reach him?'

'Your dad,' said Evie. 'I wanted to see him again.'

9

After my father died, we left Paris. We had only rented our apartment, somewhere east of Bastille, but my father had owned a run-down cottage – a *gîte* – near a Normandy beach, where we'd spent our summers. This he left to my mother, and although it proved difficult to sell at first, eventually she succeeded in parting with it. I was sad about the cottage. It wasn't until later that I understood why Evie had wanted to sell it.

Tiny, as all my parents' spaces were, the cottage had only five rooms. There was a funny mezzanine-level micro-bedroom, where I slept. The bathroom had a pea-green bath and a blue-veined sink. My parents slept next to the kitchen, in a room that overlooked a handkerchief of a garden. The fifth and last room was scarcely more than a cupboard. This is where my father drew his illustrations. It had a shelf of a desk, no wider than an ironing board; when he worked, I sat beneath it, as a pet would, listening to the scratch-scratch of his dip pen, and his irregular, drawn-out sighs. For many years, the cottage would appear in my dreams – sometimes as itself, and at other times disguised, like a gingerbread house.

If Evie thought that by leaving France behind, that by crossing the Channel one final time, our possessions sold in the Sunday markets, she would also be leaving her sadness, she was wrong. For the next three years, my mother made a vault of her sadness and buried herself inside it. I was cared for in our flat in London by my grandmother, Nana Finocchi, a tiny and fearsome Scot who had buried three husbands (the last from Argentina by way of Venice), seemingly without blinking an eyelid in sorrow. Nana slept on our sofa bed and stuffed me full of cosmopolitan goodies: shortbread, of course, and *alfajores*, the sickeningly sweet sandwiches of *dulce de leche* and cake that she brought from trips to Buenos Aires. Although she was by nature frugal, Nana Finocchi had money; the dead Argentine had dealt profitably in antiques.

'Leave her be,' she would say, when Evie spent each day in a kind of glassy reverie and a Victorian nightgown. 'She'll come out when she's ready.'

But Evie did not want to come out.

So Nana kept us afloat. It was Nana who took me to school, her arthritic fingers knotted in mine for the whole of the twenty-minute walk; it was Nana who cooked and cleaned, and it was Nana who read to me at bedtime. Along with long tracts from the Old and New Testament, which she was able to recite from memory, Nana had an arsenal of fairy tales. Tales of the selkies and the kelpies, of mermaid brides and water horses, ogres and angry fishermen. Tales that drew me out of myself completely and took me away to a place of peace and safety.

And it was Nana, and her many tales, that stayed the same, while Evie changed.

For a time, I thought she was changing for the better. About two and a half years after we first came to London, she suddenly seemed to wake up. She swapped her dole cheques and occasional stints in flower shops for a bartending job in Brixton. Evie had a Romantic's attachment to British pubs, where the carpets were stained with nostalgia and bells were rung for last orders. But it turned out not to be a good idea. Her vault of sadness opened up; the whole of London became her vault. She was still buried, but she no longer knew it.

I have no intention of going into this in any great detail, because this is not a story about that, but for the next year or so (my timeline is patchy), Evie went about the slow, steady business of drinking herself to death. She acquired a set of new, loud friends; this was unusual, for as far as I could remember the only friends my mother had ever had were Petra and my father. The friends seemed to shuffle and reshuffle; their faces changed, but not their raucous voices. I mistook Evie's merriment for joy; at first, this was easy to do, but her day-after aches and sorrows seemed to magnify whatever silent sadness had gone before. The flat smelled sweet and sour; bottles multiplied outside the door; I caught the neighbours staring at me and Nana, some mornings, on our way to school.

I will report a single, final incident. A turning point, if you like.

A Sunday morning. Nana had taken the bus to church, packed into her floral-sprigged blouse and tweed suit, her stub-heeled churchgoing shoes. I was alone in the flat. I did not know where Evie was. (By the way, I don't want, at any point, for you to try and feel sorry for me. You'll see that I don't deserve it. Also: I hate pity.) I decided to make scrambled eggs. Nana's excessive fondness for sweet things left me craving, at other times, savoury salty foodstuffs. Stilton, Marmite. A plate of eggs on toast: that is what I wanted. I must have been nine, nearly ten years old. There was no bread for toast, only some rather stale crispbread. I beat two eggs into a bowl; I took from the kitchen drawer a box of long Swan matches. And here I paused.

I was terrified – terrified – of lighting the gas.

No wraith in Nana's stories inspired as much fear in me as the prospect of a sticky ball of methane, swelling unchecked like some solar flare until it self-ignited in a burst of sudden fury, taking me and the rest of the flat with it. I had no doubt that it was possible, even likely.

I depressed the lower-left knob and twisted. At once, that sinister hiss started up, almost tuneful. I could not bear it. I twisted the dial back, so sharply I could have wrenched it off completely. I tried again, and again was thwarted by

71

the sound of it. I struck a match and blew it out. I was hungry, and I could have cried for disappointment. And then it came to me, with total suddenness: I wanted my mother. Not Nana, and not even my dead father, who would be no good to me in his present state. I wanted my *mother*.

Just then, there came a loud knock on the door.

'Alison! ¿Alison, *estás aquí?*'

It was Mrs DeAndrade. She lived a couple of floors down from us and was on friendly terms with my grandmother. It was only my insistent hunger that took me to the door; I was extremely shy as a child and I did not like to speak to people, even people I knew. But Mrs DeAndrade would be able to light the gas. She might even stay with me for the duration of my egg-scrambling, so as to turn it safely off again.

'Aliénor! Are you there, *chiquitita?*'

I went to the door. The flats in our building overlooked on the inside a large interior courtyard where, some twenty or thirty metres below, a play area and a thin crescent of pinkish flowers provided the only break in an otherwise grey landscape. The vast silhouette of Mrs DeAndrade waited against the railing. I opened the door, and she rushed in, talking at first in Spanish in her excitement, and then, realising that Nana had gone to church, in English.

'Your mother is in the river.'

Down the fire escape we went, for quickness. It was a stark, bleak day, though I can only guess at the month.

Mrs DeAndrade, ever cautious, made us cross at the crossing, something Evie never did, since it was a fair way down the road. And now we came to the concrete wall on the other side of the road that separated the pavement from the drop down to the Thames.

'*La pobrecita*,' Mrs DeAndrade kept saying. '*La pobrecita*.' *Poor thing*. I didn't know whether she meant me, or Evie.

Evie was not in the river; that was lost in translation from Spanish to English, or else Mrs DeAndrade was merely skipping ahead, and predicting that sooner or later she would be. Evie was next to the river, at its very edge, on the narrow stretch of pebbles and piled-up driftwood, of stray plastic bags and discarded bottles. She had drawn quite a crowd of watchers; we had to push our way through them, to ask them to clear a space at the railings which Evie must, somehow, have climbed over in order to get down there. Her leather trousers, sleeveless vest, jacket, bra and knickers were folded neatly on the ground. Evie stood, naked, not unlike a marble statue, with her back to the audience, facing the tide. In one hand, she held a box of Tesco wine. Slowly, she put the box down.

Then, with the air of a pleased tourist on a sun-kissed beach, she waded in.

I have no doubt at all that if she'd got very far into the river, she'd have drowned. The crosscurrents of the Thames are mighty and fearful, and Evie was no swimmer. Mrs DeAndrade always called me, as indeed she had done that morning, *chiquitita*. It meant 'little girl', but was taken from a television programme about orphans, she'd told me once. That stone-cold Sunday was the closest I came, probably, to orphanhood.

Two policemen in reflective jackets got to my mother before the tide did.

I waited until the evening before going in to see her. Her room was a crypt of unwashed clothes, of Pepsi cans and beer bottles and loose coins. A deck of playing cards was spilled carelessly on the bedside table. Evie was sitting up in bed. She was wearing her Victorian nightgown, and I thought: here we go. Back into the vault. Another wall of silence, to replace the wall of noise. She wasn't crying; Evie didn't cry much. With one hand she kept twisting at a jewelled ring in her left ear, as though she were trying to unlock something inside herself. She looked up when she saw me.

'I thought you were going to die,' I said, which was a long sentence for me, and a true one. And then: 'I want some scrambled eggs.'

She pulled me down next to her and hugged me, reaching all the way around me, holding onto me for warmth, but trying to give warmth back at the same time.

'I don't want to die,' she said. 'Not any more.'

Had it not been for Nana, who'd swept in to claim me from the police station with all the force of a miniature hurricane in a tight tweed suit, I might have been taken away from Evie. And she knew that. She cut up her Victorian nightgown, saying she'd spent too long in it, but marvelling at the delicacy of the stitching as she did so. She lit the gas burner and she made scrambled eggs for all of us. She drained the flat of alcohol, pouring it all down the kitchen sink till there was nary a drop to drink.

A fortnight later, she sent in her application to college.

10

'Nora,' said Jonah Trace. 'You heading to the tube?'

It so happened that I was one of the last students to leave the studio after Life Class. Only Megan Lattismore remained, lacing her trainers in the corridor leading to the stairs. It was the first week back after half term. A row of pumpkins, relics from Halloween, carved by the girls in Year Seven, squatted on the windowsill. Had Jonah Trace been more observant, he might have perceived warnings in their toothy snarls. It is not appropriate to offer to walk to the tube station with a student. He ought to have known that. It is not appropriate to hold her hand, however briefly, when crossing the road. And it is not appropriate to ask her out for coffee, which he had already done, once before.

What he was about to do was inappropriater still.

We went to a branch of Costa – not the usual one, frequented by Lady Agatha girls on their way home, but a smaller one in a shopping complex ten minutes away. We talked, as we usually did, about football and science fiction, mostly the *Alien* films, since we knew we had these very much in common. We talked about music and art. His favourite artists were Lichtenstein and Pollock. Teaching, for him, was more of a temporary measure; what he really wanted to do was work in special effects, though he had a fuzzy idea of how this might be achieved. And although his flatmate was called Helen, and she was indeed a teacher of French and Spanish, she was not his girlfriend, and had never met his parents' cat. He had decided to make up a girlfriend, he informed me, in order to protect himself from the advances of love-struck teens. He thought this was very amusing.

Jonah Trace was drinking a cappuccino. I had a hot chocolate, which he insisted on paying for.

'Hot chocolate, that's very French,' he commented, rather inanely. 'Your dad was French, right?'

'That's right.'

'When did he die, if you don't mind talking about it?'

'Ten years ago,' I said. 'It was an oyster. He loved oysters, my dad. Half a dozen, with lemon juice and rock salt, eaten in seconds. They reminded him of his childhood.'

I paused, then continued.

'So one evening he was out with my mum, at some bistro in Paris, and he ordered oysters. But one of them must have been bad – wrongly stored, I guess, and infected with this rare bacterium called *Vibrio* . . . *Vibrio vulnificus*. It didn't just make him sick. It got into his bloodstream, which can happen sometimes. He got these ulcers that opened up on his arms and legs, really terrifying . . . they were taking off bits of his flesh – *debridement*; I don't know the English word – horrible – and then they started talking about amputating his right arm, and my mother was crying, all wild and irrational, and saying, "But he needs it for his work!"'

'Jesus.'

'My dad was ambidextrous, like I am, so maybe he'd have been able to use his left . . . but it was too late, by that point. He went into shock. And then he died. The whole thing took less than thirty-six hours; it didn't feel real at all. We scattered his ashes on the Left Bank, by moonlight. Just me and my mum.'

All the time I'd been speaking I'd been looking down at the toggles of Jonah Trace's duffel coat; now, I looked up at him. I hoped I'd got it right: the balance of gruesomeness and pathos. I'd chosen Obscure Illness on account of Jonah Trace's obsession with horror films: as well as *Alien*, he was an aficionado of Cronenberg films like *Shivers* and *The Fly*. I thought he'd appreciate the gore, although I didn't lay it on too strong. I thought he'd be moved.

'You poor, poor thing,' said Jonah Trace.

He really did have very good teeth: I pictured a sunlit, rural childhood, full of milk and Cornish butter.

'I think you're the bravest girl I've ever met.'

'I don't feel that brave,' I said.

'You've got low self-esteem,' he said seriously. 'It's been hard for you. You haven't had things easy. When you think of . . . I dunno, someone like Annabel Ingram, in the year above you. You know who her parents are, right?'

I shook my head.

'Her dad's Anton Ingram. He's a cult producer. Made some incredible movies. And her mother was an actress, a really famous one, though I can't think of her name just now. She's probably loaded, Bel. She can do what she likes. She's privileged.'

I listened to this with interest.

'Bel's cool,' Jonah Trace went on. 'But she's never had to deal with anything much, has she? You, Nora . . . you're a proper survivor. I know I shouldn't say this, but . . . I like you. I really, really like you.' He laid his hand – a sweaty and solid weight – over mine. He was waiting, I knew, for a response.

I could freeze this frame, for a second. The art assistant sitting opposite me, a film of milk foam on his upper lip. We could be a couple of characters in a Quentin Tarantino movie. Coffee-drinkers babbling in the background; the hum of machinery.

What did my face show, at that moment? Surprise, intrigue, disgust?

I had a choice – of what to say next – and I made it.

'Jonah,' I said. 'I like you too.'

A couple of days later, he kissed me for the first time, as we sat on his duffel coat in a shady corner of Clapham Common. I had my back to a tree; he had his back to the park. Every now and again he would look around, with little, darting glances, for Lady Agatha girls, or people he knew.

It was windy, but not too cold, not yet. They were building a bonfire for Guy Fawkes Night; a man was selling hot chestnuts, and their sticky-sweet scent travelled over to us in the wind. There was a woman walking a motley collection of dogs, one of them not unlike the Rat.

The art assistant leaned forwards, towards me. He drew – he traced – a fingertip around my birthmark.

'My father always said that it looked like France. My mother said it looked like a starfish,' I told him.

He was tentative about hugs and kisses, as well he might have been – and he continued to stress that he knew that what we were doing was totally against school policy. He was very aware of that. He'd never be able to work again, he kept saying, in my school, or in any other, if we got caught.

'But we won't,' he said. 'Not here.'

He pulled me into his arms (cheap aftershave warred with Marlboro Lights), and we embraced.

I stroked his gel-greased hair tenderly, thoughtfully.

With both hands.

Other kisses followed this, and other parks, and other cafés. For several weeks, it went on like this. But he was gone by Christmas, as you know. And Jonah Trace was right: he would never work in another school again.

11

They appointed a new art assistant to replace Jonah Trace. This time it was a woman. She arrived midway through January. Her name was Sharon Alexis; she had a no-nonsense way about her and wasn't shy to tell us if our work was substandard (Annabel's third painting, of a purplish flowering tree, was turning out all the better for her suggestions, I noticed), but to my knowledge she had no interest in looking down the front of our shirts. This was, without doubt, an improvement.

I was never sure exactly how many people knew what had happened to her predecessor. Those who paid close attention to such things might have noticed that a jacket of his remained behind the door to the office in the art studio. There was no mention of him in the Farewell section of the fortnightly newsletter. But the presence of Sharon Alexis made it clear that he was not merely on holiday. The staff, presumably, would have all been told. My form tutor, Sarah Cousins, knew. I had not said anything to anyone else, but I was pretty sure that Fred and Sangeeta and Perfect had guessed that something had happened. By the mathematical laws of gossip-diffusion, the chances were that each of them might have informed, say, two or three people, who in turn would have done, over time, the same.

Nobody asked me about the Trace Incident directly until Lori Dryden cornered me, a couple of weeks into the spring term, in the library. Normally to be found sitting on the bench in the corridor with a tin of Pringles and a copy of *Heat*, as though school were just one big dentist's waiting room, Lori reminded me of a rotund fairy. Her main interest in life was in figuring out – from large, pore-exposing before-and-after shots – which celebrities had succumbed to plastic surgery. It was hard to tell whether she thought it was a virtue or a vice to reshape one's body at will. Though she seemed derisive, she once told me she had a secret bank account, which would eventually pay for a nose job. No one diffused more gossip than Lori, and I knew it was only a matter of time before she sought me out.

'Tell all,' she commanded, having steered me out of the library and into the disabled toilets, where she made herself comfortable on the floor and motioned me onto the closed seat. It wasn't my venue of choice, but a seasoned narrator will make do with whatever her surroundings.

I said, 'I don't really like a lot of people knowing. It makes me feel bad. Guilty, you know? Like I did something wrong.'

'But you didn't do anything wrong,' she said. 'Go on. A problem shared.'

So I told her, and it was – pretty much – what I had told Sarah Cousins in December, only for my form tutor I used a muted watercolour palette, while for Lori it was spray paint and glitter.

'At first I thought he hated me. It was the way he talked to me, in Life Class. Like I was useless at art, which I'm . . . well, I'm not one of the best, but I'm not terrible either. It was, like, he'd made up his mind, he had to have girls he liked and disliked, like that was OK for a teacher.'

All that Lori was missing at this point was popcorn. She goggled up at me from the disinfected floor. 'Go on,' she said.

'And I suppose I started paying attention to him, in the way that I do with people if I get a vibe that they don't like me. It's like I want to make a special effort, if I can. So I noticed the way that he was in class, with the other girls. And with some of them . . . he'd look at them oddly. A bit twitchy, if you know what I mean. Like he wasn't sure if he could control himself. I saw him touch a couple of them, a couple of times. Just on the arm, you know. The shoulder. Megan Lattismore . . .'

'Massive tits,' interjected Lori.

'Massive,' I agreed.

'So the guy was a total perv,' said Lori Dryden, keen to advance to the moral of the story.

'But whatever I'd thought,' I continued, 'I never expected him to . . . choose me. Not after the way he'd spoken to me. Then I thought, you know, perhaps he picked on me because he didn't really fancy me. Anyway . . . it was maybe three or four weeks later that I realised he always seemed to be leaving school to walk to the tube exactly when I was, even if it was different each time. He used to bring a moped to school, but he stopped. It was as if he was, like . . . waiting for me. He always seemed to be there, taking the same route to the station – you know how there's like two different ways you can go – and he started talking to me. Which is totally fine, of course. He's a teacher. But he never talked about school, just his life, and his girlfriend . . .'

'Inappropriate,' said Lori, flexing a wrist to inspect her gelled nails as she trotted out the word.

'And he asked me about my life too. My dad. What I did on the weekends. Sort of harmless . . . but sort of nosy too. If you know what I mean. Oh – and complimenting me. On the way I looked. My hair, my eyes.'

'Inappropriate,' said Lori again. 'Then what?'

'He asked me out.'

'*No.*'

'He did. In Nero. That was my mistake. I shouldn't have gone. He said he wanted to talk; I didn't know what about. We went to Nero, one afternoon, after school, and he asked me out.'

'But *how* did he say it? That is literally the weirdest and creepiest thing I have ever heard,' said Lori.

I took a moment to choose my words. It was at about this point that the script began to deviate from actual events

– as far as I can remember, Jonah and I never visited a branch of Caffè Nero together – and I wanted to be clear.

'Just that he really liked me, and he wanted to spend more time with me . . . it was obvious what he meant. He said he'd split up with his girlfriend. I don't know, by the way, if that was true. I don't even know if he really *had* a girlfriend.'

'And what did you say?'

'I said no, of course.'

Lori exhaled.

'Then I started seeing him round where I lived. It wouldn't be hard, would it, to get hold of my address? All he'd have to do was check on the system at school. There must be some kind of database. Oh, he always had a reason for being there, if we actually bumped into each other and said hi – but my area's a bit dodgy; there's not a lot going on . . . And after the second time, the third time . . . I started feeling like he was definitely, definitely following me. So . . . I tried something. An experiment. It was a weekend, a Saturday. I was out with my mum, doing a bit of shopping. Tesco, Superdrug, some Christmas presents and stuff. We were on our way home when I saw him again, on the other side of the street, far away but still definitely him: his hairstyle, his clothes. Easy to spot. It was starting to freak me out; I'm not going to lie. He didn't come up to me, probably because my mum was there. So I said goodbye to my mum, and I walked along the road and crossed the bridge. Then I carried on, along the South Bank, for maybe twenty or thirty minutes. Just walking, same pace, not looking round. Eventually I came to Borough Market. The place was rammed with tourists, vegetable stalls, burger stands, mince pies . . . I decided that if he was still following me, then it just couldn't be a coincidence, could it? I kind of weaved my way through the market and came out into this tiny alleyway, empty except for some boxes and recycling bins. It was starting to rain, just a bit; I looked in my bag for my umbrella. That's when I felt a hand on my shoulder.'

Lori flinched, with the thrilled empathy of a captive listener. 'OhmyGod,' she muttered.

'He was drunk,' I went on. 'You can always tell, can't you. He grabbed me by both arms – properly grabbed me, so that you could see the marks of his fingers even a couple of days later.'

'And what did he say?'

'I don't remember the *exact* words, but he said something like, "You say Ellen Ripley's your heroine. You *are* Ellen Ripley. You're the bravest girl I've ever met. You're fearless and proud and determined. You're a survivor. I love the way you touch the tip of your nose when you're thinking. I love the way your hair is always messy, even when you brush it. I love the way you tilt your head on one side when you're looking at your work. Both hands . . . you can draw with both hands. You speak French like it's English. Being around

86

you makes me feel . . . electrified, somehow. I just can't go on without you, Nora.'"

I judged it wise to stop there. I'd modulated my voice for Jonah's speech – not so much as to make it a parody, but just enough to give it an authentic gloss that Lori, I was sure, would appreciate. I hated to lapse into clichés, which I'd had to do, but Jonah Trace was not an original thinker.

'Holy Mother of God,' said Lori. 'And did he kiss you?'

'He tried,' I said. 'I slapped his face. And I ran.'

'And then what?'

'Well, I would have still hoped he'd get the message, you know, and leave me alone. But there was a bunch of girls from Chamber Choir, singing carols on the South Bank. A couple of them saw us, and they reported it at school. After that, of course, I had to tell my form tutor, Sarah Cousins. She asked to see the bruises on my arms. And the texts . . . he'd sent me dozens and dozens of texts. I still don't know how he got my number,' I said, getting up. 'The system, again, I suppose.'

12

The first lie that I remember telling was when I was about four years old. I attended a Montessori school near to where we lived in Paris. In the mornings, there were gentle, creative activities, many of which involved potato-printing; in the afternoons, we were laid out like sausages on mats and encouraged to go to sleep. There was a large mural of a beaming sun in a pork pie hat, from whose head sprouted thick orange rays; the word for HELLO in several languages floated in the clouds around him. A beaten-up piano stood in one corner, and there were low red tables with low red stools, where we did most of our activities. All the other children were French.

I need to describe an incident that precedes my first remembered lie. It concerns a child called Toby Lenôtre, and took place some weeks beforehand. The activity was finger-painting. We were invited to copy our full names, in different-coloured capital letters, onto long strips of white cloth. These strips of cloth had some further destination, like a wall display or set of flags, but I forget what it was.

Toby Lenôtre was the kind of child who was always leaking fluids. A ribbon of saliva dangled from his lower lip; snot bubbled permanently from his nose. I think I despised him, in a casual way. I suppose he didn't like me either, although it surprised me, at the time, to discover this. It wasn't the most peaceful of mornings, this one: you can imagine the carnage of a dozen ham-fisted children mangling their own names. But it was the kind of task that pleased me. Mme Peruvier, our teacher, had written in front of me – in solid legible capitals – my name: ALIÉNOR TOBIAS, and I'd decided on a basic but satisfying pattern alternating between red, blue, yellow and green paint. Even at an early age, I was a competent planner.

It just so happened that Toby Lenôtre, he of the leaking fluid, was sitting next to me that day. As was the habit of most of the other children, he was getting more paint on his face than on the strip of cloth in front of him, and I was concentrating on my own creation when I felt a sharp tap on my arm.

All this took place in French, but I will translate it.

'You've stolen my name,' Toby told me shrilly.

'What do you mean?' I said.

He pointed at the plastic table, where both of our printed names lay side by side:

TOBIAS LENÔTRE ALIÉNOR TOBIAS

'I have not stolen your name, silly,' I said. 'Anyway, your name is Toby.'

'It's *Tobias*. You can't have the same name as me. You have stolen it.'

'I have not.'

'Girls can't have the same names as boys, besides.'

'They can.'

'They can't. Thief!'

I imagine this went on for some time. In the end, Mme Peruvier, sensing that Toby's leakage of fluid would shortly be including tears, moved me onto the other table. I went with her perfectly calmly, and continued my painting. But inside I was really quite rigid with rage, as though a hand were balled tight in my chest.

A few weeks later, another finger-painting session was taking place. This time, the work-in-progress for each of us was a rainbow, an *arc-en-ciel*. Around the room various free interpretations were being executed, but I'd learned from my father the seven colours, and although our pots of paint lacked the wherewithal to make both indigo and violet, I was otherwise able to produce a pretty valid example of a rainbow. I was not, incidentally, motivated by wanting to please the teacher, but I did like to get things right.

Mme Peruvier was surprised to find me suddenly tugging at her sleeve in tears.

'*Il a retourné ma feuille,*' I said, with none of my usual calm.

'*Mais qui?*'

'*Toby.*'

My shoulders were shaking; she picked me up for one of her all-enveloping cuddles, and carried me over to where

I had been sitting. Sure enough, my sheet of paper was overturned, and when she peeled it away from the table, all that remained on the page was a smear – the colours I'd taken such pains to render had been merged, mercilessly, into a muddy scar.

Toby Lenôtre was high-pitched, even hysterical, in his protestations. But there were no witnesses, and where he was given to outbursts of crying and often started petty squabbles or made unfounded accusations, dribbling mucus all the while, I did not. Why should the teacher disbelieve me? I was such a placid, unflappable child. Mme Peruvier's judgement was swift. Toby was dispatched to his striped mat for the rest of the day in punishment, while I was given a sweet and a fresh sheet of paper.

I wonder if Toby, wherever he is, ever thinks now of the time he was falsely accused of ruining my rainbow. Maybe he thinks he was guilty. People do, you know. People often remember things wrongly.

Il a retourné ma feuille.

My first-born lie, but not my last.

It was Sarah Cousins who made me remember this, actually.

It was a Monday afternoon in early February, just before half term. A whole-school swimming gala was taking place at the local pool. Although I was a very good swimmer, I was not competing; I had a bad cold. So instead of being down on the poolside benches, I was up in the gallery with the girls who were having their period, the girls who were using this as an excuse, and Sarah Cousins, who was in charge of us.

Everyone in my row was working on a Valentine of some kind. Some were hand-tooling poems in silver pens onto black card; others were cutting out red hearts from swatches of velvet. I was not making a Valentine. I had no one to send a card to, even as a gesture.

'Not working on a card, Nora?' said Sarah Cousins, who was sitting next to me.

I blew my nose, shaking my head. The decibel level in the pool hall was ear-wreckingly high: the screams, the splashes, the megaphone and the whistles were reflected a hundredfold by the tiled walls. It was nearly impossible to hear my form tutor; really, the conversation was mouthed, more than spoken.

'Not even for Mr Trace?'

I glanced at her, not sure if I'd heard this correctly.

She kept her eyes on the swimmers, but her face was angled towards mine; despite the noise, and my cold-congested head, I heard the next bit perfectly.

'See, Nora. I know what you told me, back in December. I know what we went on to discover about Jonah Trace. I saw the marks on your arms, and I read those messages on your phone. But I also know what he told me. We're mates, me and Jonah. You didn't know that, did you?'

I said nothing. Nothing is always safest and best.

'How did your father die, Nora?'

I opened my mouth. Down in the pool, Lori Dryden – a surprisingly nimble athlete, given her frame – was poised, pigeon-toed, on the diving board.

'He . . .'

'He disappeared at sea, didn't he? I've heard you saying that, in the past. But that wasn't what you told Jonah. I think you had better be very, very careful what you make up next.'

'I don't know what you're talking about,' I said.

'I think you do. You're very accomplished, Nora. You're gifted. You have a way with words; you should use it wisely. Now, I'm not saying Jonah wasn't in the wrong. He absolutely admits that what he did wasn't right. But I think that the version you gave me, of what you say happened, was untrue. Do I think you're blameless? No. Not in the slightest. In fact . . .'

At last she met my gaze, with Antarctic eyes that drilled without compassion into mine.

'I think you're a little liar,' my form tutor said.

PART TWO

THE BELLE
OF THE BALL

1

You'd be surprised how few people have ever challenged me. I have a number of theories about why this might be so.

One: I choose my campaigns – both my adversaries and my battlegrounds – with care. The Trace Incident, as I came to call it in my head, was the only time I have ever called attention to myself in a significant way at school, just as the Ruined Rainbow may have been the most fuss I ever made at my Montessori nursery. That is not to say I hadn't told lies during my time at Lady Agatha's, but they were of a lesser, common-or-garden variety, more ingenious in nature perhaps than most other girls', but minor nonetheless. Bread-and-butter lies. Nothing important.

Two: I'm five foot two. If you are small and you want to be heard, you need to be loud; I am not. I speak only when spoken to, and I speak quietly. I dress blandly. I find it better to camouflage myself, like a death's-head moth, than to stand out.

Three: I have a large, shadowy birthmark, a 'characterful' mother, and a father who died in unknown circumstances. This makes me an object of sympathy and pity, and people don't like to spend too long feeling sorry for other people, if they can avoid it. Thus, for the most part, I pass under the radar.

Four: I am very, very good at what I do.

But Ms Sarah Cousins called me a liar, as we sat in the gallery and watched the swimmers.

Distress, and horror and shame. I felt those, and more, and nothing at all. I had been seen, and not just as I might choose to be seen – a girl with a birthmark and ringlet-curls, small in stature. No: my form tutor had identified and named me.

I think you're a little liar.

Her words were a wasp-sting, quick and lethal.

I was cold (and rigid, and livid) with rage. In spite of this, I still had enough of a hold on myself to do the correct thing, which was not to react. I sat next to Sarah Cousins and watched the 4x4 relay and the diving. And then, when there was a break, I smiled at her casually and melted away.

I pushed through the doors at the back of the gallery and came out onto the fire escape. I sat down, folding my arms around my knees, crumpling myself ever-smaller, like a pipe-cleaner doll. I thought of all the different and exciting ways that my form tutor might meet some kind of unhappy fate on her way home. All the poisoned oysters in the world would not do for Ms Sarah Cousins. No: she'd have to be crushed by a herd of rabid elephants, or an errant meteor, or . . . but it was doing me no good, to dwell on this. I almost felt a smidgen of respect for her, with her sheep's heart scalpel and her cut-glass voice. I hadn't seen that one coming at all; otherwise I'd have been prepared for it. I hadn't known she was a friend of Jonah Trace's; I hadn't known he'd have told her so much; I hadn't known that she would believe him. All the times that I'd been with him, I'd never seen him receive a message or a call from my form tutor. Perhaps they were staffroom buddies. The question was: what exactly had Jonah said to her? And was there – could there possibly be – any proof? A scribbled note, a text I'd forgotten to erase from his inbox? I didn't think so. But I could have been wrong.

In the days that followed the swimming gala, the walls of the Agatha Seaford Academy seemed to grow closer and closer together. Everywhere I went, my form tutor's accusation rumbled inside my ear like ocean sounds in a conch. Sometimes, I heard it so clearly that it was hard to tell what was inside my head and what was outside of it. I started to avoid the eyes of other girls. I cancelled a plan I'd made to go out with Frederika. I stopped going to the dining hall and got into the habit of spending my lunch breaks in the library instead, reading or thinking. I had a favourite space, in the furthest corner from the entrance, rather poorly lit. It was the Russian section, and little used; I liked the privacy of it. And it was there that I was sitting, on the Thursday before the February half term, working on an essay about *The Love Song of J. Alfred Prufrock*, when I had my first proper encounter with Bel.

I feel that I will always remember that poem, as a result.

I'd been working for a while, with some Strepsils and a packet of tissues at my elbow – I was finding it hard to get rid of my cold. I got up to look for some kind of reference book. I forget which. But when I returned to 'my' area, I found signs of some other presence. A paper bag from which multi-coloured sweets spilled; a can of Coke; a pack of Tarot cards, much-scuffed; a scarf with a print of fairground horses. Disturbed, I moved my things to the very edge of the table, and turned my chair towards the bookcases. This person was violating library code, and I did not want their chaos to contaminate what I intended to be an absorbing forty minutes contemplating poetry.

'All right, love?' came a voice.

'Hush,' hissed the librarian from her desk.

I looked up guardedly. It was the girl, Annabel, she of the outlandish clothing and twenty-four-hour play, and the three oil paintings, from the year above me. Was she talking to me? She sat down noisily, not looking at me, and I wondered whether she had been talking to herself. Sweets rattled to the floor like loose teeth. From her enormous bag, she pulled a sheaf of papers covered in green writing. These she began sorting through with an intolerable rustling sound. I looked down at my English file and pretended to read, but in my distress I was unable to do more than reread the same lines over and over again. Now Annabel was sending a text from her phone – another violation – and it was not even on silent; assorted beeps and clicks punctuated her other noises, and I found myself tensing up from the pain of it.

I would have to leave; there was nothing else to be done. The English could wait for another time. Now she was thumping books down in front of her: thump, thump, thump. Why did the librarian not come over to silence her? I would have done it myself, but I am not a confrontational person. I could not even bring myself to look in her direction. I was about to get up and go; I had got as far as squaring my books and zipping my pencil case in readiness when I realised pathetically that I had nowhere else to be. I didn't want to go to the lunch hall. Nor could I go to the form room, because Sarah Cousins would probably go there after lunch, to do her marking and make herself available for meaningful chats. I fancied (although it might well have been paranoia) that my three obligatory friends were less fond of me than they'd used to be, since the Trace Incident, so there was no point in going to find them.

I hesitated.

Having thumped and texted to her heart's content, Annabel now began to write. As I continued to reread those self-same lines, I found myself increasingly fascinated – and impressed – by the speed with which she was working. She used a proper fountain pen, which she dipped from time to time in a bottle of ink. This fascinated me too. My father had used a similar method. It's funny: as I write this now I find I get faster and faster, but still there's a stop-start hesitancy to the way I write. I pause, I judge myself, I correct and delete. Annabel just *wrote*, with expansive sweeps of her arm. The sleeves of her blue kimono rustled as the pen kept up its soft scratch-and-scribble, and her boot kicked against the leg of her chair, and from time to time she'd reach for another sweet and chew it with relish, and she mouthed as she wrote as though it were some kind of spiritual music. And after a while I found that it was no longer unbearable at all.

I longed to know what it was that she was writing. Surely she would get up to fetch a book, or to go to the toilets? I turned the pages of my poetry anthology at random, sometimes highlighting occasional words or phrases, but without much of a sense of what I was doing.

Annabel abruptly scraped back her chair and got up. She went over to a bookshelf and returned with a thesaurus, which she leafed through with what looked like increasing frustration. Wanting to appear busy, I carried on with my work. Sometime later, I felt sure that Annabel was watching me. I looked up to see delphinium-blue eyes waiting to meet mine.

"'Scuse me, sweetheart. D'you fancy helping me with something?' She shuffled through her pages until she found the one she wanted. Pointing with her pen nib, she said: 'Can you read from here?'

Mindful of the librarian, I read in a whisper:

'A suit of golden silk you'll wear
With silver star-flowers in your hair . . .'

'Louder,' said Annabel.

The librarian advised the room that we had five minutes left.

'Damn!' said Annabel. 'What are you doing this evening? Could you – could you possibly come round to my house? I shall be eternally grateful, and make a pedestal of roses and pomegranates for you to sit on.'

'I'm busy this evening,' I said. 'I've got Life Class.'

'Can't you skip it?'

'Shush,' said the librarian.

'How about tomorrow, then?' said Bel.

'What for, exactly?' I said.

'I need you to read more,' she said.

I paused, and then – perhaps it was the mention of reading that did it, for there are few verbs that I love more in life than 'to read' – I agreed. At once, her face lit up with the luminosity of a planetarium ceiling.

'You're marvellous!' she said. 'You're too kind. Meet you outside the gates? I'm Annabel, by the way, Annabel Phyllis Ingram, at your service.'

'Nora,' I replied. I got the impression that she had never been, and never would be, at anyone's service but her own.

'You can call me Bel,' she added.

I watched her tip her possessions into her bag and leave, light of foot in her untied shoes. She did not walk, so much as skip. I had never seen someone so comfortable in their own clothes, their own skin, apart from, perhaps, Aunt Petra.

2

Of course, as soon as I accepted Annabel's invitation I wondered what on earth I was doing. I was not in the habit of saying yes to people (with one notable exception). It had, I thought, something to do with a conversation I'd had with Evie the previous weekend. My mother had noticed that I seemed generally despondent. She took me, on one of her infrequent days off, for a manicure. Evie favoured the kind of nail bar with shouty neon signs and a cash-only register: not too fancy, a little grubby, full of old magazines.

'You can have any colour you like, as long as it's black,' she joked. She always said the same thing.

I did choose black, just to amuse her; the bottle was semi-stuck to the shelf, dusty with disuse. Only a centimetre of varnish remained in the bottle. Evie, halfway down a syrupy latte, chose pale pink. We took our bottles over to where the manicurists waited. They looked like sisters, dark-eyed, dark-haired.

I admired my mother's slender fingers, so suited to the life of a violinist, or indeed a dressmaker, which was what she had become. On the knuckles of her left hand was the word LOVE. On the knuckles of her right hand was the word HAT. When asked about it, Evie would usually say that she changed her mind at the very last minute; she realised that she could not bear to have the word HATE on her body, so the tattooist left it at HAT. And there was nothing wrong with a good hat; she herself had plenty of them.

'It's knocked the joy out of you, this whole thing with the art teacher,' she said, as our manicurists – working in perfect synchrony – soaked off the last scraps of old polish from our fingernails. 'Hasn't it?'

'Not really,' I said.

I held out my hands and watched my cuticles vanish. It was my most detested part: the cutting of the cuticles. My mother was right, but not for the right reasons.

'What you need,' said Evie, 'is a distraction. Something to take your mind off things at school. Something amusing.'

I had a brief vision of us both at Disneyland Paris: me watching jadedly as my mother stalked like Maleficent down the central avenue in one of her velvet cloaks, flaring her LOVE HAT hands, scattering terrified children in her wake. Us at *The Lion King*, singing along to *Hakuna Matata*; us shopping in Oxford Street for matching zebra-stripe onesies.

'A manicure is amusing enough,' I said. 'Promise.'

'What about a course at the Psychic School place? They keep emailing me with special offers.'

'*No*,' I said. 'Definitely not.'

'Or, even better,' said my mother, 'you need to fall in love. Love is the ultimate distraction.'

So saying, she knocked her coffee onto her lap, swore, and lost her train of thought entirely.

And so, not far from where I had once loitered in anticipation of Jonah Trace, I waited outside the school gates at the end of the next day for Annabel Ingram to arrive. Arrive she did, though curiously late, trailing scarves and bags and spilling things, as was her wont, from every pocket. It was a gold kimono today, with a white-and-silver print of Chinese pagodas.

She looked taken aback when I greeted her, as though she had forgotten. 'Oh, yes! Of course,' she said. 'Howdy. I'm just waiting for my car.'

I found this very odd. Did she have a personal, uniformed chauffeur? I didn't know what to say as we waited together by the wall. We could hardly talk about the weather. At last Bel made an exclamation and a battered Ford Focus neared the kerb; raising a silky arm in greeting, she grabbed me with the other and drew me towards it. She climbed into the passenger seat; I hesitated, then opened the rear door and got in. A boy – a man, really – of about the age of Jonah Trace was at the wheel.

'Cheers,' said Bel.

'Going home?' said the man-boy. He had a low voice and a bit of an accent, but I couldn't quite tell what it was.

'Yup,' said Bel. 'Nora, Cody. Cody, Nora,' she added.

The tobacco smoke in the car was so thick that I could almost see it; it crept into my throat like a salt-marsh fog, making me cough. I cannot stand people smoking; it is one of many personal habits that I dislike. As Cody lit cigarettes for himself and for Bel, I was beginning to be sure that this was a very bad idea.

'Thank *Christ* it's half term,' said Bel.

'I went by the theatre this afternoon,' said Cody, as we joined a queue of cars at the traffic lights.

'Did you see Lex? Can we use the space?'

'He says if we lock up and don't trash it, then OK. But there's no running water, no heating.'

'Doesn't matter,' said Bel.

They continued their conversation, which excluded me. It seemed to involve printing programmes and making sure various people knew what was happening on a certain date.

'Darling,' said Bel. 'We are being very rude. I am sorry.' She swivelled around and bestowed a glittering smile upon me. 'Tell me all about yourself, Nora,' she began.

'This traffic is shit,' said Cody.

'Take a detour, then.'

'What kind of detour?'

Bel banged her head lightly against her headrest, as a child might do. She threw her cigarette out of the window, opened the glove compartment and fished out a packet of sweets. 'I don't know. You know these things.'

Her phone rang; the ringtone sounded like old-fashioned carnival music.

'Azia, honey!' said Bel, picking up.

I couldn't hear the voice on the other end, but it was obviously not good news: Bel continued to bang her head as the conversation continued.

'I know, I know,' she was saying. 'Thurston called. This week of all weeks, for heaven's sake. Have you seen her? How did she look? Well, I hope she's at death's *bloody* door. Maybe I'll send Cody round to break her legs.'

I looked at the back of Cody's head, but he did not react to this; I presumed it was a joke.

'It was a joke,' said Bel, at that moment. 'Anyway, sugar, I must go. I have a car-guest. And a Plan B. I'll tell you later.'

She hung up the phone, stuffed another handful of sweets into her mouth, swivelled round again and winked at me.

'Never attempt anything without a Plan B. That's what my dad always says.'

Bel lived on a hill-slope street in Wandsworth, not far from the common, called Rosewood Avenue. It was long and winding, and full of tall, grey, terraced houses, set back from the road and rather Gothic in appearance. Issuing various instructions to Cody about where she wanted to go later on, and at what time, Bel got out of the car, not looking out for traffic as she did so. Then, holding my hand, she led me down the black-and-white tiled path to the door. It amused me to see that a key was kept under a potted plant.

'Home!' she yelled.

She pulled me over the threshold, and the hall was as much like Alice's well as anything I'd ever seen. A long mirror gave the impression of greater space; an apothecary cabinet on the opposite wall overflowed with curious, nonsensical items. Directly in front of us was a flight of stairs; she led me past them and down the hall to a big, somewhat dilapidated kitchen.

'Welcome,' she said. 'I think everyone is out.'

The floor of the kitchen was black-and-white tiled, as the path to the front door had been. It was as though visitors were expected to jump into a game of chess in every room. Spider plants in wicker baskets hung from the ceiling, as did one of those large, rather frightening clothes-drying racks. There was a red cooking range, a free standing fridge, a large painted dresser and a central island with a scarred surface. On one side, a rectangular dining table stood beneath a crowded windowsill, and beyond it a flight of steps led down to a conservatory full of rattan furniture and more spider plants. Beyond, I could see a garden with a small pond at the end.

Bel poured me a tumblerful of gin, adding tonic and ice and a slice of lime. 'First drink of the day,' she said.

While her back was turned, I was able to pour most of it into the sink and refill the glass with water.

I longed to see every room, but she led me upstairs, chattering manically all the while. Up to the third floor we went. Splashing gin every few steps, Bel opened a door at the top of the house.

'This is my lair,' she said.

I was reminded of Evie's room in her darker days. Every surface was decked with clothes and scarves; necklaces lay on the floor in little heaps, as though stowed there by magpies; hats were piled in corners. In the corner was a four-poster bed, an antique one. A plaster model of a Venus flytrap sat malevolently beside it. Theatre programmes littered the floor, and posters for films and plays of which I'd never heard covered the walls. Next to the window was a full-size skeleton dangling from a metal stand. It wore a striped tie and a chain of Hawaiian flowers. The air was stale.

'Cheers,' said Bel. She touched her glass to mine, then climbed onto her bed, pulling apart the heavy chintz-like curtains as she did so. 'Come in!' she said. 'Come into my parlour. I don't bite.'

This was very much not my kind of thing. As I've said before, I don't like cuddles, proximity, sharing and so forth. But I felt the inclination to do what she did. So I giggled and climbed up, kicking off my trainers.

'Tell me everything, Nora. What's your middle name?'

'Alison,' I said.

'Favourite colour?'

'Blue.'

'Star sign?'

'Virgo.' This last I said randomly, reaching for the first zodiacal element that came into my head. I didn't see why I should divulge my real one, which was Pisces.

'Why are you wearing black nail varnish?' asked Bel.

'Because it's cheerful,' I said.

She smiled; I noticed that she was missing a tooth on her upper left side. Sometime later I learned that she'd killed the nerve with regular cigarettes.

'D'you have any pets?' she said.

'None.' I thought of rat-dog Oscar, and was glad of this.

'We have a cat. Cleopatra. You'll meet her later. What's your secret weapon against the world?'

'I'm sorry?' I said.

'What can you do? What's your best thing? The thing that makes you completely *you*, the thing only a Nora can do?'

This was not a question I felt I could answer. It was far too intrusive. 'What's yours?' I retorted.

'I,' said Bel, 'am a child of the theatre. It's in my bones, my blood and my soul. In fact, that's what I wanted you for. You know the thing you read to me in the library? Well, it was an adaptation of Cinderella.'

I nodded. '*Cendrillon*,' I said. I used the French name for it; my father had read me Perrault's fairy tales many, many times.

111

'D'you like fairy tales?'

I nodded again.

'I just adore them,' said Bel. Her eyes had grown rounder and rounder until I could almost see, reflected in them, the princes and castles and monsters of her imagination.

'I had a story-tape of them, when I was little,' she said. 'The woman reading the stories, her voice was like yours: so calm. She sounded a lot like my mama. They used to make me feel so safe.'

I did not know the recording she meant, but I could imagine well enough the kind of voice she was remembering. 'You said you wanted me to read some more,' I said, prompting her.

At once, she leaped up and rummaged through the bag at the foot of her bed until she found the green-inked manuscript. 'Yes siree. I certainly would. From . . .'

She ran her fingers down a page.

'. . . here. That'll do nicely. Just read until I tell you to stop.'

'OK,' I said. 'Are you sitting comfortably?'

She wriggled down under the duvet, clutching a stuffed leopard and her tumbler of gin, her eyes fixed on my face. 'Fire away,' she murmured.

I scanned the page, and began to read. The adaptation was all in verse, light and sparky. It was a pleasure to say aloud, and I read the whole of the page, and then the next, until Bel said:

'Nora, Nora. Your voice . . . it's magical.'

'Would you like me to read more?' I said.

'Not from the page. Can you . . . I just really wanna hear the whole thing now. Not in verse, not a play script, but the story. Like on the tape. D'you think you can do that? You know, in your own words.'

For Narrative Nora, there is no more tempting invitation.

'Once, long ago, there was a man who married for a second time, and she was the haughtiest, most arrogant woman you ever saw . . .' I began, keeping my voice low and rich and consistent.

I told her the story of Cinderella. Sometimes, as I was speaking I became my father, with his French-accented whisper; at other times I was Nana, in full storytelling mode. At other times, I was someone else entirely, someone I didn't know.

After a while, I realised that Bel was asleep. I waited until her breath was a gentle rush and fade. Then I prised the tumbler from the crook of her elbow and removed my leg from beneath her hand. There was a rash of cigarette burns around one of her wrists: it looked more like the markings of frequent accidents than deliberate action. I picked my way through the clothes – Bel might act like a child, but she had a large quantity of very expensive underwear, I saw, much of it from Agent Provocateur – and left her bedroom, closing the door quietly behind me.

3

When you are alone in an unknown house, and your hostess is dead to the world, and you wish to explore but are not so well acquainted with the family that it wouldn't look very odd if anyone came back and caught you poking around, you must allocate your time very carefully.

That is a truth universally acknowledged.

I looked first for a bathroom; a guest can always legitimately look for a bathroom. The door opposite revealed only a linen cupboard. I went down the stairs to the floor below. Here I discovered the bathroom that must be used by Bel. There were more black-and-white tiles, and more spider plants. A claw-footed bath with a brass curtain rail took up most of the space; lined up alongside the edge were some antique-looking toys: a red, smiley-face apple, a diver on a board, a set of plastic ducks. The cabinet was not locked, but I found only the usual medications. I blew my nose and caught sight of my reflection, watching me in the mirrored cabinet door. For a moment, it looked like my birthmark was on the wrong side, which startled me; then I saw that it was the shadow of one of Bel's kimonos, slung over the top of the door.

Next to the bathroom was another door, locked.

I went down another flight of stairs. Film posters, framed and unframed, met my eye at every angle. I studied them. Evie and I watched a lot of films, and a lot of television too. But I did not feel my knowledge was comprehensive; I had not heard of all the films on the posters, although I felt that I should have. There were, however, a few that I knew were 'cult' films, particularly from the late 1980s and 1990s. I lingered to look more closely, hoping for a pattern to emerge.

And by and by, it did.

One name stood out among the small-print of personnel at the bottom of most of the posters: Anton Ingram. He was credited as producer or executive producer each time. This, surely, must be Bel's father. Of course! I remembered Jonah Trace saying as much. I noted it in my head, along with some of the film titles. I would look him up, as soon as I got home. A large poster in a heavy frame featured a stately Georgian manor house, fringed with pinkish-purplish trees. *Jacaranda*, the film was called. I'd heard of it, but not seen it. I looked for Anton Ingram's name, but it wasn't there.

Down, down, down I went. The carpet was soft and yielding under my socks. From the landing below I could see another bedroom, which must belong to her parents. This I did not venture into, though I saw from the doorway more of the same: plants, books, textiles, art from abroad. A set of decorated masks, mounted on a wall.

A clock chimed from somewhere. I stirred. Should I go home? How long would Bel sleep for? While I considered what to do next, I returned to the ground floor. I had Bel's tumbler and mine: the perfect excuse to go into the kitchen, to wash them up. I did this first. There was a stack of unwashed crockery in the sink. As I washed the glasses, I studied the pictures on the wall. Much of it was artwork done by Bel at different ages; each picture had been labelled in a careful hand. There was another name too: Darian. Was that a boy's name, or a girl's? I wasn't sure. I was gratified to see that at the same ages I'd been a better artist than both of them. There was a marked difference in styles: Bel's work was splashy, imaginative and bold, while Darian's paintings were cautious, well-executed and small in scale.

A sudden streak of movement. I looked round: a fat tortoiseshell cat had appeared at the cat flap in the conservatory door. Padding into the kitchen in the liquid, soundless way that cats seem to have, it oozed around my legs while I washed up the tumblers. With its hollow purr, it was quizzing me, I thought. *What are you doing here, Goldilocks? Sleeping in the beds, eating all the porridge?* I was starting to think that the cat was right. I'd better get going. I didn't know if Bel was expecting me to still be there when she woke up. She'd wanted me to tell her a story, and this I had done.

But perhaps I would just finish my self-guided tour, before leaving.

Nora Tobias, Reader of Houses, worked on.

The living room was painted a mustardy colour. In this room, I imagined, drinks parties might be given and parlour games played. A carved chess set rested on the coffee table. There were books on Japanese art and Gothic literature, on gardens, on fashion and on film. The walls were stained with patches of damp, but the television and sound equipment looked expensive. So did the furniture.

In this room, the family photographs were plentiful. One shot showed a dark-eyed, brown-haired man in a green suit and a tall blonde woman in a long, pale dress, standing in the middle of a field; there were others of these people separately, and much younger. The woman was exquisitely beautiful. She was so beautiful that she did not even look real. She was the kind of person that Evie would want to dress. This must be the famous actress that Jonah Trace had mentioned to me. She'd been on some of the film posters too, and some of the theatrical ones. Phyllis Lane, she was called. And was Phyllis not Annabel's middle name? I wondered how old Phyllis Lane was now, and whether she still worked.

There were pictures too of Darian, a boy a little older than Bel, and of Bel herself. I tracked their progress through the years, from white-haired toddlers to raggedy, scuff-kneed children, Bel always in some kind of outlandish attire, Darian watchful and withdrawn. For a while longer I looked, an interested museum visitor. Evie and I did not have many family pictures. It was a sad fact that Evie, in moods ranging from mad to miserable, had destroyed a lot of photographs of my father – it was hard for me, nowadays, to recall his features with any clarity.

'Hello,' said a voice.

I turned. There was a man sitting in a chair by the fireplace. I felt a bolt of cold shame, akin to that I'd felt at the swimming pool when Sarah Cousins challenged me. Had he been watching me wandering about the room as though it were mine? I supposed he had. But the man was getting up now and smiling, holding out his hand to shake mine. He did not look offended by my presence.

'You are a friend of Annabel's?' he said. 'How d'you do. I'm Anton.'

'I'm Nora,' I said.

The first thing I thought was that he looked old, older than most people's fathers, certainly older than mine would have been. He was in his sixties, at least. Very tall. He had sparse grey hair, longish, and a beard, and a face I can only describe as strong, definite, almost stern. He was wearing a checked, open-neck shirt and dark jeans, and he was reading something on bound A5 paper that I guessed was a script. He had a faint lavenderish scent that reminded me, strangely, of France.

'Have you been offered tea?' he said.

'Gin,' I said.

He raised his eyebrows. 'Come. I shall make some.'

In the kitchen, he filled an old-fashioned kettle with water and set it on the stove, saying: 'Are you part of Bel's little project that she's working on?'

'I don't think so,' I said. I wished that I were able to come up with more impressive things to say, but I felt, for some reason, hugely intimidated by this man.

'What are you studying at school?' he asked, as he set two mugs on the counter and added tea bags.

This was better: it was no problem for me to talk about literature. I told him which texts I was reading in English and French, and he listened with what seemed like interest, asking intelligent questions that showed me that he knew the books. Before long, I could tell that he was marking me in his mind as a suitable friend for his daughter.

'I wish Annabel showed as much aptitude as you do for learning,' he said. 'She makes very little effort at school. She has a brain, but not much interest in using it. Of course, we didn't set her a good example. Neither her mother nor I went to university. Her mother went to LAMDA, and I went straight into the business. Annabel has a place at drama school, but I'd like her options to be wider than that, which is something she doesn't seem to appreciate.'

I sneezed, which saved me from having to respond to this. It seemed oddly confessional.

'You're not well,' said Anton. He removed the Earl Grey tea bag from my cup. Reaching for a chopping board, he sliced half a lemon finely and put the pieces in the cup, adding hot water. He pushed it towards me, along with a jar labelled *Miel*, saying, 'Careful. Hot. This, and perhaps some honey, will do the trick.'

My father would have done exactly that, for me or Evie or Nana. Hot lemon and honey, every time. I appreciated it.

The front door banged and footsteps could be heard in the hall. Then into the kitchen came the boy I'd seen in the photographs in the living room. It must be Bel's brother, Darian. He was very tall, with dark gold hair and a lean face; he looked like he seldom smiled. He was wearing a slate-coloured hoodie, jeans and trainers: none of his sister's elaborate costumes. He seemed not to notice me.

'This is Nora, a friend of Bel's,' said Anton.

'Hi,' said Darian.

'Are you out tonight?' asked his father.

'I have a gig later.'

'Supper?'

'Sure.'

The hot lemon was just the thing for my scratchy throat and tired sinuses. I sipped it, leaning in what I hoped wasn't too awkward a fashion against the big oak table. The cat curled up in a wicker chair and watched me. In turn, I watched as Anton melted butter in a pan, and fried tiny pieces of onion, and added rice and wine and some amber liquid from a saucepan, while Darian did the washing up. There was something calming and symphonic about the scene.

'Lettuce,' said Anton.

Darian got some out of the fridge. 'Where's Bel?' he asked.

'Asleep,' I said.

'I am not,' came a voice, and Bel walked in. The hem of her kimono dragged along the kitchen tiles. She saw me and looked pleased. 'You're still here, sugar.'

She poured a glass of red wine from the bottle and walked over to pet the cat, moving with the absent grace of a foil-wrapped ghost. I noticed her father's look of disapproval, and the way the look was mirrored, briefly, in Darian's eyes.

'What are we having for supper?' said Bel.

'Risotto.'

She shook her head. 'I want a short-order of pancakes with maple syrup.'

'Well, you are more than welcome to prepare them for yourself.'

'I wanna go out,' she said.

'Where to?'

'Somewhere elegant, with white napkins and a dessert trolley.'

'The Savoy?' asked Darian, squeezing the other half of the lemon into a cup, and adding olive oil.

'Yes.'

They all – father, brother and cat – ignored her.

'Can I help?' I asked.

'That's very kind. You can lay the table,' said Anton. 'Cutlery in the dresser, napkins in the drawer, glasses in that cupboard on the left.'

Finding the cutlery, I was momentarily paralysed by anxiety. Were you supposed to eat risotto with a fork, or a

121

spoon? Should I lay out both? What about knives? I did not want to reveal my lack of culture, my fatal ignorance. But I did not want to ask. In the end, I opted for a fork and a spoon, setting them together, rather than at right angles, and hoping that was correct.

'Set a place for Mama,' said Bel.

So I laid the table for five, while Anton stirred the risotto and Bel lolled backwards like an off-duty clown in a wicker chair. Darian had gone next door; I heard piano music, so expertly played that I thought it was a recording, coming from the living room.

'Ready,' said their father. 'Nora, come and sit.'

Bel came and sat down next to me, bringing the cat with her.

'Should we not wait for your mother?' I said to Bel in a whisper.

The cat squirmed fatly on her lap, shedding a cloud of fur.

'Oh, Mama's here,' said Bel.

She nodded towards the windowsill, which held stacks of unopened letters, a camera, a box of worming tablets and an earthenware pot. I looked up, half expecting to see Phyllis Lane through the window, tall and blonde, perhaps pushing a bicycle, her hair full of stars. But there was no one there.

'She's in the jar. Cheers, Mama,' said Bel, raising her glass.

Darian and Anton raised their glasses likewise. I did not, because I wasn't sure whether I was supposed to.

I saw Bel looking at me, with her eyebrows quirked as

though in a silent challenge. I wondered whether she wanted me to be shocked, or surprised, that they kept their mother's ashes in the kitchen. But I wasn't. It was the sort of thing Evie might have done, although my father was buried in France.

'Dig in,' said Anton.

It was a delicious risotto. He had added some cheese – goat's cheese, I thought – and a handful of spinach. I tried not to eat too fast. They ate with forks, I saw, so I took care to copy this. Despite her protestations, Bel finished her plate in seconds and was now helping herself to more, though I noticed she had not taken any salad.

'Mama died on an aeroplane,' said Bel, from the stove. 'She choked on a peanut.'

'Cashew nut,' said Darian.

'She hated flying,' said Bel.

They did not seem particularly perturbed; I understood this. Their pain had been translated, over time, into the realms of anecdotage. It must have been many years ago. I noticed that their father said nothing. I wondered if they nodded their glasses to their mother, in her jar, every night, or whether it was a show they put on for visitors.

For a while there was silence. I didn't mind it; Evie and I often ate in silence.

'Daddy,' said Bel. 'I thought you'd like to know my production is going just . . . swimmingly.' She said this with heavy emphasis, but I didn't think it was meant ironically.

'That's good to hear, beauty,' he replied.

'Rehearsals all next week,' said Bel. 'Performance on Monday after half term. You will be there, won't you? Darian, I need you too, for the music.'

'I might have a recital.'

'I *need* you,' she repeated. Her glass was once again empty. 'You wouldn't let me down.'

'I've got to go. We're sound-checking at eight.'

Darian put his plate in the sink and left. He and his sister were tremendously unalike, I thought. But they did not seem to hate each other the way that some siblings did. The cat curled itself around my leg, and I sneezed again.

'Bless you,' said Anton, to me. Then, 'Bel, where are you performing?'

'St Michael's hospital. The children's ward.'

He nodded. 'That was a good idea.'

'*My* idea.' Her eyes were glinting again. 'You are coming, aren't you, Dad?'

'Unless things go awry in Berlin and I get held up, I shall be there. I look forward to seeing what you've come up with, you and Azia,' said Anton. 'And now, girls, if you'll excuse me, I have a call with LA.'

Bel reached over and ate the rest of my risotto, while the cat looked on.

4

The business. A call with LA. Performance. LAMDA. Production. A child of the theatre.

These terms were used so easily by the Ingram family. But to me the glamour of them was almost palpable: they were like gilded party streamers, or birds of paradise. They dazzled me, these phrases, those people. Although Evie worked in television, I never thought of that as Show Business, as such. The Ingrams, now: they were one of those families in whose DNA the business, as Anton called it, ran deep and unsullied. Every available space in that grey Gothic house was loaded with the stuff of performance: scripts, leaflets, tickets, posters, programmes, old reels of film in metal cases. The longer I spent there, the more I saw, and the more intoxicating I found it.

After supper, Bel dragged me back upstairs to her bedroom.

'Now, sugar, what size would you say you are? Extra-super-tiny? I wonder . . . Ah! Take off your clothes.'

Not quite knowing how to say no, I found myself taking off my shirt and trousers. I stood there in my underwear while Bel dug around in boxes and chests. I despise being naked in front of people; I had not been naked in front of anyone for a very long time. That I had never been naked in front of Jonah Trace goes without saying.

'Nora, you're a doll,' Bel was saying. 'I could just *eat* you. A marzipan mouse of dainty deliciousness.'

As she spoke she was lacing me into a kind of basque, lilac in colour and looped with a silvery design, as though fairies had gone to work with calligraphy pens. It was small and extremely uncomfortable; the hooks nicked my skin in places as she did them up. With one hand Bel tugged the elastic from my hair; she fanned it out over my shoulders.

'Left foot, right foot,' she chanted.

I obeyed, picking up each foot in turn, allowing her to bring a bundle of gauzy turquoise fabric up to my waist and secure it with a safety pin. Now she was smoothing the skirt down; her hands passed deftly over my hips. She seemed to be enjoying herself. The skirt was pleated and iridescent and even in the dull light of her room it glowed with semi-precious other-wordliness. I glanced at myself in the mirror. Against my better judgement, I was quite pleased with what I saw. Bel had turned me into a wingless sprite. My hair was a burnt-toast cloud against my shoulders. I admired my collarbone, and the way the basque triangulated into my waist, making my hips seem wider. When anyone I knew dressed up in this kind of excessively girly way I felt nothing but casual loathing, but there was something so strange about my reflection that I felt peculiarly liberated. I could have been anyone.

'That will do very nicely,' said Bel. 'Oh! Shoes you must have. What size?'

'Four. But I don't wear heels.'

She sorted through a mountain of assorted footwear and brought out some velvet slippers.

'These,' she said.

I did not like the idea of old shoes, as much as I did not like the idea of old clothes. And yet I still did not argue. I put them on.

'You shall go to the ball,' said Bel. She wrapped one arm around my waist. The pressure of it caused the hooks and bones of the corset to bite a little deeper. 'Although, in point of fact, that's your line.'

'My what?'

'Your line. "You shall go to the ball." Say it!' she commanded.

'"You shall go to the ball",' I said slowly.

'More on the "shall". Less on the "go".'

'You *shall* go to the ball.'

'Now say: *"You shall go to the palace ball, and you'll be the fairest one of all."*'

I said it.

Bel squeezed me again. 'Perfect. Just perfect,' she said.

She had changed too, though I hadn't noticed. I saw that the clothes she had dressed me in matched her own: she was wearing a blue kimono now, embroidered with dragons and starry-leaved trees, and underneath it a vest and layered skirt not unlike the one she had chosen for me. She stood a good six inches taller than me in her trainers.

Looking out of the window, she said: 'Cody's here. Good. Got everything?'

I wanted to change back into my old clothes, but I didn't think this was going to be viable. Sweeping them into my rucksack, I followed her as she tripped down the stairs. She jumped the last few steps of each flight.

'See, Nora,' she explained, as we descended. 'This production of *Cinderella* is something I'm putting on for some children in a hospital, as I was saying earlier. I've called it *The Belle of the Ball*. And one of the cast members has dropped out. Wretched Steph, who plays the Fairy Godmother. I'd do it myself, of course, but I'm directing, and I'm the stepmother too, and I'd have to rewrite the final scene without the Godmother in it, which would ruin it rather. It's only a small thing, but it's fearfully important that it all goes well. I have to be able to concentrate. So, I thought, when I saw you in the library – I mean, look at you! You *are* a fairy! Even that mark on your face is . . . so special. You know?'

I was amused by her roundabout way of auditioning me: summoning me to her house, asking me to tell her a story. I would come to understand that Bel had her own way of doing things, and it wasn't always straightforward.

'It's only a few scenes. Two rehearsals at most! And the performance Monday after next. I'll pay you in wine and candy. I'll make you a pedestal of finest crystal. Just say you'll do it. Please?'

I thought about it. Part of me, of course, wanted to say no at once, out of habit as much as anything else. That was the Norian way. But part of me, inexplicably, did not.

There was no sign of Anton as we left the house. Bel clattered ahead of me down the path. It was fully dark now, and drizzling. She had picked up the bottle of wine that had been open at dinner, I noticed, though there wasn't much left.

Cody was leaning against the car, smoking a cigarette. What did Bel's father think of him? I wondered.

'Y'all right,' he said to us both, in greeting. 'Where to?'

I didn't feel great, I said, and I wanted to go home.

'Nonsense,' said Bel. 'Come for a drink. Lift your spirits with spirits! Take us to the Battersea Bridge Hotel,' she said, clambering into the car.

5

It was a wedding. That much was instantly clear. Although two elderly women looked askance as we came through the door in our finery, the doorman (a little thrill chimed in me at the sight of an actual doorman) waved us immediately towards the lift, next to which there was an ivy-covered board bearing the legend MR AND MRS EGENHAUSER, in a just-married heart. The Battersea Bridge Hotel was medium-sized, but fancy: the floors were pinkish marble; the walls were mirrored; Art Deco chandeliers hung from the ceiling in the lobby.

Bel stopped by a circular tray on a small coffee table. She picked up a glass with a semicircle of orange twisted at the rim, and drained it. 'Screwdriver,' she said.

A glowing light announced the arrival of the lift. As the doors parted, Bel leaned over and kissed me on the lips. I don't know why people always describe the taste of a kiss, although for the record I think she tasted of smoke and the remnants of other people's drinks. There were other, more prevalent senses at this moment. The smell and feel of her hair as it fell about my face, for example. It was as though a tent were collapsing on top of me. Her lips were softer than Jonah Trace's, but only a little. After the first jolt of excitement came my usual dislike of having my personal space invaded, and although I suppose I allowed her to kiss me, I made no attempt to kiss her back. I could feel her laughing as she pulled away, doing a kind of pirouette-curtsy, and dived into the lift. Hoping that the two old women had not seen this little tableau, I paused and then followed.

On the way up to the seventh floor we were silent. I felt that she wanted me to challenge her, to ask her why she had kissed me; I also sensed that to do so would somehow be the wrong move. I needed to accept it for what it was, whatever that might be – a lightning-strike of attraction (unlikely), an act of pure randomness (more likely), a piece of performance art (likelier still). It would not be cool to enquire.

Then Bel said, 'Have you ever done any acting?'

'A bit,' I said.

'Have you won any awards?' she asked.

'No,' I said. 'Have you?'

She looked coy. 'Of course.'

I had an idea that this was untrue.

'There's a project coming up that I'm excited about,' she said. 'Top secret at the moment. I can't say too much, but . . . Oh, Nora. It could be the best thing that ever happened.'

We arrived, and came out of this lift to the drumming

of rain and the babble of guests. It was a sprawling, glass-roofed space; sparkling doors led out onto a terrace from which you could see the night-time astronomy of the Thames. There was a canopy protecting the wedding guests from the rain; heaters emanated an orange glow, but there were few people actually outside. Waiters and waitresses bore trays of canapés on green fronds, while others circulated with bottles of champagne. In good weather, it might have been magical.

A woman with an auburn bun and a clipboard asked for our names.

'Annabel Ingram plus one.'

'I don't see you.'

'We're with the band.'

'Oh. Hang on.' The woman turned over a page. 'Here you are.' She drew a line through Annabel's name and gave us a glacial smile.

Bel pushed me through the door. I hesitated. The glacial smile had unnerved me; that and the fact that there had been no plus one next to Bel's name. I was a stranger, an uninvited guest at a wedding, as unwanted as a dark fairy at a christening. I was suddenly aware that it was past nine, or possibly even later, and I'd told Evie I wouldn't be home too late. I didn't like the thought of her worrying.

'I should go,' I said.

'Honey, we only just got here!' said Bel.

Under the yellowy lights, her hair looked less white and

more golden. I could see people looking at her, the way they might observe an unusual sculpture. She took me by the elbow again. Now she was leading me through the crowd. Every woman, it seemed, was some kind of fairy. Some outfits were more conservative than others; some people wore masks and headdresses; there was a sprinkling of wings. The men, by and large, wore suits, but I spied a handful of donkey-ears. The room was heavily upholstered in greenery and twinkling lights. I looked for the bride; I saw a tall girl upholstered in a fishtailed monstrosity with a garland of azaleas and guessed that this must be the unfairylike Mrs Egenhauser.

'It's supposed to be *A Midsummer Night's Dream*,' Bel said. 'I love costume parties. But I coulda done this *so* much better.'

She said this quite loudly; a couple of official-looking fairies took notice of this insult and frowned. Bel found a fuchsia-coloured drink and drained it neatly, professionally. She took no notice of the side-eyeing men in their dark, expensive suits, of the official-looking fairies. These people were presumably not her friends. A quick assessment of the crowd told me that Bel would have no more time for them than she would for most of the girls at Lady Agatha's.

I looked around for the band. In the corner was a low platform, flanked by speakers, and on it a quartet of players. A girl sat astride a wooden box that she was pounding with one capable hand. A dark-skinned boy was playing upright bass. I saw Darian, sitting at a Yamaha keyboard, an iPad propped beside him to show the score. He was playing with quiet concentration. I felt that he was one of those people who could abstract himself entirely from any situation in favour of the inner spaces of his mind. A second girl, about my height, in a dark-red dress, was singing about moonlight in Vermont. Her voice was rich and low and rather good, I thought, though I do not have much of a musical ear. People were dancing in a self-conscious way on the small square dance floor, wings clashing, while others staggered about with drinks and cameras, or phones, photographing themselves with the usual tiresome narcissism.

'Penny for them, sugar,' said a voice, and I looked up to see Bel smiling at me.

I replied truthfully: 'I was thinking that I'd rather die than be the kind of person who takes a selfie.'

She screamed with appreciative laughter. I was relieved that she did not try to kiss me again. 'Come on,' she said.

She elbowed her way through the wedding-goers with not so much as a pardon-me, dragging me along behind her. When we got to the platform, Darian looked up and saw us, and I thought that his face took on a slightly mask-like quality before he acknowledged Bel with a smile. The band were mid-song, and I expected Bel to hang back a little to allow them to finish, but she bounded onto the platform, knocking over a bottle of water next to the singer's feet and causing her microphone stand to teeter precariously.

The singer swayed to the left to allow Bel to squeeze by her, still looking out towards the wedding party as she sang.

I hung back, watching. Bel flung her arms around Darian's neck, pushing him along so that she was sharing his seat. It amazed me that he was undisturbed by this, even beginning what sounded like a complicated piano solo at that moment. Now she was reaching across him to fiddle with his iPad; I watched him shake his head, admonishing her. She leaned down and brought up a hip flask, which she shook experimentally and then drank from. His dark blond and her yellowy-gold were two tones from the same palette. Their pale faces, his so still and hers so mobile, mirrored each other. I watched Bel jostle and nudge and fidget while he played and felt a ripple of envy. I had occasionally wished for a brother. Feeling for my phone, I sent a quick text to Evie, reassuring her that I'd be home later on.

The song came to an end. The singer murmured something about taking a break and undulated away in her dark-red dress. Darian got up. He was holding Bel's arm in a slightly controlling way and I got the impression that he was trying to encourage her to leave the stage. Bel was shaking her head and gabbling into his ear. Then she turned to the bassist, as though for support. The drummer tilted her head back and laughed. Bel blew her a kiss; Darian shrugged. The bassist played a rolling cascade of notes; the drummer joined in with a wicked grin. Darian looked undecided for a moment, then mouthed something to the other musicians and something else to Bel.

'Just one,' he seemed to be saying. 'No more.'

Under the shifting tones of the spotlights, Bel's face changed also, becoming watchful, knowing, open and closed at the same time. It's hard to put into words, exactly. I'd come to know it well as her 'performance' face. Adjusting the folds of her kimono, smoothing her hair at her temples, Bel sashayed towards the mic stand, caught hold of it with both hands and began to sing. It was a song I didn't know, about loving someone who loved you and taking a vow. It seemed appropriate enough for a wedding, and Bel sang it well. She didn't sound like a professional singer, the way the red-dress girl did, but there was something so arresting about the way she stood on that small stage, as the musicians built a wall of harmony behind her, that quite a few people on the dance floor stopped dancing and watched her. Some even clapped and whistled. I noticed that Darian too kept his eyes on Bel the whole time. Bel raised her arms like a priestess. She singled out a man in a bow tie – I realised that he was Mr Just-Married Egenhauser himself, with his bride twirling beside him – and twinkled a verse in his direction. She hummed and chortled and whispered into the microphone as though she were telling it intimate secrets. I watched her, mesmerised.

Then Bel sang:

'Love the one who loves you
Though she looks like a cow;
You married her for her mo-ney
But who cares 'bout that now?'

What happened next was very quick and I imagined that Darian had done it plenty of times in the past. Before the bride and groom could realise that Bel was making up new words (she was drunk enough to be slurring her consonants quite a bit), Darian caught the other musicians' eyes and they brought the song to a close with a roll of percussion and an up-and-down rattle of piano keys. The lights changed again and a booming playlist took over as Darian steered Bel down from the stage. She looked gleeful and lit-up. I recognised the feeling exactly, I realised. It was the *up*ness I always felt when I'd done something with a measure of success, the heady rush of pride and joy that sometimes was swiftly followed by a desperate need to find something to match it.

'You are literally unbelievable,' Darian was saying.

Bel did a little shuffle with her feet. 'Rubbish. They loved me.'

'You're bloody lucky no one heard what you were singing. I'm going out for a cigarette. I don't want to see you here when I return.' He looked over at me. 'Nora, please take my sister away.'

'I wanna stay and sing more,' said Bel.

The rotating disco ball on the ceiling flecked her face with iridescence.

'I'm not going to ask you again,' said Darian. 'Don't make a scene. Not here. Not while I'm working.'

She pirouetted twice and came to an uneasy rest against the speaker, which wobbled. 'All right,' she said. 'We'll go.'

Our progress to the exit was slow. Bel collected several more drinks on the way. We had barely been there an hour, I thought, although it was hard to judge. It had been entertaining, in that the episode – corset, song and all – had taken me out of myself, and I realised that this was what I sorely needed. Now, though, my head-cold was spreading like a cloud. I wanted a book and my bed, and pyjamas that didn't dig into my sides.

'Now for more drinkies,' said Bel in the lift. 'I know just the place.'

'I can't,' I said. 'I've no money, and I have to get home. My mum . . .'

She took from her kimono pocket a neat bundle of twenties. 'Darian has provided,' she said. 'He always makes sure they get paid at the beginning of the night. Now, *where* is Cody and the godforsaken car?'

She'd taken the band's wages. She must have got it out of her brother's pocket while she was onstage.

'Have you taken all their money?' I said.

'Oh, sugar, of course not,' said Bel. 'Just the barest *fraction*. Now, Nora, you *are* going to do the play. Aren't you?'

'I don't . . .'

'Oh, go on. I . . . I implore-ya, Nora!'

I could see that she was pleased with the half-rhyme, because she swung me around and around in the Art Deco lift, chanting it like a refrain.

'I have an essay to write . . .' I protested.

'But think of the poor ill children!'

'I really . . .'

The two old women were still in the lobby when we came out of the lift. With a pot of tea on a silver tray between them, they were huddled over a game of Gin Rummy. I longed for a moment to be able to stop and join them, but – singing *Moonlight in Vermont* loudly and tunelessly – Bel swept me out into the night.

6

My mother makes an excellent breakfast, and the morning after the afternoon with Bel that turned into evening that turned into night, I was very, very glad of it. She took one look at me as I emerged from my bedroom, and then went to our local Tesco. On her return, she served me eggs over easy on toasted muffins, with bacon and mushrooms on the side, and a pint glass of Tropicana, loaded with ice, and a mug of coffee.

I'm not a drinker, for so many reasons. But Annabel Ingram ground me down, turning my noes into maybes and my maybes into yeses. From the red wine to the Screwdrivers and then the Bellinis and then whatever we drank at the place after that, and the one after that one . . . at some point I'd even downed three shots of pepper vodka. Tequila, straight out of the bottle.

Whisky.

I was, frankly, disgusted with myself.

'I'm going to wait until later,' said Evie, 'to ask whether I need to be worried about anything.'

She sat down next to me with her cup of tea and *Seamstress Quarterly* or whatever it was that she was reading. She isn't much of a reader, in general. Indeed, she seemed to be more interested in staring into my face, like a forensic pathologist, while I ate.

'Evie,' I said. I took a mouthful of bacon, exquisitely eggy. 'Could you stop staring at me like that?'

'When I said you needed a distraction, I didn't mean one whose chemical compound is C_2NO_5H,' said my mother inaccurately.

'Trust me,' I replied. 'This is not going to be a habit. I went out with a girl from school. There were cocktails. She kept buying them . . . I didn't want to be rude.'

'Easily done.' Evie dunked a ginger biscuit in her tea. She may not be the most imaginative person in the world or, dare I say, the deepest thinker, but one good thing about her is that she isn't easily alarmed. She doesn't set curfews or check pockets for contraband items. She's not an eaves-dropper or a phone tapper. Just because she has had a major problem with alcohol doesn't mean that she thinks that I, by nature or nurture, am bound to endure the same struggle. Frankly, I worry far more than she does that I am fated to be like her. Or like my father.

'Just as long as you weren't . . . you know. There's having a good time and then there's using booze to deal with stuff. I should know. All that shit that happened with your art teacher. If you need to talk about it . . .'

I understood what she was trying to say.

'Really. I'm OK.'

I completed the cryptic crossword – including one very tricky anagram – on the back page of the newspaper, just to prove it.

Evie invited me to go for another manicure, but I declined. She threw on her velvet cloak and disappeared, saying she was going to look for some fabric in Berwick Street. Did I want to go with her? No. I didn't want to go to Soho; I had grainy memories of having been there the night before, in a bar with a beaten-up piano. I remembered Bel standing on top of the piano with a lampshade on her head, performing a number from an old musical. Then there had been a Polish restaurant with a live band. It was there, I was pretty sure, that the pepper vodka appeared. There had been other vodkas too. Plum and honey and others that I didn't recall. We had eaten thick stew and plates of buckwheat. Bel had called for more of this, more of that, even though we had both eaten already, at her house. Two men had sent champagne from a nearby table, and before I knew it we'd been joined by several people with strange names and stranger mannerisms, and I couldn't be at all sure whether Bel knew them, even vaguely, or whether they were entirely random additions to the night. But beyond that I had little memory. What had I been doing? What had I said? The shame of not knowing was hot and viscous.

Getting home. That was something I couldn't remember at all. A night bus, I thought. I hadn't been driven home, I was sure. Had Bel got bored of me, and sent me away? That was a possibility. More likely I had decided to leave.

One thing I did remember was Bel pleading, her voice pitched in an upwards spiral: 'Oh, Nora, Nora, I implore-ya . . . *please* be in my play.'

This at midnight, at 1 a.m., at 2 a.m. Promises of pedestals, of course. She seemed to have a passion for pedestals, though I didn't know why.

After Evie was gone, I ran a bath and soaked myself as one might pre-launder a soiled sheet. There were little cuts on my chest, as though the Midsummer fairies had pinned me down and dug in their nails. I couldn't work out what they were, and then realised: they were from the bones of the corset-thing. My throat was sore from talking over loud music. I had a bruise on my right shin. I tried to remember how I could have gotten it. Perhaps I'd fallen getting out of a taxi, though I couldn't be sure. And where was the corset-thing? I found it in a heap beside my bed, and wondered how best to wash it. Evie would know.

Later on, I went for a walk. My path took me across our estate, across a couple of main roads and down to the river. The Thames always calms me. The greyish February air was cool and quite refreshing; I walked briskly, trying to clear my thoughts. The churning nausea was gone, but the horror of amnesia remained.

I sat down on a bench and watched the river go by. A couple of tugboats were making their peaceful way upriver;

on a long and brightly-lit boat, music was playing. I lost myself in the river, imagining that I was no bigger than a single molecule of water.

And all of a sudden, it came back to me, like a fruit-machine jackpot on the P&O ferry – my response to Bel, while the Polish band played raucously in the background.

'*All right. I'll do it.*'

Just then, my phone vibrated with a text. I was reminded of the many messages there had once been from Jonah Trace. Fond and friendly texts, to begin with. Intrigued. Later, quite passionate; obsessive, even. Confused texts. Angry texts. And, just before Christmas – a single, final epitaph on the gravestone of our doomed relationship: *I didn't want things to turn out this way.*

Involuntarily, I sighed. I'd be very surprised if he ever got in touch with me again. Those texts, I reflected, had been a linchpin in my version of events. Evidence of great value. They'd been very useful – edited, of course, to show him in the most unfavourable, stalkerish light. Furthermore – and this was crucial – Jonah Trace had no texts at all from me. I'd been careful to delete them all from his inbox, not too long before I called time on our relationship, lip a-tremble. Then came the event in Borough Market – stage-managed with care, planned to perfection – where he confronted me. As I knew he would do. And that was the end of it. No, Jonah; you may not have wanted things to turn out as they did, I thought. But none of it – ever – was about you, or what you wanted. I sighed again, as though the memory of the Trace Incident would leave my body in a cloud of carbon dioxide, and be gone. There was still, at the back of my mind, a hint of anxiety about Sarah Cousins and what her suspicions might be. But I was sure – pretty sure – that the episode was over.

Looking down, I saw that the message was from Bel.

Rehearsle on Tuesday at midday, it said. There was an address, and then a row of kisses. I thought it was charming – and perhaps a little daft – that Bel, an actress, was unable to spell 'rchcarsal'.

I had got the impression, on the Friday night, that Bel hadn't thought much of my clothes. And indeed, I had always made a point of not caring what I wore. But on the day of the rehearsal, when I surveyed the contents of my chest of drawers and saw the dark trousers, the long-sleeved tops in earth and stone colours, the pale T-shirts and vests, I realised they would not do.

I rummaged in Evie's room, unearthing a pair of purple dungarees, the legs of which I rolled up a couple of times, and a shirt with a print of penny-farthings. (I'd noticed that Bel liked patterns). Evie's shoe size was much larger than mine; in the end, I went to Brixton market, early the following morning, and bought some pink-and-white Converse that were similar to those that Bel wore. Then I scuffed them for an hour in the park, so that they would no longer look new. I looked in the mirror and felt disgusted with myself. But it was better than the old-clad alternative.

I knew the play was based on *Cinderella*, but since Bel had not sent me any kind of script to read, I'd been keeping myself busy over the past few days with other kinds of research. It seemed, from looking at the Internet Movie Database, that Bel had done only some short films for graduating directors and two series of a teen drama that had been shown on a satellite channel. I managed to see a few clips of this online. Anton Ingram's list of production credits was so long that I limited myself, for the time being, to those which had received awards or nominations. I did something similar for Phyllis Lane. For three days I watched two or three films per day, keeping notes in a notebook of anything that particularly grabbed my interest.

And so it was that, dressed in my different clothes and feeling much better acquainted with the work of the Ingram-Lane dynasty, I came to Bel's rehearsal.

It was a pub called the Four Horsemen, in a part of East London I'd never been to before. This, it turned out, was the space Cody and Bel had been discussing when I first went home with her. The pub stood on the corner of a wide, lonely street, next to a warehouse full of office furniture. The windows on the ground floor were boarded up; I wasn't sure if I'd come to the right place, but seeing one of the doors standing open, I went in. Inside, the air smelled of old beer (I was reminded of Evie's drinking days) and had the blood-numbing chill of a place that long stood unheated. The barstools were stacked beneath a dartboard. There was a heap of unopened letters on the bartop.

There, at the bar, was Cody. He was eating a Müller yogurt with a plastic fork and filling in a crossword at the back of a tabloid paper. By daylight he looked older, perhaps older than Jonah Trace. He had thick, dark hair that curled tightly around his scalp, and crows' feet at the corners of his eyes.

'She's upstairs,' he said.

He nodded towards a door on the window side of the bar, marked in tarnished gold UPSTAIRS. I went up a gloomy staircase, where every inch of wall space was covered in flyers for plays. At the top, another door. For a short, strange moment, I couldn't help feeling that this was a trap of some kind. It wasn't a rehearsal; there was no play. This pub was a makeshift temple. Bel was a High Priestess. I would open the door to find a votive altar. With a cackle and a scream, Bel would sacrifice me, and perhaps some other people, to whatever god or goddess she worshipped.

Then, shaking my head and telling myself that I'd been watching too many movies, I opened the door.

The room was larger than I'd imagined it would be, with spotlights on the ceiling. There were perhaps ten rows of seats, on increasingly raised levels, with a narrow central aisle. There was a small stage. The walls were burgundy in colour. The floor was polished, but there were black rubbish sacks dotted about, oozing debris. A dark-skinned girl with a long, dark plait curled around her shoulder like a pet snake was sitting cross-legged in the front row with a scroll of papers. A boy in a white shirt, black trousers and a pinstripe waistcoat was standing at the window, rolling a cigarette and talking on his phone. And on the stage were four people, two boys and two girls. Bel was perched on the edge of the stage in another kimono, a green one with dragons on the sleeves. Seeing me, she leaped up and came dancing over, hugging me as though we had known each other for our lifetimes.

'Here she is!' she cried. 'It's Nora, our eleventh-hour fairy – the cleverest, sweetest little darling you could ever imagine.'

The girl with the long dark plait smiled at me. 'I like your dungarees,' she said.

'This is Azia,' said Bel. 'She's my co-writer, the narrator too. Over there on the phone is Thurston. He's producing. And these are Jess and Chris and Zubin and Paige. Jess is Cinderella, Zubin and Paige are the stepsisters, Chris is the prince and I'm the stepmother, as you know. We're not having a father because there's no one to play him. And you, of course, are the Fairy Godmother!'

The boy in the waistcoat, having finished his phone conversation, came over and poured some whisky into a hip flask from a bottle in the corner. He smiled at me, and I saw: good dentistry, good education, good manners. 'Would you like a drink?' he said.

He spoke with an American accent. I shook my head.

'How is Steph?' said someone.

'Do not mention that girl's name to me again,' said Bel. 'Who has a spare script for Nora?'

'I do,' said Azia, and she handed me a stapled A4 booklet. 'Bel, it's hardly Steph's fault that she's ill. Glandular fever is no joke. We don't want any infectious illnesses anywhere near the ward.'

Bel shrugged; I could see that she had taken Steph's desertion personally. Then she smiled. 'It's much better to have darling Nora.'

'Do you act?' said the girl Jess, in a tone of voice I didn't much care for.

'Nora has trodden the boards hundreds of times!' said Bel. 'She's been Eliza in *My Fair Lady*, and Grizabella in *Cats*, and the Nurse in *Romeo and Juliet*.'

I waited for someone to challenge these blatant falsehoods, but no one did.

'There's very little time,' Bel added. 'We must get started at once.'

'Did Bel explain why we're doing this?' said Azia, as we sat down in a circle and prepared to do a read-through. 'The play is for children, you see. The children's ward at St Michael's hospital. My mum is a registrar there.'

'And I want to do a performance *here* too,' said Bel, with a wave of her sleeve and a hungry, heart-set look that I would come to know very well. 'But the bastards are tearing it down. It's been condemned. I think we should stage a protest.'

'Let's just stage the play,' said Azia, 'and go on with our lives.'

Even as I write this now, I can feel the bubbles of terror in my marrow at the thought of standing up, assuming a voice, assuming an expression, saying lines, being seen, being heard. I must have looked comically afraid to anyone who had been watching me; I hid it as best I could, taking the opportunity to read through the whole of the play, *The Belle of the Ball*, while I waited for my first scene.

The play wasn't very long – six or seven scenes – and I judged that it would last no longer than half an hour. Overall, Bel (or her co-writer Azia) had stayed very faithful to the feel of the original French version. There was something rather elegant about the old-fashioned words, and the simple, pleasing way in which they rhymed. I supposed nowadays it was more common to make *Cinderella* into a comedic pantomime. Here it was a wistful love story; it was a tale of a troubling second marriage, conflict between sisters, thwarted hope and mistaken identity. I enjoyed the simplicity of it. She'd dramatised it beautifully, I realised. I felt a little shot of jealousy. Was Bel good at everything she turned her hand to, as well as being magnetic to men, and mesmerising to look at, and the daughter of famous people besides?

It did not seem fair.

I felt hands on me: Bel had appeared and grabbed me round the middle. She placed her palm on my stomach. 'Breathe into *here*,' she commanded. Her hair smelled of smoke and sandalwood. 'You're much too tense in the shoulders, sugar. Diaphragmatic breathing; that's what you need to practise. I'll show you properly, later. Now – this is your scene.'

Trying to do as she'd shown me, I breathed into my middle, and then said: '*Oh, little Cinders, why so . . .*'

'Not so fast,' said Bel. 'Don't gabble.'

I breathed again, and said:

'*Oh, little Cinders, why so sad?*
Could it be a dream you had –
A nightmare, filling you with woe?
Tell me, dear, what ails you so?'

Bel chuckled. 'Much better,' she said.

Jess and I read through our scene, and after that I wasn't needed again until the finale. We had a short break and then rehearsed the play fully. It wasn't hard to learn the choreography of my scenes, and once I was sure that I wasn't making a fool of myself I found that I was able to relax.

'A natural,' said Bel. 'You're a natural. Just as I suspected.'

She herself was a revelation. As the sneering, domineering stepmother, she projected a haughty hideousness that transformed her completely. It was hard not to look at her

151

constantly, although I tried my best not to. As we ran through the play from beginning to end, again and again, I lost awareness of time and was surprised when Thurston shrugged himself into a tailcoat, threaded a rather sorry-looking carnation into one buttonhole and announced that he had to be somewhere by three thirty.

'My mother's getting remarried,' he said. 'I'll be disinherited if I don't attend.'

'Who to?' said someone.

'Her divorce lawyer,' he replied. At this, he upended the contents of his hip flask down his throat, adding, 'But they didn't stipulate what state I ought to be in.'

Later on, Cody was sent out for supplies and we had a picnic on the stage: bread and olives and stuffed vine leaves from a tin. Heavy red wine. I took only some small sips, but was glad of the warmth in my throat. The room was very cold.

'To Cinderella!' said Bel, raising a plastic glass. She touched my glass with hers. 'To my eleventh-hour fairy. I adore-ya, Nora.'

When she looked into my eyes, I felt as though her passion – for performing, for living – was spilling into me, beguiling and unstoppable. She didn't know me well enough, I kept thinking, to be able to say with certainty that she 'adored' me. And yet she seemed to believe it.

We met again a few days later. It was, said Bel, the Dress Rehearsal, and I could see that she had gone some way towards organising costumes. I would wear my fairy outfit; Cinderella's sisters had been similarly kitted out from Bel's wardrobe, while the remainder of the cast had been equipped with various charity-shop findings. It was only a short performance, but Bel behaved as though we were preparing for a six-month run at the Globe. It was this intensity that I found so attractive about her; I think everyone else did too.

We spent the whole day in the upstairs theatre at the Four Horsemen, and I found that by offering to accompany the individual people who went out on various errands, I could find out quite a lot, quite easily. I think they all appreciated my willingness to step into their production. And so they talked to me quite freely. From Zubin, whom I accompanied on a trip to buy coffees and muffins, I learned that he and Azia were involved in the same Youth Theatre group. Jess and Chris had acted with Bel in the twenty-four-hour play under the railway arches the previous year And Bel and Azia – as I'd already guessed – were great friends.

An hour or two later, I went out for bottles of water with Paige. Paige was intelligent, dry-witted, and rather shy. She too had acted with Bel in the past, in the teen TV drama. She didn't do much acting any longer; she was in her first year of an English degree.

As I'd hoped she would, she told me about Bel. Bel was brilliant at some things, useless at others; she'd been kicked out of several schools, the most recent one a fancy boarding school — one of those places with horses in a paddock, vegetable gardens — in Shropshire. It seemed Bel found it difficult to commit to things. Her predicted grades were poor, despite her intelligence.

'Why doesn't Bel act much professionally any longer?' I asked.

'Well,' said Paige. 'She's got her A-levels to do. But to be honest, she has *form*. I don't know how much I should tell you about it. Let's just say she wrecked a very expensive set.'

'Accidentally?'

'Bel always said so to me, yes.'

'What are her parents like?' I asked. I didn't want to let on that I knew much about Bel's family, although by that time I had read several books about Hollywood, which contained quite a few anecdotes about Anton Ingram, and a biography of Phyllis Lane, to say nothing of the progress I was making with their film catalogue.

'Oh, didn't you know? Her mother was Phyllis Lane. She died years ago.'

I ummed in a noncommittal way.

'And her dad's a famous producer. He's the reason why Bel's doing this. He thinks she can't get it together, and she's out to prove that she can. Or something.'

Darian arrived towards the end of the afternoon. He sat at the side of the stage, with a laptop and a portable hard drive. Glimpses of the screen revealed a complex canvas of numbers and lines and what looked like the skeletons of elongated fish. I thought I had never seen such total concentration.

During a short break, I went over to see him. 'May I hear some of your music?' I asked.

He looked up, startled by my appearance. 'Sure. But it's not quite right yet. And it's not music as such. Soundscapes.'

He handed me the headphones and I put them on.

'That's the intro,' said Darian.

'It's . . . magical,' I said.

'Yeah, that's what Bel wanted. *Something magical*, she said. It's not properly mixed down yet. I'll do that this evening.'

He played me three other short pieces, designed to fit in between the scenes. As I watched him tapping the keyboard, adjusting an echo here, a beat there, I surprised myself by feeling quite emotional. I was *moved*. I am drawn to passion: Darian, whose sister was as loud and dynamic as he was solemn and withdrawn, was obviously passionate about what he did. In their own ways, they all were.

That night, as I went through Evie's wardrobe again, wondering what else I could usefully purloin, I asked myself how I could remain friends with these people, when the play was over.

7

Marking the register in the morning of the day of the performance, Sarah Cousins said:

'Pleasant half term, Nora? What did you get up to?'

'Not much,' I replied.

She folded her lips into a smile. It wasn't a nice one. I wondered whether she still saw Jonah Trace, and if they ever talked about me. I wondered if she had shared her opinion of me with any other members of staff. The way she looked at me, sometimes, made me very uneasy.

Sarah Cousins had various announcements to read out before assembly.

'Those of you doing English, coursework must be handed in before midday to Ms Sullivan's pigeonhole, or sent electronically if you prefer.'

I froze. I'd forgotten – not only to bring in my coursework, but also to finish it. It was almost impossible to believe that I could have done such a thing.

'All right, Nora?'

I nodded. I'd have to go and find Anneka Sullivan and explain. Perhaps I'd say that I'd been ill, or – better – that a family member, like my Nana, had been unwell over half term; Ms Sullivan would surely believe me, if I were convincing enough, and extend the deadline. Quietly, I started running over the exact way that I'd express myself – a little distracted, on the verge of frustrated tears, but not overplaying the distress. Yes. I barely listened as Sarah Cousins read out the rest of her notices. There was an announcement about next term's Lower-Sixth play, which was to be Ibsen's *A Doll's House*, advising us that auditions would be in the first week of April, and a note of thanks from a local charity for which Lady Agatha girls had recently raised money.

As I stood in the chapel, twenty minutes later, half singing some plodding Lenten hymn, I found myself looking cautiously along the pews, trying again to sense which girls, if any, were looking at me differently. It would be too much to hope that no one had overheard that conversation between me and Sarah Cousins. Even though the swimming pool had been an echo chamber of shrieks and splashes, there was still a chance that we had been witnessed. And if it had, there would be rumours. And those rumours could have spread like measles over the half-term break.

Sarah Cousins called Nora Tobias a liar. It must be to do with Mr Trace.

A little liar, she said.

Lori Dryden was reading *Closer* inside her hymn book. A couple of people were coughing into Kleenex; the school was a petri dish of diseases. Only Megan Lattismore looked up as my gaze swept along the line, and she did look back at me with a funny quizzical stare, the emotion of which I just couldn't place. I looked for Bel, who would be standing with the Upper Sixth at the back of the chapel, but remembered that she'd said it was unlikely that she'd come into school before the performance. There was too much preparation to do, she said. The hymn slowed to a ragged close and I shook myself, mentally, promising that I would never again forget to finish a piece of work. As Caroline Braine at the lectern intoned something from the Bible – Jesus in the wilderness – I began to rehearse my lines for *The Belle of the Ball*.

It was just as I was leaving the chapel that I stepped into the path of Mr Drake, the Director of Studies, a kind of second-in-command to the headmistress. He apologised, the way people do after a near-collision.

'So sorry,' he began.

And then he did a double-take, obviously realising who I was. It was impossible to misread the disapproval on his face as he hurried past me. Looking around, to see if there had been any witnesses, I caught sight of a couple of girls, hands cupped in readiness to whisper. They saw me and shrank back into the shadow of the cloister. In a red rush of embarrassment, I made my way out, as quickly as I could. I began to rehearse my lines again.

I took the tube on my own to St Michael's hospital, as soon as the school day was over. Riddled with nerves, I sipped repeatedly from my water bottle. I fiddled with my hair, my nails. My right hand, always the less steady, shook as I fanned my script. As I often did at times of stress or boredom, I anagrammed words at random. I have always liked anagrams. Unlocking the secret meanings in things gives me an odd kind of satisfaction. My father showed me how to do it.

Annabel Ingram, I wrote.

Banana Gremlin.

Darian Ingram.

Daring Airman.

By the time I got to the children's ward, I felt calmer. I did not know much about hospitals in the UK; Evie and I never required their services. Since my tale about the poisonous oyster was a work of fiction, I'd never been inside a French hospital either, other than to have my tonsils removed, aged four, something I scarcely remembered. St Michael's seemed like a place where all the senses were on high alert: the overhead lights were bright; the smell of disinfectant and a hint of something darker and more morbid seemed to seep from all surfaces; voices chimed over the ping of the lift doors. Up to the fourth floor and along a walkway I went, and then down a short flight of stairs, and when I saw Zubin and Jess at a water fountain I was relieved to see people I knew.

Zubin said, 'Everyone's in there, setting up.'

A pair of swing-doors bore a sign above them saying

'Playroom'. Through the tinted glass I could see Bel, in her green kimono. I pushed through the doors. Bel was ordering Chris and Thurston to rearrange the long pink-and-blue sofas. Her hair was piled on top of her head and she was wearing glasses, which reflected small white stars from the overhead lights. She saw me and waved. Darian knelt in the corner, where a television on a trolley had been pushed away from the wall. Cody was nowhere to be seen.

'I want them as close to a semicircle as you can get them,' Bel was saying.

Paige and Azia were flipping different switches on and off, while Bel issued further instructions. Everyone was talking at the same time.

'Going to need another four-way adaptor . . .'

'Try now.'

'That won't work. What about an extra lamp, just offstage?'

'Does anyone have a small table?'

I decided there were too many people helping already for me to usefully offer my services. In the biography of Phyllis Lane that I was reading (*Life in the Fast Lane*, it was called) it said that before a show, Phyllis would always, without fail, take a moment alone to prepare. I sat in an orange armchair in which a plush Elmer the Elephant was resting, and studied my lines.

At twenty past five the children came in. Some were dressed; others wore dressing gowns and slippers. Some bore the obvious signs of unwellness – a shaven head, a plaster cast – though no child coming had a high risk of infection, Azia had explained to me. I had been so absorbed in the play that I had not given much thought to the children. Now, I was overcome with shame that they had not been in the forefront of my mind at all times. Nurses with name-badges pinned to their chests were helping them onto the sofas; those that could not walk were wheeled in their chairs to the front. Paige and Jess were handing out little programmes on folded pink cards.

'Come and sit here, Felix,' said a nurse, helping a pale boy onto a sofa.

To hear my father's name, so unexpectedly, made me jump.

He'd have been pleased to see me perform, but of course he'd never had the chance. I thought about Evie, and what she'd said, that night back in October – how she'd gone to the Psychic Awareness Course because she'd thought, somehow, that she'd find out how to 'reach' him. At the time I'd been, I suppose, shocked. When Felix died, Evie at first was angry, not sad. Sadness came later, and lasted longer. But never before had Evie wanted to try to 'reach' him, as far as I knew. But now I was beginning to see how she might be feeling. My parents had loved each other. I'd loved them. They'd loved me. We had been a perfect triangular unit. To want my father to be some-where, somewhere reachable – to want to be able to find him, through whatever means – that was, perhaps, quite understandable.

I looked at the little boy, Felix, and hoped that the play would not disappoint him.

'Practising your lines?'

It was Azia, smiling down at me. Her hair was in two plaits today, perfectly symmetrical.

I nodded. 'Is that your mother?'

A tall, elegant woman was standing at the back of the room. There was a grey-haired man beside her, partly in shadows, and I realised that it was Bel's father.

'Indeed,' said Azia. 'Only for these kids would she allow me to take a break from my A-levels.'

I have learned enough about performing, by now, to know that it goes by more quickly than you would imagine. Bel – a totally transformed Bel to the one who pranced and sulked, who stole money and danced on tabletops – motioned us into our places, and someone turned down the lights, and the children were hushed.

Then Azia, dressed in a black T-shirt and jeans, stepped forward and said:

'Won't you listen, if you please,
To a tale of magic and mysteries,
A tale of wishes, love and dreams –
Where nothing is quite as it seems.

Long ago, it all began:
There was a kindly, widowed man . . .'

And on it went. Even now, months later, I can remember every word of the script, but of the performance itself I find I cannot remember much. Those twenty-five minutes went by in what seemed like a flicker of a racing pulse. I remember only small things: the audience bursting into laughter at Bel, galumphing around in stepmother garb, and a thrill of excitement when the slipper fit onto Cinderella's foot; how the music seemed to fit the actions on the makeshift stage so perfectly. And how dark it was in the audience, with the two bright lamps in our faces. There was no need for a proper stage, or professional lights or speakers. The room was alive with make-believe.

Lady Agatha's, and all it contained, seemed incredibly distant.

The children clapped with real pleasure at the end. We took another bow. The boy called Felix was sitting absolutely still, and gazing at me with a kind of quiet reverence. It made me feel uncomfortable at first. I smiled at him. He stared a moment longer, and then smiled back, and it looked like a tiny sunrise.

'And now,' said Bel, 'we must have an after-party.'

'Certainly not. It's *Monday*,' Azia said. 'I have stuff to do tonight. Mum will take us to Pizza Express. Is that after-party-ish enough for you?'

It was not.

Cody was carrying armloads of props to the car. Bel turned to him.

'Darling, call Giacomo. See if he's in.'

'Bel, you can't expect him to—'

'It'll just be a few of us. We'll bring our own booze. We'll be quiet as . . . hibernating hamsters.'

Her lip was beginning to tremble. This was little-girl Bel again. The hospital car park was growing dark. The others said their goodbyes and disappeared.

'Nora,' said Bel, throwing her green arms around me. '*You'll* come out and party with us, won't you? I know! How about that place in Waterloo where they do the jazz improvisations? Darian can play for us. We'll drink whisky sours and toast the performance. It's bad luck not to. You must, you have to. Without you, the play wouldn't have *existed*!' Her fingers clutched, almost painfully, at my shoulders. 'You were marvellous too,' she added.

I replied: 'No. *You* were.'

'We'll have you home by midnight, with a coach and footmen.'

I feigned a moment of deciding, and then I said, 'Sure. I'd like that. Just let me text my mum.'

I looked in my bag for my phone, thinking: *Pass Go. Collect £200.* In Monopoly, that's all you need to survive another round. To pass Go, and collect £200. I didn't care where we were going: a boat, Pizza Express, a jazz club or a prison cell. It was all the same. I would make it so that there was a next time, and another £200.

But when I turned on my phone to text Evie, I saw that she had already texted me.

Azia was saying, 'One hour I'll come for. No more.'

'You can come for *five minutes*,' said Bel. 'Nora, honey, you ready?' Her American accent was back: a sign that she was happy.

I looked at their expectant, beautiful faces.

I said: 'My grandmother's very unwell. Nana. In Scotland. I'm sorry. I have to go home.'

8

From one hospital to another in twenty-four hours.

To my embarrassment, I cried all the way out of London, hot loose tears that I was unable to control. My shame was rooted in the fact that I knew I was crying for several reasons, and it felt wrong to use my Nana as a pretext. I *was* crying for Nana, of course. But I also cried because I wasn't sure if I had done enough to cement a friendship between me and Bel. She'd barely smiled when she said goodbye, jumping into the car with no backward glance, no further farewell. I must have offended her by leaving, even though I'd had a very valid reason. I felt almost frantic with despair. And while Evie drove and the rain sewed seams down the windscreen, I cried more.

Nana's frailty had crept up like a weed, subtle and binding. Dwarfed by her curtained cubicle and hi-tech bed, she seemed frailer still. Her cheeks had been bleached of their usual rosy blush. I thought of Nana's arteries, sludgy with her beloved *dulce de leche*; I thought of her battered Mars bars – Nana and Evie were the only people I knew who willingly ate battered Mars bars.

Nana was awake when we got to her bedside, and quite lucid. She held out a hand for each of us, and we kissed her on both cheeks, one at a time.

'You can't bring flowers in here,' said the hefty duty nurse. 'They spread diseases.'

'Then you shouldn't have a sodding flower shop on the ground floor,' said Evie, but she stowed the cellophaned daffodils under the bed. We had also brought grapes and dried cherries, *Private Eye* and *Hello!* magazine. We sat on either side of the bed and willed Nana not to die. But we could see that she wasn't far from it; they might discharge her in four days or a week; there might even be some kind of operation they could do, but she was going to die, sooner rather than later. One of the reasons we knew this is because she seemed so at ease with the thought; in her small accountant's notebook she had written a list of hymns and the telephone number of her vicar.

And now it was Evie's turn to cry.

'Evelyn,' said Nana softly. 'I want you to know that I was quite, quite wrong about your wedding dress. I told you on no account to get married in black.'

Evie smiled through tears. 'You certainly did. You threatened not to come to the wedding.'

Nana blinked her pale eyes. She went on, taking trouble with each word as it came: 'You were the most beautiful bride. In your long black dress. Like a mermaid, you were.'

'I was wearing white underwear,' said Evie.

The woman in the bed opposite looked at us over the top of her paperback.

Now Nana turned to me. 'And you,' she said. 'Dearest Nora. Never stop being yourself, duckling.'

'Dearest Nana,' I replied.

I folded both my hands into her outstretched one, thinking how many times I had done this before: held my Nana's hand. I thought of the years she spent with us, sleeping on the sofa, living out of her suitcase, looking after me and the flat while Evie was unable to function. There was no problem that couldn't be solved with prayer, or a piece of shortbread. Nana had secured us, solid as an anchor, for those anchorless years after my father had died. And now she was unsecured, and floating. Now her hands needed the strength in mine, and not the other way around.

We stayed overnight in a small hotel near Glasgow Royal Infirmary. I discovered when I unpacked my bag that I had not brought my phone – I would have to wait until we got home until I could speak to Bel again. And I could have cried again, for disappointment.

When I woke up the following morning I knew, somehow, that Nana was dead. I stood at the window, not wanting to wake up my mother, wanting the last sleep she had before learning this news to be a long one. The rain was coming down again, slate-grey and slanting. My reflection appeared to me in the glass, and she looked to me like a stranger, casually inquisitive, peering in.

But Nana was not dead, not yet. The hospital would keep her a while, making changes to her medication, monitoring her progress. We waited to be told things, not knowing when or how each piece of information would come. It altered our perception of time: now each day was a milestone, bringing new hope or new despair, and the days were name-less and numberless. Evie booked me a flight home at the end of the week, since I couldn't miss too much school. She herself would stay as long as she had to.

Then we went to Aunt Petra's house.

It was not too far – perhaps three quarters of an hour from the hospital. We drove through Dunbartonshire to Argyll and Bute, around rocky coast and through dormant villages, while the rain drummed on the roof of our ancient car. Evie was calm, but her fingertips tapped at the steering wheel, keeping time with the rain. I kept an eye on her pallid profile as the sea lochs stretched out alongside us, silently asking her the questions I'd been asking, on and off, for ten years.

Are you OK?

And: *What will we do if you're not?*

I rolled my head to the side in a pretence of sleep. If Nana died – when Nana died – I would lose my only ally. Without Nana, there would only be me, checking whether Evie was OK.

We followed the edge of the Gareloch, dotted with sail-boats and the odd yacht, then we passed a naval base – so huge and forbidding that all I could think of was the unstoppable onset of war. After a while, the roads grew narrower and more winding; we came through two or three smaller villages, turned off the road down a tarmacked drive, and came to a gate marked 'Seat of Tranquillity'. Reedy grasses grew up around the gateposts; here and there an army of nettles had been cut back, to make way for those who needed to cross the threshold.

'We're here,' said Evie. She reached over and hugged me. 'It will all be all right,' she said. '*I'm* all right. I promise you.'

But I am not the only one in my family who can tell lies.

9

My ability to tune into the feelings of my mother is strong. Blame the fact that I had no other company after the death of my father. Blame the fact that our flat on the eighth floor of the housing estate is small and spaceless; blame the fact that her grief nearly gobbled her up, and it scared me.

People talk about 'getting over' the death of a loved one. As though death is a hump in the road that you leave behind. I did not think death was like that. From what I'd seen, death was sticky, like semi-dried blood; it got all over your hands, whether you liked it or not. And the more that you loved someone, the stickier it was. I loved my dad. I sat under his desk while he worked; I brought him his small cups of coffee, and his much-adored *palmiers*. But Evie loved him more. Of course, I am not Evie, but I think I can say that: she loved him more. And although she didn't speak about him very often, and although we left France behind, and although she had made no tomb of his possessions, there was no question of her forgetting him, or getting over his death.

He did not say goodbye, you see. To either of us.

But I don't want to go into this now. My point is this:

I am very tuned in to my mother, and I had a feeling that she was going to do something different, and possibly dangerous.

And I was right.

We'd been staying with Petra and Bill for two nights, maybe three. Visiting Nana by day, playing board games by the fire in the evening. Petra had put me in the attic, which had a low sloping roof, a collection of hideous porcelain dolls and a sofa bed that looked more uncomfortable than it actually was. Although he had no shortage of baskets all over the house, Oscar, for reasons he kept to himself, insisted on sleeping with me.

That night I woke up – straight up, as if someone had cracked open the blinds or smacked me on the side of the head. I was out of breath. Maybe I'd been dreaming about falling. I sat up; Oscar growled at me sleepily.

I got out of bed, listening.

It wasn't raining, for once. Maybe I'd been woken by silence. An owl hooted, somewhere quite far away. I put on my slippers and dressing gown and opened the door to the attic. There was a minuscule landing just outside, and a tiny, curtainless window. Through this window you could see the driveway at the front of the house and, over to the left, the octagonal studio.

And in the studio there was a light.

I did not think it was burglars. I'd been into the studio, and there was nothing to steal but a pile of fraying yoga mats and a carved Buddha. I shut Oscar in the attic, in case he misguidedly thought we were going for a night-time walk, and went down the stairs, slowly, avoiding the floor-board that creaked and the rumpled carpeting. Snores floated from Bill and Petra's room, but masculine snores, I thought. Evie's room was down at the opposite end, where all the paying-guest bedrooms were. Her door stood partially open. No snores, and no breathing. I went over to the bed. No Evie.

What were she and Petra doing in the studio in the middle of the night?

I made my way down to the ground floor, glad of my slippers on the cold damp stone. Not drugs. Playing music, perhaps. My pace quickened a little. Not drinking; surely not drinking. My mother would never. And Petra would never let her. I went out through the kitchen door and around the back of the house. A pathway led to the studio, some fifteen or twenty metres away. The private secluded studio.

Not for the first time, I reflected that I am in many ways much less of a teenager than my mother is. Here I was, like a stout matron, about to break up their party. Whatever they were up to in there, they were doing it very quietly; I could hear none of the shrieks and giggles that usually accompanied Evie and Petra's conversations. Maybe they were having a KFC. With all her devout commitment to vegetarianism, eating a bucket of breaded chicken was definitely something that Aunt Petra would need to lock herself away for. Bill Quick hadn't eaten meat since 1994.

But my radar was pure and incredibly clear: *something is up with Evie. Check on her now.*

They were kneeling on round meditation cushions at the centre of the room. Each in her own way looked rather uncomfortable: Aunt Petra is too wide, and my mother is too tall, to kneel with ease on a small round cushion. Three candles burned in front of them; there were further clumps of candles, always in groups of three, in the octagon-corners of the room. The air was misty and pungent: jasmine, geranium, something I couldn't identify.

When I opened the door, they both opened their eyes and jumped.

And then, in a way that was almost funny, they both said, 'Nora!'

I stood on the threshold in my dressing gown, feeling like Mrs Danvers in *Rebecca*. 'What are you doing?' I said.

'Close the door,' said Aunt Petra. 'Come in. Grab yourself a cushion.'

I closed the door and stepped forward a pace, no more. 'Mum?' I said. I never called her 'Mum'. I hoped it would jolt her.

She was looking guilty and pleading and obstinate, not quite meeting my eye.

'We are opening a channel of communication with the

Spirit World,' said Aunt Petra, with the glib air of someone reciting from a book.

'You mean,' I said, coming closer, 'you're trying to contact the dead. My dad. Am I right?'

'The Spirit World,' said Aunt Petra again.

'On the basis of one half-baked seminar!'

'It was a two-day course. They have an excellent reputation . . .'

I said to Evie, 'I thought you didn't believe in it. I thought you said it was nonsense.'

She was still looking guilty and pleading and obstinate. Now she got up and came over to me and bent down to hug me; despite the enormous difference in our heights, it still seemed that she was the child.

'I wanted to try,' she said, so quiet I could barely hear her. 'I couldn't resist. All this with your Nana, and thinking about him, still thinking about him so much, after ten years . . . I just wanted him to tell me why. You must understand.'

'I do understand,' I told her. 'I do. But this is really dangerous. Stupid and dangerous.'

They both seemed to be considering this.

'Perhaps she's right,' said Aunt Petra. 'We ought to have someone to guide us, a professional medium. It's always best with three people, so they say.'

But that wasn't what I meant. I was thinking of the wall of sadness, of the vault inside Evie that could open up again and swallow her. And there would be no Nana to coax her back; there would just be me. I couldn't allow Evie even to attempt it, whatever they were about to do.

'What exactly were you planning?' I said.

'What they taught us,' said Petra. 'To open the chakras, one at a time. To find a place of great stillness. To wait . . . Evie was going to speak to Felix, to see if he was out there.'

'And then?' I said patiently. 'How was he going to respond? You don't have a Ouija board, do you?'

Please could they not have a Ouija board. Please. I'd seen horror films, even if they hadn't.

'Writing,' said Evie. She had something in her hand; she held it up. It was one of her cloth-covered notebooks with hand-cut pages, a biro clipped to the spine. 'They call it automatic writing.'

I wanted to explain to them, in words of one syllable, what – ideally – should happen next. We would blow out the candles; we would go back inside and make hot chocolate, or Ovaltine or whatever Aunt Petra had mouldering away in her cupboards, and then we would go back to bed. But as I planned this all out in my head, I thought: but I'm supposed to leave on Saturday morning. And they'll try again. I can't stop them from trying again. And then I saw that Evie was crying once more, those helpless, colourless tears.

'Evelyn, don't cry,' said Petra, struggling up from her

cushion and coming over to join us. We stood in a huddle, three witches of different sizes, in the candlelit dark.

'What if I do it?' I said. 'You tell me what to do, and I'll do it. You said I'd be good at it, with my imagination. All the chakras and stuff.'

Why they agreed to this, I am also not really sure. Personally, I think that Petra was more afraid of the Spirit World than she claimed to be. As for Evie . . . I think she understood that I didn't want her to venture into territories she might not come back from.

Also: I had no intention of doing anything other than putting on a performance. It would be a very convincing one.

10

Stopping just short of clapping her hands in delight, Aunt Petra took charge of the choreography.

'We'll rearrange the cushions in a wider circle, just so,' she said.

Outside, a wind had started up, and it was wailing against the walls of the studio. Under my dressing gown, I felt ripples along my skin; it was late February and the studio was cold. I could feel my breath coming in miniature snowdrifts. The points of the candles winked and danced. While Evie dried her face and hugged her knees, Aunt Petra explained to Nora the Non-believer how to open and close the chakras. This was long and complicated, and I will give only a few of the details here. She told me to imagine a focus of energy at seven points of my body: the base of my spine, my sacrum, my solar plexus, my heart, my throat, my 'third eye' on my forehead, and my crown. In order to be fully opened up to the possibilities of what lay beyond my own body, I needed to imagine each chakra opening up like a flower. Some people found it helped to concentrate on the colours: red, for the root chakra, was first.

It was difficult, and it was also easy. I listened to Petra's instructions, to the wind and the sound of Evie's shallow breathing. Keeping my eyes closed, I followed what Petra was saying. I pictured the flowers – strange, geometric balls of petal and light, with bound-up energy cycling inside them like writhing ribbons. I pictured opening up each one, letting the ribbons of energy reach out and around me: beanstalks, beams. To picture each flower – each chakra – was easy to do. To keep concentrating was not. Never have I more fully realised the expression: suspending your disbelief. And yet, I did not want to suspend my disbelief. Or not entirely. I needed to stay in control. I needed to be able to make up something good for Evie. Something believable.

'And now moving up to your solar plexus,' murmured Aunt Petra. 'The solar plexus is yellow. A yellow flower, like a buttercup, opening up . . .'

Beyond the flowers – they had glossy, vinyl leaves that extended into miniature points – was a universe of absolute darkness. I congratulated myself for doing this on Evie's behalf. Even though she claimed her imagination wasn't as good as mine, I wouldn't trust Evie alone with the flowers and the darkness. At first, it seemed like it had a strange beauty. But the longer I stayed there, opening up each flower, the darker the darkness became.

And we hadn't even met any spirits yet.

Picture me now: eyes shut, wrapped in my towelling dressing gown, holding my mother's notebook in one hand and a pen in the other. Assume that my chakras are on high alert and that my mind is a big, blank page. I am ready to receive a message from the Great Beyond.

This is how I hope I appeared, to Evie and Petra. But inside, I felt physically altered: chest hot, mouth dry, head curiously light, as though I were coming down with a serious fever. My heartbeat kept doubling and halving, doubling and halving. All of a sudden, I found that I could see a tightrope, travelling forward and into the distance. And there, on the tightrope, on a small, shiny unicycle, was *me*, cynical Nora. And I kept my eyes trained on myself, as I balanced on the tightrope. I could not lose sight of myself. I don't know what I'd been expecting, but I was beginning to find it stranger, more alienating, more frightening than I could have imagined. It was like My Little Pony gone horribly, horribly wrong. I was right: a person could get trapped there.

'Evelyn,' said Aunt Petra. 'I think you should talk to Felix now.'

And so my mother, as husky as a forty-a-day smoker, started to speak. Some things she said in English, others in French. For a while she talked about costumes, things she was planning for her next job; it was as though she were on the phone to him, filling him in about her day. Something funny that Mrs DeAndrade had said on the stairs. How beautiful I was getting, and how brave I was. (At this, I winced; the tightrope shook. She was referring to Jonah Trace.) Then she began talking about Nana; how she'd never heard the phrase *myocardial infarction* before, and now it was all she could think about, over and over; how he'd always been so sweet with Nana, driving her to the church on Sundays although he hated to drive.

'And will you look out for her, please? I don't know how it works. I don't know when she'll come. But I know . . . she'll be so glad to see you. You and Brando and Boots.'

Brando and Boots were Nana's long-deceased collies. I noticed that my mother had left out all of Nana's dead husbands. That was probably for the best. Nana hadn't seemed that keen on any of them.

'I love you,' said Evie. 'I'm sorry . . . I'm sorry that I was so angry.'

All the time she was talking, I wrote in the notebook, keeping it close to my stomach, curled in my hands. Sometimes I swapped hands, as I do when I'm under any kind of pressure; I do it in exams without realising. I was doing it now. It was getting harder and harder to focus on the image I had of myself on the unicycle in the middle of the tightrope. It was getting harder and harder to keep myself from falling off it, and into the flowers and the deep. Feeling sick and light-headed with the effort, I kept myself travelling forwards. My mother's voice faded in and out, then gradually stopped.

'I think we should bring her back,' said Aunt Petra, the great expert. 'Nora, love. Nora?'

'I'm going to be sick,' I said, before I could stop myself.

181

I felt the rush of air as my mother moved towards me.

'No. Wait. I'm OK,' I said, taking control of myself, bit by bit.

'Don't open your eyes just yet,' said Aunt Petra. 'The chakras must now be closed.'

From head to foot, we went through the same process, just in reverse. I shrink-wrapped each flower with iron-clad haste. Never again, never again, I was thinking. Never again will I do something so rash and so stupid. Between the unicycle and the edge of the tightrope there had been less than a millimetre; one blink, one slip, was all it would have taken. I thought about everything real: the sofa in our living room that Evie cherished like a pet, Oscar's whiskery rat-face, the big iron gates of my school. Real and material. Real and safe.

I opened my eyes.

On the page in front of me were three or four lines of writing, almost unrecognisable as mine.

'A natural. She's a natural,' Aunt Petra was saying, as Bel had done. 'So smooth, the way she was writing. That's the beauty of youth. Although I fancy Nora has a very old soul.'

Slowly I tore out the page, and gave it to my mother. She read it in silence. Then she read it aloud.

'*I am very proud of you, Evelyn. I watch over you and Aliénor all the time. Alison will be all right, I promise you. Do not be afraid. I wish I could tell you why I am gone. But there are some things that are hard to explain. One day, Evelyn, you will understand. In the meantime, think of the red and white kite on the beach.'*

'"I am gone",' said Evie, repeating. 'He always said "I am gone", not "I have gone". It was really him. He was really there. It even . . . it even looks like his writing.'

She was tearful, lit-up, sad-happy.

'Did you see him?' she asked.

'No,' I said. 'What I saw was a kind of unending darkness, with these ribbons of rainbow-coloured light all around me, and vague shapes, sort of floating.'

I did not mention the tightrope, that thin link between me and sanity that I'd needed to hold onto for dearest life.

Aunt Petra was nodding intelligently. Could they really believe it was that easy?

'But I heard his voice,' I said. 'It was *definitely* him. Quiet at first, but it got louder. What did he mean about the kite? What kite?'

'You were too young to remember,' said Evie. 'We were all on the beach one day, the one near the Normandy cottage. We found a kite, half-buried in the sand. We thought it was broken, but it wasn't; it just needed a bit of repairing. It was half-red and half-white. He said it was just like us: me and him. He was red, I was white. Like Lancaster and York. Together we were whole. And we fixed it, and we made it fly.'

And now Aunt Petra was crying. I realised the only person

who hadn't cried was me. I could have cried with exhaustion. I could have cried with relief: they believed me completely. Even about the kite – the kite had been important, a vital, credible detail in what was otherwise a pretty predictable note. I remembered the kite well enough, but I was only about two at the time. I knew that Evie wouldn't have thought it possible for me to remember something from so long ago.

I had succeeded; I had succeeded so well that I could at that point have carved out for myself a career in taking money from fools, for passing on more messages from those who had died.

We blew out the candles and went back to the house. Aunt Petra made hot chocolate, and I drank a whole cup of it. Then I kissed them both goodnight, and climbed upstairs to the attic. The things I do for my mother, I thought to myself. But I was pleased, because I knew, in the tuned-in way that I had of knowing things about Evie, that I had averted whatever crisis might have been about to happen. Nana would die, sooner or later, but the wall of sadness would not be an impossibly high one; the vault would not bury her for ever.

Evie had forgotten, in her joy and her tiredness, to ask for her notebook back. And that was good. Because I had only shown her what I'd written with my left hand, as I focused on the tightrope that spanned the flower-filled void.

On the opposite page was something else, something I only noticed afterwards – and luckily did not show Evie or Petra. The writing was cryptic, inexplicable and messy. I had no memory of doing it at all. But I must have done. With my other hand.

O angry flame.
Attention, Aliénor.

Oscar made way for me, grudgingly, as I peeled back the blankets and sheet. Before I turned out the bedside light, I looked at the words again. They sent a cold little current along my limbs.

Attention. It held a different meaning in French, I knew. It meant 'beware'.

A message from the Spirit World, Petra would declare, I was sure. But from which spirit, if so? And why? It could only be Felix Tobias. And that had implications I couldn't bear to consider. No. Séances were show business. Everyone knew that. Wherever my father was – and I wasn't sure he was anywhere, but personally I imagined him on a Normandy beach, paintbrush in hand – I hoped he was, finally, happy. I'd achieved what I'd set out to achieve, which was to convince Evie of this. No one had been present in the octagonal studio but the three of us and the carved Buddha.

I tore out the page, crumpled it up and threw it into the wastepaper basket.

As I fell asleep, I saw myself once more on the tightrope, aloft and wavering, while the flowery chakras swirled underneath, with their energy fronds reaching out like the tendrils of man-eating plants. And the darkness . . . the great and borderless darkness . . . and the sound of the wind on the walls . . .

And faintly, almost like laughter, somewhere far, far below me, a voice that may or may not have been mine, screaming.

PART THREE

JACARANDA

1

Whether training a dog, embroidering a handkerchief or burying a husband, Nana had always been a person of great resolve. For a day or so more, she hovered on a tightrope of her own. And then she stabilised. It seemed she had decided not to die, after all.

'Don't *ever* scare me like that again,' said Evie, after Nana had been discharged and we'd brought her back home. My mother seemed to glitter with an inner light. I was sure I knew why, and it wasn't just because Nana was still with us. From time to time, Evie would look at me and twinkle with pride.

I placed my lips on my grandmother's powdery cheek, and was glad that it felt warmer than it had in the hospital; it was as though lifeblood were flowing through her again, if only for the time being. Nana put on *Murder, She Wrote* and looked about for her knitting.

'Goodbye, Nana,' I said. 'See you soon.'

'"Blessed are the pure in heart, for they will see God",' she muttered. 'The Book of Matthew, 5:8. Stay true to yourself, my girl.'

* * *

'Dad told you, didn't he?' said Evie, after a period of silence on our journey home. She'd decided to drive back with me, after all, now that Nana seemed to be on the road to recovery.

'What?' I said.

'About Nana.'

'Ah, yes,' I lied. 'He did.'

'You knew she was going to be all right,' said Evie, regarding me as a devout pilgrim might look upon a beloved temple.

I pointed out that according to the laws of physics, Nana wasn't going to be all right for ever.

'But he told us she wasn't going to die. Not then. Nora Alison Tobias, I think what you did was the most bloody amazing thing I've ever bloody seen. It made that whole psychic workshop totally worth it, after all. Petra would never say so, but she's massively jealous. She'll keep practising now, just see if she doesn't. The way he told you about the kite. That *writing* . . .'

She waved her tattooed fingers as she spoke. It was raining still, the slow lane of the motorway barely moving. At her mention of the writing, I suppressed a wave of revulsion.

'I think you should do it again,' said Evie.

I couldn't think of anything worse.

'But just imagine what else you could find out. You could try to talk to Grandpa! Or Brian from the Rolling Stones. Or the captain of the *Titanic*. Ask him why they didn't spot the iceberg earlier.'

To this I said nothing.

'Or Dad, of course,' she said, as though she'd forgotten the reason for doing it in the first place. It was very Evie, this: a vault of sadness, a veil of flippancy to cover it up afterwards.

Controlling myself as best I could, I said: 'Mum. I did it once, for you. I think twice would be stupid.'

She reached over and put her hand on my arm. 'Sorry. You're right. These things always take their toll, don't they? You do look a bit shattered.'

'He said he was OK,' I went on. 'And I think that's all we can really ask for.'

As I report this conversation now, a few months later, all I can think about is how much we were leaving unsaid.

It was late on Saturday night by the time we got back. After nearly a week away, London felt louder and stranger than ever. The river was jumping with parties on boats, the air alive with sirens.

Straight away, I went to find my phone. I imagined all the things that Bel might have found to say in her messages. Congratulations on my performance in the play, for a start – or if not congratulations, then at least thanks, for my helpful part in it. Perhaps an invitation to go out with her, or round to her house. Then maybe there'd be a couple of anxious follow-ups – why wasn't I responding? Was I OK? What about my Nana? The volume of these would go up and up as the days went by. I prepared myself, as the texts and notifications came in, to reply at once and explain that I'd left my phone behind. I might even call her, if she had left me a significant number of messages.

The first text was from Thurston, and it did indeed thank me for my part in *The Belle of the Ball*. I deleted it by mistake in my effort to close it quickly. Then there were five or six messages from Perfect, with details of all the homework I was missing. Perfect hated to miss an assignment. High-pitched beeps came from the living room: Evie was checking the answerphone. I listened, in case for some reason Bel had rung the landline, but knowing that she wouldn't have done. Petra's voice bleated fondly, asking if we'd got home safely. Then another woman's voice. It sounded work-related. I looked at my phone again. Switched it off and back on.

There was nothing from Bel; not an iota.

'Oh,' I said aloud.

'What's wrong?' Evie stood in my doorway, less pallid than usual.

'Nothing,' I said. 'You OK? Any news? How's Nana?'

'There *is* news,' she said slowly. 'I've been offered a job in Romania. A vampire movie.'

'That's amazing,' I said. 'You've got to take it.'

'I dunno,' said Evie. She wandered over to the balcony door and looked down through the cast-iron bars towards the river. 'It feels like the wrong time to go. Leaving you on your own, and Nana sick . . . I'd have to get a flight on Monday. I could be gone for a few weeks. Five or six, even. Away for your birthday. It's too much right now.'

But I urged her to go. To work with vampires – with bodices and cloaks, with silk-lined coffins and doublets and hose, or whatever was needed – was Evie's Grail, and she had to take it. Mrs DeAndrade had spare keys. I could stay with a friend, if I got lonely. She could come back, if she had to. We could speak by phone and Skype.

In the end, she agreed.

So all the next day Evie unpacked and repacked her cases. I was impressed: she seemed practical and full of purpose. The prospect of losing Nana was not the same as the loss of my father, I realised. Nana's life had been as rich and layered as one of her beloved *alfajores*, and we knew that when she eventually died, she would be at peace. I saw that Evie had drawn, in red biro on the inside of her wrist, a small kite. A minicab came to get her at three in the morning, and I got up to wish her good luck.

'I hate goodbyes,' she said, kissing me on the ear.

I went to school a couple of hours later full of anticipation. Bel's timetable I knew as well as my own; her form room was on the floor above mine, and I found a reason to go there before registration. But I did not see her there; nor did I see her bag. I had already decided that her lack of messages was down to impatience – she would want to see me in person, I decided, to thank me. I wondered where she was.

Then it came to me: the Art and Design Centre. More than likely, she'd be there, working on her portfolio. Hurriedly, I made my way there, brushing aside the ghosts of my dealings with Jonah Trace as I went down the stairs, and the doubts that squirrelled up and down in my consciousness about who, exactly, knew what. Those doubts were liable to kindle wildfire, and do all kinds of mischief. I couldn't allow this to happen.

Sharon Alexis was cleaning brushes at the sink. 'Help you, Nora?' she said.

'I'm looking for Bel,' I replied.

'She was away most of last week,' the art assistant said. 'Haven't seen her today, either.'

And now it all made sense – Bel was, of course, ill. I hoped she hadn't caught a cold from me. I'd feel bad if that were the case. It was more likely, though, that she'd gone out partying too many times. I pictured her in her conservatory, halfway through some kind of hangover-healing eggnog in a vintage cup, or a many-plated breakfast.

But as I was going back upstairs, there she was, coming down. The usual clatter of trinkets accompanied her. She was, for once, not wearing a kimono, but a leather jacket and flared jeans. The whites of her eyes were pinkish; her nose likewise.

'Oh, hey, honey,' she said. 'How's your grandma?'

I was so pleased to see her that I could have almost reached out to hug her, but something in her manner stopped me.

'She's stable,' I said. 'Out of hospital. How are you? Have you been ill?'

She sniffed. 'Heartsick,' she said.

I realised she'd been crying. 'How come?'

'It's just . . . there's something I want, desperately, more than anything. And I can't have it.'

'I'm sorry,' I said, and I was. 'Can I do anything?'

'I don't even want to talk about it,' she said, brushing past me.

I wanted to follow her down the stairs, catch her by the arm, ask her what the matter was. But I did none of those things.

'Has anyone ever done anything that broke your heart?' came a muffled voice from below me.

Yes, I thought. Yes, they have.

I caught up with the rest of my class, who were already winding their way to the chapel, and Sarah Cousins gave me another unsympathetic look.

All that week, each time I saw Bel it was the same – a light greeting, an airy farewell. No hugs. No confidences. No plans for the future. What was wrong with her? Was it something to do with the play? As far as I could tell, *The Belle of the Ball* had been well-received by children and hospital staff alike. So why, in the words of the Fairy Godmother, was Bel so sad? What was it that she couldn't have? Who, or what, had broken her heart? I found myself quite preoccupied by it all.

Then, to make matters worse, Lori Dryden came to me with some unpleasant news.

'There's a rumour going around that you honeytrapped Mr Trace,' she told me one break time, her mouth full of KitKat.

'I don't even know what that means,' I said.

It was true: I didn't. Was 'honeytrap' even actually a verb? I thought it was an undercover operation, something you saw on TV crime re-enactments. But Lori, who no doubt was spreading the rumour as well as receiving it, said it with relish, and I saw at once what she was trying to say. The tagline had shifted; the victims had swapped sides. Now Jonah Trace was the injured party, and I was a honeytrap. A ruthless, manipulative teen fatale. *A little liar.* In other circumstances, I might have thought it was quite an attractive word. And indeed, it was almost apt.

'People are saying you led him on,' she said, watching me closely from underneath mauve-shadowed eyelids.

'Who's saying that?'

'Can't reveal.'

With no time to waste, I began to cry, dramatic and shuddering. I ran my hands over my upper arms, as though to calm the angry bruises that had been left there by Jonah

Trace's fingers. I was helpless and unable to control my tears, and I knew that Lori, who had never seen me cry, would be suitably shocked.

She laid down her KitKat, but went on chewing as she drew me into a close embrace. Through the wall of her cheek I could hear the sound of crunching, like a combine harvester.

'I never thought it was true,' she said mildly.

Evie was gone, but far from the thrill of freedom that I usually felt when I had the flat to myself, I fell into a quicksand of gloom. My conversation with Lori lingered and spread, like damp on a wall, absorbing me. It wasn't just the thought of what people were saying. It was the thought of what I had done. He deserved it, I kept thinking to myself. He did. I might have engineered certain situations, but he allowed it to happen. He *wanted* it to happen. For someone like my father, goodness and evil, right and wrong, were polar opposites, with not an inch of slippage between them. But I didn't think it was as simple as that.

I forgot to eat. I slept on one side of my bed, pressed up against the wall. The boiler kept breaking down, and I missed the bristly, whiskery Oscar, who was warm, though infuriating. I found no pleasure in reading. I dawdled on my way into school. I would have stopped going altogether and spent my time instead wandering along the South Bank, or staring at the river. But I couldn't afford to do anything else at school that might have caused trouble. They seemed not to want to investigate the Trace Incident further, in spite of my form tutor's misgivings, in spite of the rumours, presumably because they'd found he'd done similar things with other girls at other schools. I had to be grateful for that.

But still I did not feel safe.

In the evenings, I watched movies, continuing my research into the Ingram-Lane dynasty, even though I didn't know whether Bel would ever call me again. I went through old albums, looking at the darker spaces where photographs of my father had been. And I thought of my Felix Tobias fairy tales that I told, so fluently and with such ease that I barely connected them any longer to the person they were meant to be about.

He disappeared at sea.

He was poisoned by an oyster.

He died in a crash on the Métro.

It was funny, I thought, that I should tell such lies about my father, a person for whom truth was very important. I remembered a time when I'd brought him a sketch of a clock tower that I'd drawn. He said it was magnificent, studying it closely, following the pencil strokes with a finger.

'Did you use a ruler? These lines are perfectly straight,' he said.

My father frowned on using a ruler when doing an observational drawing. I assured him fervently that I had not.

'Now, Aliénor,' he'd said, with a sadness so clear that it pained me deeply, 'you know that it is wrong to lie . . .'

I sat on the balcony in my coat. I lay in the bath, while the tap dripped onto my ankle. I stood at the bathroom mirror, watching myself and trying not to think about the tightrope and the flowers, and the long, long fall into darkness.

And although I despised myself for it, because it was maudlin and teenagey and self-absorbed, I would stand at that mirror and think: *I do not know who I am.*

2

March the eleventh was a Saturday, and also my birthday.

I woke early with a sharp, winded jolt. I'd been dreaming of the flowers. The tightrope in the darkness, and the flowers, and that indecipherable message, lettered with my right hand: *O angry flame. Attention, Aliénor.* I splashed water onto my face and made myself breakfast – toast, yogurt, coffee, more than I'd usually eat – but the dream still clung to me, the way savage and messy dreams do. Then Evie called from her trailer; even though the line was poor, she belted Stevie Nicks' *Edge of Seventeen* down the phone with such gusto that I laughed aloud, and finally the dream was gone.

'How are you?' she said.

'I miss you loads,' I said. 'But I'm fine. The weather's all right. A bit changeable.'

While she told me at length about the joys of hooking corpulent C-list actresses into waist-hugging corsets, I opened a small pile of cards. There was one from Petra and Bill, another from an old friend of Nana's, and a third from my French godmother, whom I seldom saw. Nothing from anyone younger than forty-five. Nothing from any of my former obligatory friends. This was not unexpected. But it made me feel something I did not often feel, because over the years I had taught myself to delight in solitude.

It made me feel lonely.

I thought for a while. And then I reached for my mobile and, with care, wrote a text to Bel. It was simple enough, the kind of message I never sent to anyone, ever.

Howdy, it said. *How's tricks?*

Then I sat back with a book and waited.

Almost comically quickly, my mobile rang.

'Nora, honey, it's me. I'm having a party and I want you to come,' she said.

There was no mention of why she'd been ignoring me at school. Heartsick Bel was gone; I wondered what had changed. I presumed it was connected to the party, and her reasons for giving it.

'Green!' said Bel, having given me some directions that seemed vague in the extreme. 'Wear green. Bring anyone you like, and a bottle, of course. *Two bottles.*'

From eight, she'd said, but I waited until closer to nine before I set out on the tube. I had two bottles of wine, one red and one white, bought with some of the cash that Evie had left. I'd carefully planned the journey – two tube changes, and then the overland, and then a fifteen-minute walk. From where we lived, it was well over an hour. It felt like the apex of bravery to be going to a party alone.

The dress code caused me some concern. Evie owned plenty of green garments, but I didn't like the idea of wearing something eye-catching as I walked through an area of Outer London – somewhere near Hampton Court – with which I was unfamiliar. I was therefore wearing close to my ordinary clothes – jeans, a black vest top, a denim jacket. My concessions to Bel's code were a shamrock badge of Evie's from her bartending days and a turquoise-and-yellow checked scarf that I'd found at the back of her sock drawer. Green eye-pencil lined my upper lids. Part of me wanted to wear something outrageous, something Bel-worthy. But I just didn't have the courage for it.

The tube carriage smelled of alcohol and anticipation. The residue of the day hung heavy in the compartment, a thousand exhaled breaths clogging the humid air.

'You're early for St Paddy's day,' said a tanned man in a beige jacket, raising a brow at my shamrock.

I smiled and looked again at my map of London, trying to learn by heart the route I would take to the party. *Constantine's Wharf*, Bel had said. *Walk through the gate. Fourth boat from the end. Morgan le Fay.* I had never been to a houseboat before. I wondered if there would be rats.

As I was leaving the station I saw Thurston coming up the stairs, with a white-tooth grin and a tan that said Money.

'Long time no see,' he said, kissing me on the cheek. He was wearing a Kermit the Frog T-shirt under a black blazer, and as we walked he regaled me with anecdotes, many involving vodka and poor behaviour on the slopes of a Canadian ski school. After some time, we turned towards the river – *follow the river*, my father said in my head – and came to Constantine's Wharf. I could see a round, overgrown island not far away, which surprised me, because I hadn't known there were any islands in the Thames.

'Bel's famous for her parties,' Thurston told me, as we neared the row of houseboats. I looked at the names: *Strange Fortune* and *Rover's Revenge* and *What Moonlight* and *Idaho*.

'Who owns the boat?' I asked.

'Giacomo,' he said. 'You know him?'

'No.'

'He's one of Bel's exes. A musician. This is it, here.'

And sure enough, we had come to the fourth boat from the end. It was a barge of some kind, I thought. *Morgan le Fay* was painted in white on the dark-blue hull. Music – the squawking of digital ostriches, to my ear – flowed densely from the speakers on the deck. There was smoke too, and for a moment I thought the boat was on fire, but it was dry ice from a machine. Thurston took my hand and helped me across the gangplank, and I stepped onto what felt like hay. I looked down. Streamers of ivy and clumps of ferns were heaped all over the deck. A girl in an aquamarine sequinned tailcoat was leaning over the rails, warbling into her phone. The door to a kind of upper chamber was propped open, and from inside came more smoke and louder music, and a mist of green light, like some toxic ether. I felt an urge to turn around and flee, but Thurston still had a hand on my arm, and I steeled myself. I took off my jacket, which showed off my neck and shoulders and arms, and walked in.

The upper room was empty; it had a table and chairs, and bits of musical equipment and instruments in cases. There was a steering wheel of polished wood. I remembered the right word for the upper room: wheelhouse. There was a short flight of very steep stairs, and I let Thurston go down these first, since he knew where he was going. I had a sensation of crossing some boundary between living and dead, land and sea; maybe it was the thought of water all around and beneath, or maybe it was the feeling of walking into something that couldn't be known.

Below was a dark oblong room with a leather banquette at one end, a kind of kitchenette at the other, and small rectangular windows. I saw Bel at once. She was wearing a man's suit with flared trousers in bottle-green velvet, a cream shirt, a lime-coloured bow tie, a bowler hat. She was sitting on the kitchen counter and singing *Ten Green Bottles* with much merriment. Azia, her hair tied up in a green scarf, was dancing with a tall boy I didn't know. Everyone else, apart from Thurston, was a stranger. I could not see Darian. Some people looked much older. Characterful, colourful people they were, with many-toned hair and elaborate voices that made their origins hard to identify. Their movements were grand and expansive; the small space made them seem grander still.

They wore leather and animal print; they wore fishnet stockings and false eyelashes and high, high shoes, men and women both. And a lot of green, as per Bel's instructions.

I went over and talked to Azia, who was now adrift between dancers. She seemed pleased that I was there. The music was so loud that it was hard to hear, and we went up onto the deck for a while, which was a little better. I knew the kinds of things she liked to read, and it was no trouble to mention two or three writers that I thought she would admire.

Later, as I was coming back into the wheelhouse, Bel cannoned into me. Her eyes were glittering and unsteady. She wrapped herself around me, singing into my ear.

'Nora, I adore ya,' she sang. 'I'm sorry I was so tragic all of last week. Everything's better now. Daddy . . . well, he sort of changed his mind about something important. You'll see.'

I'd never seen her quite like this before, glib, almost gibbering, though over-glazed with a queenly grace. What she'd taken, I don't know; I imagine a blend of substances, tailored to her particular desires. I didn't know the party guests well enough to say whether their states were substantially altered by chemicals, but there was enough evidence – dark-coloured liquid in a wrought silver chalice, sipped and passed on; powders in thin lines on upturned mirrors – for me to assume that most of them were high on something. I found it alarming, unnerving. I was just starting to think that I had to get home – the last train would be leaving soon – when a bell clanged and Bel climbed back onto the counter with a glass of champagne in her hand.

'Ladies and gentlemen, *Meine Damen und Herren*, boys and girls and halflings and all my darlings,' she said. 'Welcome to my party. On Giacomo's boat. Thank you, Giacomo.'

'What're we celebrating?' called someone from the corridor, where there was a disorderly queue for the bathroom.

'Hush now,' said Bel. 'I'm just getting to that. We are gathered here today, because . . . but let me tell you the entire story, my loves. Once, long ago, a couple of years after Mama died, our father secured the rights to *Jacaranda*. For those of you who are ignorant simpletons and do not know, *Jacaranda* was a prizewinning novel that was adapted into a movie directed by Vincent St Clair and starring Ken Harmon and Susan Lorrimer and . . . my mama – *our* mama, I should say, Darian, sorry – in her first major feature. *Jacaranda* was hailed as a great English love story. Hers was a small role – that of Clementine, the daughter – but it was the role that set her on her path to greater stardom and for which she was nominated for an Academy Award as Best Supporting Actress. She was nineteen at the time of filming. In fact, it was when he saw this movie that our father fell in love with her – so he says – although they didn't meet until many years later.'

As Bel spoke, the room was totally silent. I moved away from a rowdy guest, wanting to hear her clearly. She held out her empty glass of champagne and waited for someone to refill it. Someone did.

'Ta,' she said. 'So, as I was saying, Papa bought the rights to *Jacaranda* nearly ten years ago. He got different people to write treatments and scripts. None of them right. Then he had some meetings with a writer-director called Gabriel Glass, and Gabriel wrote a script and it was *perfect*. Now Papa has raised money from all kinds of different places, they have the script and the director and two major names attached as the stars, and I have promised on pain of death not to mention who they are just yet. Ladies and Gentlemen, *Jacaranda* has received, officially, a greenlight!'

To this there were cheers, though I felt they were out of pleasure at Bel's happiness rather than genuine excitement. I found Bel's little speech quite fascinating. She seemed so lucid, so word-perfect. Was there any more exciting phrase in the English language than *the path to greater stardom*? I'd yet to hear it, if so. I watched Bel's poised, angular, pearlescent face, as she said:

'There's more.'

A cry of 'more, more!' echoed around the room. Green bulbs glowed from two wall lamps, and I realised, quite late, the point of the dress code. Looking about the room, I saw Darian, his gold hair combed straight back over his head, sitting on the banquette and watching his sister with an expressionless face. Hers was anything but expressionless, of course.

Managing to look coy, wistful and proud, all at the same time, Bel said: 'Now, as soon as I found out that the movie was greenlit I sat down with Papa and I said to him: "Daddy, there is nobody who can play the role of Clementine as well as I can. You *have* to let me play her." And, d'you know what? He told me he'd been thinking the *exact same thing*. Principal photography starts in the autumn, once they've worked out their budgets and schedules and whatnot. I'm going to be Clementine. And I'm going to do an incredible job!'

Azia said, 'Well, I never.'

The music came back, raucous and thundery. Bel took a bow. Slipping through the crowd, I waited to use the bathroom. It was a tiny, alarming place with black walls and a black toilet, a headless doll suspended from the light cord and a skeleton – like the one Bel had – jammed under the window. By the time I returned to the party, the room was heaving with formless green debauchery. Azia was nowhere to be seen. Bel was sitting on the lap of a boy with long black hair who I presumed was Giacomo, the owner of the boat, drinking from a jar. I checked the time. Ten past midnight. I'd missed the overland. Probably the tube as well. I'd have to take a bus, though I hadn't a clue which, or how long it would take me.

A hand on my shoulder. 'Are you OK, Nora?'

It was Darian.

'I'm fine,' I said. 'Just tired.'

'I can't give you a lift anywhere,' he said. 'I'm sorry. I have to stay here. Perhaps—'

The sea-green-tailcoat girl came over and claimed him, weaving busy hands around his neck.

I climbed the staircase back up to the deck. Night twinkled through the small round portholes of the wheelhouse, which was deserted except for Zubin, asleep in a chair. I sat on the floor and took out my phone. The battery was flat. I didn't have a bus map. I would have to guess. If Thurston were still there I might have been able to charm him into escorting me, but I hadn't seen him. Perhaps he was in one of the bedrooms. The air was sharp and cold and I wanted my jacket, but I hadn't seen that either. I didn't want to go back downstairs. I felt very tired. Every time I tried to galvanise myself to get going, a fear of being alone in the London night stopped me.

Perhaps Zubin had the right idea. I climbed into the other chair, and I was, like him, just small enough to fit well inside the seat. I didn't have the inner tranquillity that he clearly had, however, because the noise, the smell of smoke and dry ice, the instability of it all made it hard for me to fall asleep. But the greenlight party raged on and on until the noise dwindled, and eventually I must have slept.

3

'I'm afraid there's been a misunderstanding. You did well, sweetheart. You and your troupe in the children's ward. But one good deed does not a reformed character make.'

Before I opened my eyes, I knew that it was daylight, and from the solidity of whatever I was lying on I realised that I was no longer on Giacomo's boat. A nudge of fur at my ankles told me that an animal was present. Opening my eyes, I saw the tortoiseshell cat and realised I was on the sofa in the Ingrams' conservatory, under a crocheted blanket. Some way away at the kitchen table were Bel and her father, speaking quietly, with a teapot between them and plates of toast, untouched. The earthenware jar containing the remains of Phyllis Lane sat thoughtfully on the windowsill, looking on.

'Daddy,' Bel was saying. 'But you *said* . . .'

'I understand why you want to play this part.'

'It's *my* part. I can do it justice. *Only* I can do it justice.'

'This is not school,' said Anton, buttering toast. 'This isn't some threepenny costume drama, a play you've decided to put on in the middle of the night, amateur dramatics in the village hall or even a performance for sick children that you've cooked up out of the kindness of your heart. These are serious people. This is serious money, with serious expectations to go alongside it. Look at what happened at your school last year.'

'I was exceptional in *Cabaret*. Everyone said so.'

'You were so late for one of the performances that they nearly had to cancel it.'

'That's not true.'

'And what about *Teen Spirits*? You can't say that was an overwhelming success now, can you?'

The conversation was a rapid back-and-forth, and I got the sense they'd played the scene many times.

'They were going to ask me back for a third series,' Bel began.

'Only because they couldn't prove that it was you who flooded the set,' said her father. 'The problem, Annabel, is that you have no sense of responsibility for anything.'

'How can you say it's not my part when you told me I could play her? I had a party to celebrate! A greenlight party!'

'This is exactly my point. It's not about parties, awards, red carpets or greenlights. This is not about what you tell your friends, Bel. I did not promise.'

'You said YES.'

'Yes, I would think about it. That's all I said. You chose to interpret this in your own way.'

'You. Said. YES.'

I kept very still as I listened, not wanting them to know that I was awake. I was surprised that Bel herself was up. She couldn't have had much sleep. I didn't feel like I'd had much, myself. How had I got here, from the boat to the conservatory? I closed my eyes and continued to feign unconsciousness as their conversation went on.

'Your predicted grades are appalling,' he said.

'Oh, come on, Dad—'

'Your lack of intellectual ambition is something I find quite deplorable.'

'I have plenty of ambition. My ambition is to play Clementine in *Jacaranda*.'

'And then?'

'Drama school.'

'Along with a thousand other people. All just as hungry and full of ambition. You'll have nothing to fall back on if you leave school with no qualifications.'

Silence.

'I'll get better grades.'

'I don't believe you.'

'For Chrissake, Daddy. I *promise* you I will. But you have to promise me too.'

The scrape of a chair; I opened a subtle eye to see Anton walking over to the range, where the kettle was whistling. My throat ached for tea.

'It's not as simple as that. One thing you don't want in this business is a reputation. Sure, directors will go out and party with you and have a good time. But you'll find after a couple of years that you just won't get the parts you want. People won't want to work with you if they've seen you off your face too many times. Or, indeed, if you commit acts of wilful vandalism.'

Another pause, and then: 'Sure,' she said. 'Sure, Dad.'

'So there will be no more parties on boats, automobiles, in circus tents or nuclear bunkers, or anywhere else you manage to dream up,' said Anton Ingram, as he poured water into the teapot. 'I'm not proposing a curfew here. Just an observation of principle. Convince me that you can pass your exams, show the occasional spark of altruism – those sick children were a nice touch, but I could see what you were doing – and live like a healthy human being and not a coffin-dwelling wraith, and—'

'Oh, man.'

'Don't "man" me, Annabel.'

'Sorry.'

'What do you think? Can you do all those things?'

'I can. I definitely, definitely can.'

'Promise?'

'Girl Guides' honour. Cross my heart and hope to—'

'Then,' said Anton with robust dramatic timing, 'I shall think about it. Careful of the hot water.'

My neck was bent at a strange angle. I unbent it; the cat slithered off me and Bel looked over from the stove, where she and Anton were mid-hug.

'Hi, sugar!' she said. 'Just in time for breakfast.'

'Good morning, Nora,' said Anton. 'I'll see you later,' he said to Bel, kissing her on the cheek. 'We'll talk more. You look very like your mother when you argue with me, incidentally.'

'It's all going to be magnificent,' said Bel, eating jam out of the jar with a knife.

Darian, who had come into the kitchen not long after, rolled his eyes. 'You're an idiot,' he said. 'I didn't realise when you borrowed the boat that you were intending to tell everyone you had the part. He'll never give it to you.'

'He will.'

'Why did you say that he already had, in front of everyone?'

Bel rolled a cigarette, although I noticed she did not smoke it immediately. 'I was getting the universe to sort it out,' she said. 'I was making it real. If you say things enough times, they become true, you know.'

Darian said, 'Giacomo says you owe him two hundred and thirty quid, incidentally.'

'For what?'

'All the stuff that got broken.'

'Nonsense,' said Bel. 'What are a few old plant pots between ex-lovers? It was hardly much of a party, anyway. A very small gathering of intimate friends. Anyway, I practically own that boat. He named her for me and everything.'

I could hear Anton on the phone in the living room, and

wondered if he was speaking to some mysterious financier, or even Mr Gabriel Glass himself, about *Jacaranda*. Could it really be as simple as that? Was Anton really able to promise a part to his daughter? Later, conversations with people who knew about such things would inform me that yes, he could; for a producer as powerful as Anton Ingram, it really was that simple. Although the big parts required big stars in order to secure funding – whether from the BBC or a bank or a media investment company – a relatively small part like Clementine, suitable for a début performance, was certainly something that he could give to whomever he chose.

'D'you really think he's going to let you be in the movie?' said Darian.

'Why the hell not?' She licked the knife with relish.

'Your history, for a start.'

'We've already discussed that. I need some OK-ish grades, though.'

'He'll probably get you a tutor,' said Darian. 'God help the tutor.'

'No,' said Bel. 'I can't deal with that. Having to be at home at the same time every week and watch them squirm and stare at the clock and feeling so incredibly stupid. I have a *much* better idea.' She smiled. 'Now I shall go for an energising jog in the park. Wanna come, guys?'

But Darian wanted to practise the piano, and I said I wasn't much of a runner.

I could see from the way that Darian was covering his toast with Marmite and then cutting the slices into ever-smaller rectangles that something was bothering him. I didn't feel that I could ask. Instead, I asked him if there was somewhere I could charge my phone.

'Behind the kettle,' he said. 'Just unplug the juicer. No one uses it anyway. There's a whole bunch of chargers there, in the drawer. Any good?'

'Perfect, thank you,' I said, taking one.

What I really wanted was a toothbrush, but I didn't feel that I could ask this either. A few minutes later, however, he went out and returned with a towel, a toothbrush (new, in packaging) and a tiny shampoo bottle of the free-gift variety.

'Bel's shown you where the bathroom is, yeah? If you want to take a shower. Not that I'm suggesting you, ah, need to take one. You know.'

I thanked him for his excellent hosting sensibilities, to spare his blushes. I heard piano music when I went upstairs: tight, mathematical scales that climbed and fell with jumpy ferocity. It seemed to me that Darian Ingram had few ways to express how he felt.

When I came back to the kitchen there was no sign of Bel. Darian was in the garden, smoking. He looked round at me, and smiled in a way that felt beckoning, so I went to join him. He offered me a cigarette; I shook my head.

The air smelled of damp earth; there were some little buds peeping up through the soil in the flower beds.

'Did you enjoy the party?' he asked me.

'Honestly,' I said, 'I'm not much of a party person.'

'Me neither. What do you like?'

'Reading,' I said. 'Reading and swimming, mostly.'

'Do you have exams?'

'A-levels next year. Nothing this year except coursework.'

'Look,' he said. 'She's going to ask you to, like, help with all her work. Writing essays and notes. Revising. There's, what, two and a half months until her A-levels. I don't want you to get dragged into all this.'

I asked him what he meant.

'It's just a power game between Bel and Dad. This is how they've always been. She asks for something ridiculous; he promises it on certain conditions. Or he bribes her with something to get her to change her behaviour. That's how we got her off Valium. And shoplifting. Sometimes neither of them gets what they want. Sometimes they both do. But Bel survives. And that's all Dad cares about.' He stopped, looking embarrassed. 'I shouldn't be telling you so much.'

'It's OK,' I said.

'The point is,' said Darian, 'you should get out now, while you can. Don't be taken in. That's all I'm saying. Bel's all about what she can get.'

The cat leaned over the pond and swiped for a fish, letting out a scratchy yowl that made us both jump. We stayed in the garden a while longer, not saying much, until Bel came clattering around the side of the house in purple running shorts and said, with what I presumed was sarcasm, that she hoped she wasn't interrupting anything important.

4

Darian had known Bel all her life; she'd been a part of mine for a matter of weeks. I had no doubt that he was right. He had warned me. Clearly he was a rational person, worth listening to. I think, at that moment, it might have been possible for me to make my excuses and walk away.

But I didn't.

Sure enough, after Bel returned from her jog, she did indeed suggest that I might be able to help her with what she called 'organisational matters'. In return, she promised, as she always did, 'a pedestal', this one of rainbows and quartz and chrysanthemums, if I remember correctly. This might seem like an odd sort of exchange – unfair, really – since she was offering a made-up object of no value in exchange for so much. But what she was really offering was *herself*. Her time, her affection. And it was an offer I couldn't refuse.

I began to adjust the patterns of my daily existence to suit hers. For the rest of the spring term, Bel and I spent our lunch breaks in the library, our heads close together as I helped her first to make up the considerable academic ground that she had lost, and then to create and use revision materials for English and History. Even with Art and Design I helped her, by mimicking her bold sketching style with my left hand, and filling page upon page of her sketchbooks.

We met after school. Sometimes we even met before – eating eggs on toast in the local greasy spoon and chatting both sense and nonsense. Since Evie was still in Romania, I started spending Friday nights at Bel's house, and occasionally I'd stay over until the Monday morning, when Cody would appear out of nowhere to drive us to school. Bel had a relative who would periodically send her money, and when this happened, the theatre was what she wanted to spend it on. We saw plays by Shakespeare and Arthur Miller and Tennessee Williams, sitting in the cheapest seats, but having – I thought – the most fun. I'd never really gone to the theatre; it was too expensive for me and Evie unless as an exceptionally special treat.

As good as her word, Bel neither held nor attended a single party.

Just as I'd suspected, she was not at all stupid. It was laziness and lack of drive that had resulted in her poor grades thus far, not lack of ability. I was no teacher, but I could see that she was making real progress. Her verbal memory was very sound, and although her essay technique was poor I found that if I wrote model essays that showcased exactly how to treat a particular question, she was able to reproduce them with ease. By and by we found we didn't need to work the entire time, after all. We'd talk, and dress up; we'd read to each other in the garden and make up strange things to eat and drink. I told her about the death of my father, choosing Mysterious Disappearance as the story I felt she'd appreciate most, and she listened in soulful silence. I told her about my mother, and about Aunt Petra. I even told her about the séance in the octagonal studio, and the Chakra Flowers of Doom (not the entire story, of course, but a version of it).

Bel was entranced. 'How did you know it was him?' she said, at once. 'It could have been a demon, you know, pretending to be your father.'

Like me, Bel had seen a lot of movies.

'I need you to do it again,' she'd say sometimes. 'Get into your trance, and talk to my mama. Ask her whether Daddy is going to let me play Clementine.'

But I wouldn't allow myself to be persuaded.

Announcing that tar and tobacco were wrecking her acting voice, Bel stopped smoking. She went running on the common every week; at least, that is what she said she was doing. She took to drinking a concoction of beetroot, pineapple and kale that I found totally undrinkable, but that – she claimed – would purify the blood. Her eating habits remained erratic, as did her drinking habits. But by and large, I could see that Anton's challenge had been taken up.

'Have you ever seen *Jacaranda*?' Bel asked me, one Friday

night as we sat in the conservatory, a bottle of red wine between us in a nest of crisp packets.

I fancied that she wanted to be the one to show it to me for the first time, so I said that I hadn't. I had, of course. Twice.

'Oh, but you must see it! Then you'll know – you'll understand, straight away, why it's so important to me.'

We went downstairs to the basement, to what Bel grandly called the Cinema Room. It was more of a den, a small study with book-lined walls, a velvet sofa and a Persian carpet. A projector was mounted on one wall, and a pull-down screen took up the whole of the wall opposite. Bel rummaged through boxes of DVDs until she found *Jacaranda*; even in the dim light, the purplish flowering tree on the front of the box was unmistakeable.

'Mama was nineteen when she played Clementine,' said Bel. 'She used to say that Ken Harmon came onto her the whole time they were filming. One day she just couldn't stand it any longer and spiked his coffee with laxatives. Nora, darling, d'you think you could run upstairs and fetch the vino?'

The opening credits were rolling over syrupy violins when I returned with the wine. Bel was stretched out on the sofa; she curled her legs up so that I could sit beside her and I felt her hands threading through my hair. It was the sort of thing I hated, but she did things like that so often – although, thankfully, she had never again attempted to kiss me – that I found I'd got rather used to it.

The words: *And introducing Phyllis Lane as Clementine* appeared on the screen, and Bel caught her breath theatrically.

'I never tire of seeing her name in writing,' she said. 'She always wanted to be an actress. Her real name wasn't Phyllis. It was Pauline. Her father was a butcher, you know. He was horrified when she said she wanted to go on the stage. But my grandmama supported her. She took on extra sewing for three years in order to pay for my mother to go to drama school. Sometimes she worried that Grandpa would never forgive her. I tell you, Nora, you don't want to get on the wrong side of a man with a meat cleaver.'

I made encouraging noises as a shot of an English coastal village, seen from above, lit up the dark room. I'd heard some of these stories before; they changed from telling to telling and I was never sure if Bel herself could tell the grains of truth from the flowers of embellishment. In so many ways, Bel was a much worse liar than I was. I always knew when I was lying, whereas I think that Bel didn't. I hated it when people talked during films; it had been one of Jonah Trace's most irritating traits. After a while, however, Bel stopped talking and we let the film transport us back in time to the Devon coast in the inter-war years, to a failing marriage and a falling-down house, to murder and intrigue and rich orchestral music . . . and to Phyllis Lane, who played the part of the smart young daughter, Clementine, with verve and depth and luminosity.

I'd thought it before, but as I watched Bel as she watched her mother, I thought it again: Bel's acting style (the sheer, ferocious, all-or-nothingness of it) was very similar. Perhaps Anton Ingram really did intend to offer his daughter the part.

At the end of the movie, Bel wept real tears. 'And what did you think?' she said.

'It's amazing,' I said. 'So moving. Also quite funny in places. I see why your dad wants to readapt it. Certain scenes – the ballroom one, and the treehouse among the yew trees where they find the key – I can just imagine them, not the same, but sort of updated.'

'I just love Mama's hair in this so much,' said Bel. 'How d'you think it would suit me?'

I looked at her sideways, comparing her profile with her mother's. In keeping with the period, Clementine had a shortish bob that shone like the proverbial spun gold. Phyllis's hair was a whiter shade than Bel's, but – as far as I could tell – of a similar thickness.

'Your bone structure's the same,' I said. 'And your nose. I think it would look fine.'

'Nora,' said Bel. 'Do you know how to do hair?'

And so it was that early the next morning Cody was dispatched to the shops for dye and professional scissors, and while Bel made up her beetroot-and-kale drink I plotted my course of action. Highlights, I decided, were the thing to do here, rather than an all-over tint. They'd look more natural.

'Let's use Dad's bathroom,' said Bel, when Cody returned. 'It's bigger.'

Bel had been eight when her mother had died, and Darian nine, but Phyllis Lane's long absence was not that easy to discern when we opened the door to the bedroom that she and Anton had shared. A cotton kimono with an indigo print hung from an embroidered screen, as though its wearer might be changing just behind it; a set of hairbrushes and combs were stacked in a pot on the vanity table; I was sure, without looking, that the wardrobes that took up an entire wall would contain as many gowns as the Ugly Sisters' dressing room. Now, finally, I understood why Bel wore kimonos so often. Of course: they had belonged to her mother.

The bathroom was just off the bedroom. It was tiled all over in grey marble. Bel dragged the dressing-table stool into the bathroom and put it next to the bath. She emptied the shopping bag into the sink. Cody, quite intelligently, had bought a kit from Boots, rather than the individual products I'd specified.

'Got everything you need?' asked Bel.

'Pretty much,' I said, fitting a perforated shower cap over her head and opening the sash window to let in air. 'The scissors aren't great. We'll improvise.'

I'd made up the peroxide mixture and painted three or

four clutches of her yellow-gold hair, drawn through the holes in the shower cap, before it occurred to me that we should have done a strand test – Evie was always going on about taking care with hair dye. Apparently Petra's face had swollen up once when she'd tried to become a redhead and she'd spent twenty-four hours in hospital. I communicated this to Bel.

'Nonsense, darling,' she said, in her American voice. 'I'm not bothered by a few poxy chemicals.' Her phone rang. 'Can I pick it up?' she said.

'You may,' I said. 'Just don't hold the phone right next to your head.'

'Giacomo!' she said. 'Howdy, sugar. No, I'm at the salon. We can talk.'

A low rumble of discontent from the speaker.

'Honey, I don't . . . are you *sure* they were broken at the party? But which ones? Those old ferns were dead anyway, surely. The mirror was cracked already. You know that. And as for the carpet . . .' Bel remonstrated for some time. When she hung up, she said, 'Goddamn Giacomo wants me to pay him money.'

'Are you going to?'

'He should be pleased to host parties for me on his boat. They give him the illusion of popularity. He'll forget about it. He's just mad because I wouldn't sleep with him. Why would I do such a thing? Never do anything twice, that's what I always say.'

The easy way she talked about such things always unsettled me. I focused on drawing more of the gold strands through the shower cap, painting them precisely with the lavender-coloured liquid, my hands working, as they sometimes did, in absolute synchrony.

'Did *you* sleep with the Art Man?' she said. She gazed limpidly at me in the mirror. Not taking my hands from her head, I looked back at her.

'What art man?'

'The sad-puppy-faced one with the toilet-brush hair.'

'You mean the art assistant, Mr Trace,' I said, unable to stop myself laughing at her description. One of the things I liked most about Bel was her total lack of interest in our school.

'Yes. The Art Man.'

'No,' I said.

'Why not?'

This was dangerous territory. What did she think had happened, between Jonah Trace and me? What should I tell her, I wondered – the official version of events, or something closer to the truth? I almost fancied telling her the truth, just to see how she reacted. But it would be giving too much away. Bel was still a student at Lady Agatha's, and she wasn't especially discreet. It wouldn't be safe to tell her.

'Why do you think I might have?' I said evenly.

'Well, sugar, there was obviously *something* going on.

227

I saw you guys, sneaking into the café off the high street. I saw the way he looked at you. Mind, he looked at nearly everyone that way. The guy was a creep.'

'Indeed,' I said. 'I certainly didn't sleep with him.'

'What *did* you do?'

'Nothing. What do you think I did?'

'Relax. I'm not trying to put you on the spot, sugar,' she said. The cool blue eyes gleamed in the mirror. She seemed to be appraising me, somehow. 'I was just thinking, you know. If it had been me . . . I'd have given him, I dunno. A taste of his own medicine.' She winked.

I said nothing. Nothing is always safest and best. Even to Bel, whom I counted as a friend – a very good friend. It was a risk I wasn't prepared to take.

'How much longer?' asked Bel.

'We're nearly done,' I said, and we were.

'God, I look mad,' she said, surveying the shower cap and the pulled-through purple strands.

'It'll be beautiful,' I said. 'Trust me. Now we need to wait for a while. Half an hour, maybe a bit more.'

She smoked a cigarette out of the window, saying that just one wouldn't hurt, and for a while we watched the cat digging up bulbs in the flower bed.

'Daddy wanted to get married again,' she said, à propos of nothing. 'A few years ago. I scared her away.'

I busied myself at the sink, washing away the purplish traces of dye, making sure there was no stain.

'Holly, she was called,' Bel went on. 'She was all right, really. I was horrible to her. Really horrible. Horrible to everyone. I stole a lot of money from my godfather and I just spent it and spent it. Took everyone out for dinner, went to Rome for the weekend with Giacomo and stayed in a five-star hotel . . . so many drugs, Nora. Jewellery and vintage clothes and . . . oh, I can't even remember. I paid back what I could, of course, over time. Dad never found out, thank God. But then I got kicked out of the stupid fancy school that Dad had sent me to. I hated it there. I came home and Holly just couldn't cope with me. In the end, I think Dad realised I would only change my behaviour if he got rid of her.' She looked round at me. 'That's why I always liked *Cinderella* so much,' she said. 'It was the father getting married for the second time to this awful woman that did it for me. I used to read it aloud all the time to annoy her.'

Then she shook her head. 'Heavens,' she said, 'Memory lane!'

Her voice had changed back to its theatrical tone, and I realised that for the last few minutes she'd been speaking in what must have been her true voice. (Much later, I would realise something else: all the put-on accents she habitually used were taken from the films of Phyllis Lane. They were her mother's voices.)

And then she sat with her back facing the sink and I washed her hair, twice, and conditioned it, and after that

I cut her hair with toenail scissors, whose blades I thought might be sharper than those of the inferior scissors that Cody had bought, and after that we went upstairs to Bel's bedroom to dry it.

'It's quite incredible,' said Bel. 'I look just like Mama did in *Jacaranda*. Do you think this will be enough to convince Papa?'

'I don't know,' I said. 'We'll have to see.'

At this she gave me a joyful, rib-cracking squeeze; laughing, I returned it.

'Let's play a game,' said Bel. 'Truths.'

'No dares?' said Azia, arching backwards so that her upper half hung down towards the carpet. She gave a catlike yawn, and then pulled herself up again.

'Can't be arsed with dares,' said Bel, yawning too.

It was a quarter to midnight; I was attending something I'd scorned so easily for most of my teenage life. A sleepover. Some film about witches flickered on Bel's laptop, whose screen had a disfiguring spider-web crack. Unfinished tubs of Häagen-Dazs oozed a sugary dribble onto the cover of Bel's bed; a bottle of Amaretto, taken from the downstairs drinks cabinet, was lodged between us. We had lit candles around the room, just as Evie and Petra might have done. It was exactly the kind of scene I'd have had no patience for, once upon a time.

'Truths it shall be,' said Azia. 'Let's start with Nora.'

'I don't want to go first,' I said.

'But we know the least about you,' said Bel.

'That's not true,' I protested.

'Go on,' said Azia.

'OK,' I said, drawing a fingertip down the ridge of my nose.

Bel leaned forwards. 'What is the worst thing you've ever done to someone?' she said.

I wondered if this was an invitation to tell them about Jonah Trace. Too bad; I wasn't going to recount it. I told them instead about Toby Lenôtre and the Ruined Rainbow.

'Not good enough,' said Bel at once.

'It's true,' I said mildly.

'Perhaps, but it can't be the worst thing that you've ever done.'

'OK,' I said. 'Fine. I'll tell you another story.'

One had just occurred to me; one I thought would show me in a less severe light.

I told them the story of Rita Ellory.

Rita was the Brown Owl, the woman in charge of the troupe of Brownies Evie forced me to join a few years after we moved to England. Brownies had been a significant part of her own childhood, and she had a fixed notion that I would enjoy it if I participated for long enough. Though still in her vault of sadness, she managed in one of her more lucid periods to find a pack that met in a community centre not far from where we lived. The wooden floor sported a fairy ring made of hideous polystyrene toadstools. I was a Sprite. My Sixer was called Zoe; she had a pointed, bossy face, like a pecking chicken. I didn't like her much. But I reserved my actual hatred for Rita Ellory, Brown Owl.

Rita was not a woman who liked children; what she was

doing, running a Brownie pack, was not obvious at the time. My theory now is that she was waiting to sniff out a husband: some put-upon father, longing for a release; a rich divorcé with a nice car. The first thing she did was to challenge the reading record I submitted to go with my Booklover badge.

'You can't possibly have read all these books,' she sneered.

Toby Lenôtre, shrill as a burglar alarm, wailed, all the way from Paris: 'You have stolen my name. Thief!'

My face, of course, betrayed nothing. She was similarly dismissive to other girls, which somewhat defeated the ethos of Brownies as a whole. The other thing Rita Ellory did was pick on us – any and all of us – about our looks, our bodies, and she did this in a curious way. It would sound almost affectionate at first, the way a fond if misguided grandmother might speak. But everything she said had a hidden thorn: a barb that sank in deep and took hold, and might only be found much later.

'Ah, look at your little legs,' she'd say to some diminutive Elf. 'Look at you, running along on your fat little legs. This little piggy went to market; this little piggy stayed home.'

She'd give a piglike snort, and play around with the phrasing, waiting to see if she got a reaction. Rita Ellory was adept at looking for weaknesses, for gaps in our girlish defences. I was always glad she never knew that my father was dead (she wasn't interested in absent fathers, who couldn't be flirted with). But she could take the piss just enough out of a regional accent to cause its owner to say little, in shame; she faked concern for eczema and bitten nails; she had a range of remarks about braces. And she had a field day with my birthmark. She was always looking for interesting things to compare it to, and since she was not an imaginative woman, this process was dull, as well as painful. My policy was to not respond in any way to her comments and this, over time, made her comments more outrageous.

'Has anyone ever told you it looks like a tea stain?' she finally said, as we were getting ready to recite the *Oh Lord Our God* bit, before we went home.

I glanced towards the door, where the mothers and nannies would soon be appearing. I looked for Evie. There she was, uncharacteristically wearing a velour tracksuit in a shade of piercing blue. It was possible that Rita Ellory had not seen her.

'I'm sorry?' I said. 'I didn't hear you.'

'Your face,' said Rita more loudly. 'It looks like someone has dumped a leaking PG Tips tea bag over your eye, doesn't it?'

I counted on Evie to catch what Brown Owl was saying. As it happened, Evie couldn't; she was too far away and too deaf, although she told me afterwards that the expression on Rita Ellory's face was enough to convince her that something was not right. But another mother, with hearing less impaired by a decade in Goth clubs, did hear her, and reported her words at once to Evie. Evie sailed in, as stately as ever despite the velour tracksuit. She seized me by the hand, denounced Rita Ellory with a foul-mouthed tirade, and stalked out again, dragging me behind her. I never went to Brownies again, and I did not miss it.

But that was not the end of the story. As far as I was concerned, Rita Ellory had not been punished at all.

'So what did you do?' said Bel, with her hungry look.

'I made a list of things I knew about her,' I said. 'There wasn't much. She wasn't married. She lived somewhere near Imperial Wharf. I didn't know her address. But I did have her phone number. I copied it into my notebook, and I kept it.'

'And?' said Azia.

'I kept the notebook in the back of a drawer. And I waited.'

'How long?'

'I waited for five years,' I said. 'Just waiting, and thinking. I needed to come up with the right thing. I wanted some time to elapse. So, finally, I guess quite a few years ago now, I had about a hundred cheap business cards made. You know the ones; you can do it on machines, in shops or at service stations. I uploaded a picture.'

Bel uttered a peal of laughter, guessing. 'No,' she said.

'What did you put on the cards?' said Azia.

'I don't remember exactly. Something like this: BUSTY, MATURE BLONDE OFFERING MASSAGE AND MORE. CALL

RITA ANY TIME NIGHT OR DAY,' I said, remembering perfectly. 'And her phone number, of course.'

Azia was smiling and shaking her head. 'Five years,' she said. 'Her number might have changed.'

'Oh no,' I said. 'I checked that. I called her, once, and hung up. Just to be sure.'

'You thought of everything,' said Bel, with manifest glee.

'I stuck the cards up in phone booths, all around London,' I said. 'It took me a couple of weekends to really spread them around. I guess a lot of them would have been taken down . . . but I just hoped she got called enough times to really disturb her. She so much liked disturbing other people. Those are always the types that can't take it themselves.'

Bel lit a rare cigarette, as though tired out by the excitement of listening.

'I can't believe you waited five years,' said Azia again. 'I will never get on the wrong side of you, Nora.'

I smiled at her, modest. We may not have been playing dares, but I dared them, nonetheless, not to believe me.

'Your turn,' I said. 'Bel. Go on.'

Pouring herself another glass of Amaretto, Bel appeared deep in thought. 'I guess I really did wreck the set of *Teen Spirits*,' she said.

She told us the story. It involved a stolen security pass, paint, bags of flour and a hose that was left on overnight, long after the revelling cast had gone home. Azia and I listened in silence.

Then Azia said: 'Does your dad know all this?'

'Sort of,' Bel said ruefully. 'I've always said it wasn't my idea. But, well, you know. There was absinthe involved.'

'But why did you do it?'

'Oh, I was just pissed off with everyone. The director mostly. He kept asking for script changes. One afternoon they cut all my best lines. I saw red. And then I saw a whole lot of other colours.'

The following morning, Azia and I went to the tube station together.

'You know last night, when we played Truths,' said Azia.

'Yes,' I said.

'What Bel said. It wasn't the whole story, you know. It wasn't just that they cut her lines. It was what the director did afterwards. She went for a drink with him, to discuss her part, she thought. He was married, in his forties. I forget his name. Anyway, he tried it on. I think he even put his hand under her top, or something. She was furious.'

'I see,' I said. I thought about Ken Harmon and Phyllis Lane on the set of *Jacaranda*. Clearly, Bel and her mother differed from me in the way in which they enacted revenge. 'I wonder why she didn't say so.'

Azia shrugged. 'People don't always tell you everything. Even in a game of Truths. In fact, I wouldn't call that the worst thing that Bel's ever done. She's done so much worse than that. The funny thing is I'm not sure if she'd remember it like that. I almost wanted to start the game again, just to ask her. I've known Bel for thirteen, fourteen years, and sometimes I still feel like I'm figuring her out. Sometimes I don't know what she's aware of, if you know what I mean.'

'What did she do?' I said.

Azia paused to tie her hair back.

'She attacked someone. A girl at her previous school. Tried to strangle her with a scarf.' Azia wound a green-and-purple bandanna around her head; I noticed she glanced down at it first, as though she were trying to understand how it would feel to strangle someone with an item of clothing. 'They kicked her out, of course. Amazingly, the girl didn't press charges. I think schools always try to hush things up internally.'

Thinking of the Trace Incident, I nodded.

'Emily, she was called, or Amelia,' said Azia. 'I only met her once.'

'But why did Bel do it?' I was curious now.

We had come to the tube station, where we would go in different directions on different lines.

'She never said,' said Azia. 'I love Bel, love her to pieces, as my mum would say. I tolerate lots of her madness, and God knows, maybe I join her in some of her mayhem. But I can't stand violence. It terrifies me. So I never asked. With Bel, you know, it's just possible . . . that there was no reason at all.'

6

Ever since *The Belle of the Ball*, I'd been feeling a certain desire to get back onto some kind of stage. It was the look on the little boy's pale face, after the performance; the sudden light when he smiled at me; the way he had clearly been taken out of himself for the short duration of the play. I wanted to do that again, and again. Of course, every story is a performance. So is every lie. But the lighting and directing, the programmes and the costumes, the massed audience and the thrilling wave of applause – those things were all new to me, and I found them intoxicating. I started to want acting to become a part of my daily life. I was not sure how. I didn't want to study costume, like Evie; I wanted to be on the stage, under the lights, saying lines that weren't mine.

And so, when Sarah Cousins read out a reminder from the drama department about auditions for the Lower Sixth production of *A Doll's House*, I hesitated for no more than a few minutes before I decided to try.

I'd been thinking for a while that I was getting very detached from life at school. I had allowed a kind of alienation to set in, after the Trace Incident. Sarah Cousins,

I was sure, now hated me; you had only to listen to her clipped, nasal, questioning voice as she said my name to know that. I felt like a translucent question mark hung over me as I walked across the courtyard, or down to the art room for Life Class. (Yes, I still went to Life Class.) I imagined people saying: 'Do you think she did . . . ?' And with that, I felt a real, solid shame. Not for what I had done, but for the fact that people suspected me of doing it. The Trace Incident had been a performance of a kind, I realised. Maybe it just hadn't been good enough.

I dodged the attention of the headmistress. When I wasn't with Bel, which was often, I did my own work; I had occasional conversations with my teachers about what I wanted to study after Sixth form, but I was unable to furnish them with any definite plans. I was waiting for my mother to come back from Romania, I kept saying.

All this, I realised suddenly, had an unfortunate side effect. I looked *guilty*. My inability to engage with anyone or anything at school other than in the most passive ways made me look like I'd done something wrong. And that was the last thing I wanted. No: I needed to get involved, promptly, with some school-based event. Not just swimming; carving up the lanes with my butterfly strokes every Friday was hardly a team activity.

And then came the reminder. *A Doll's House*. Auditions. Monday at 4.15.

At first, I thought: no. And then: why not?

The drama teacher, Mrs Tomaski, had an office in a trailer near the car park. Auditions for plays, as far as I knew, were always held there. Taller even than Evie, Mrs Tomaski was massive-chested and wide-hipped and motherly, with a helmet of dark grey hair, and talked in the booming voice of a Professional Thespian. She called everyone 'dear', mainly because she was incapable of remembering names.

'Hello, dear. Come in, and welcome,' she bellowed, when I showed up at the trailer door sometime after school. I'd waited until the line of girls had dissipated; I did not care for an audience yet.

'Now, *you* I don't know in the slightest,' said Mrs Tomaski.

'I'm Nora,' I said.

'Yes, dear: everyone will read for Nora. But what is your name?'

'Nora,' I said. I could see this might go on for some time. 'Nora Tobias,' I added. 'I'm in Twelve C.'

'Ah: your actual *name* is Nora!' The penny had dropped. 'How funny. Have I taught you, dear?'

'Yes, in Years Seven and Eight, for a term,' I said. I wasn't surprised that she didn't remember me; she wasn't the type to take particular notice of my birthmark, and I had done nothing to distinguish myself during the brief drama modules I'd taken. Wallflower Nora had definitely not volunteered to step into the limelight.

There was a slight delay, while she looked for the photocopies she'd been using for the auditions. 'Thought I'd seen the last of you girls. Put the pages down somewhere . . . but where? A-*ha*, they're under the cat.'

A ginger tom, fatter even than the Ingram family's overfed tortoiseshell, was displaced from a faded sofa while Mrs Tomaski seized a plastic sleeve full of printed sheets. She handed me one and told me to study it for a while. Did I know the play? I said I did not. Tactfully, she went to the kettle and began making tea, humming under her breath. She offered me a cup, which I thought was very courteous. Clearly, if there was any gossip about Nora Tobias the Little Liar, Honeytrap Extraordinaire, in the staffroom, it hadn't reached the decorated ears of Mrs Tomaski. I started to relax. I focused with intent on the words before me. Here was another Nora. As I had become the Fairy Godmother in *The Belle of the Ball*, now I would become Nora Helmer, wife of Torvald. Although I'd told Mrs Tomaski that I didn't know the play, I had by this time read it three times.

'Are you ready, dear?' said the drama teacher.

I began to read.

When I'd finished, I could tell that Mrs Tomaski was pleased. She didn't say much, but her expression was easy to interpret.

'You have a lovely way of *speaking*, dear,' she said.

A few days later, Mrs Tomaski posted the cast list on the drama department's intranet page, just before term ended. Even though I knew I'd impressed her, I was not expecting to be given a part. It is always better not to have expectations. But she'd given me the role of Nora, even though I had so little experience.

Evie called that evening and was overjoyed to hear the news.

'To see you coming out of yourself, sometimes,' she said rather cryptically. 'It's very pleasing.'

I realised that, for all the many long days I'd spent worrying about my mother's wellbeing, I'd never considered that she might also, occasionally, have been worrying about me.

7

The Easter holidays came around, and Bel's hard work was rewarded with a much-improved set of reports. Anton took us all out for a celebratory dinner to a Japanese restaurant that Bel loved. Darian held my chair for me in a gentlemanly way as I sat down, and I noticed Bel notice this. There was a quick flicker across her face of something like annoyance, but it didn't stay long. Summoning the waitress, Bel demanded mixed sashimi and miso soup, and tofu deep-fried to a honeyed crisp, and aubergine with sesame sauce. Anton and Darian drank Tiger beers; Bel drank sake and I drank water.

I looked round the restaurant, watching a man hunched in solitude over a bowl of noodles. Evie was due back at the end of the holidays, and although I missed her a good deal, I realised that I would also miss the freedom I'd had to stay over at Bel's, to live life as she did, answering to almost nobody.

'Salmon teriyaki,' said Bel.

'I think we've ordered enough to be going on with,' said Anton. He was looking quite relaxed that evening, the lines around his eyes not so pronounced.

'What beautiful daughters you have,' said the waitress, bringing more beer.

'Just the one daughter,' said Anton, nodding at Bel. 'And one son,' he added.

'Don't you think I look like Mama?' said Bel, when the waitress had gone.

'Very like,' said her father. 'As I've told you before.'

Darian was playing a piano scale on the tabletop. He looked at Bel as she patted her hands over her hair, and rolled his eyes. Then, taking a dollop of wasabi, he dissolved it with care in the ceramic dish of soy sauce. This wasn't Bel's way; she liked to smear it all over whatever she was eating, ingesting too much, and then wheeze and cough in a kind of hybrid of agony and delight.

'That wasn't necessary, though,' Anton went on. 'As a gesture.'

'What d'you mean?'

'Making your hair like Mama's. It wasn't necessary. Because . . .' He brought out from beside him a thick booklet of white A5 paper, solidly bound. JACARANDA, it read, in Courier font, together with the writer's name, GABRIEL GLASS, and the date, and the words FIFTH DRAFT.

'Daddy!' said Bel.

'You've earned it,' said Anton. 'I just want you to read it through, for now. Confidential as ever, of course. Read it and let me know if you still want the part.'

'Want it!' said Bel, in a full, small voice. 'Of course I *want* it.'

'There's a couple of people I'd like you to meet, but we'll talk about that another time. For now, I just want you to know that all your efforts have not been in vain.'

'Does this mean it's definite?' asked Bel.

He smiled, handing her the script. 'It's a definite . . . *maybe*. You still have your exams to get through.'

'A toast,' said Bel. 'To *Jacaranda*.'

'To *Jacaranda*,' her father solemnly replied.

Darian took a long sip of beer. Wryly, he raised his glass too. It seemed the Ingram family were always drinking toasts of one kind or another.

'Oh, and to Nora too,' said Bel. 'I nearly forgot.'

'Indeed,' said Anton. 'I don't think you'd have managed those grades without your loyal Nora.'

'Nora is playing the lead in a little school production of *A Doll's House*,' Bel said, patting my arm. 'So clever.'

'Indeed?' said Anton, again. 'Well done, Nora. That's excellent news.'

I couldn't help but feel that I was being very subtly patronised. Darian, meanwhile, gave me a smile that managed to be both sympathetic and conspiratorial. I returned it gratefully.

Seeing us, Bel said, 'Get a room, kids.' Her hair eddied from side to side as she laughed.

* * *

Raw fish does not agree with me. That night, staying over at Bel's, I had another dream about the flowers. I was walking, with difficulty, through a dark place with an uneven floor. The flowers were strewn like corpses to my left and right. A faint shimmer came off them. Red and blue, green and yellow, orange and turquoise and indigo. I knew with certain dream-knowledge that this was a place of indescribable danger. The flowers swelled bigger and bigger as I passed, until eventually there was no path ahead. And now the thorny, ribbony tendrils came reaching around me, caressing my legs, my waist, steadfast as straitjackets.

And then the flowers were gone, as though they'd never been there, and I was lying on a trolley in some white-lit hospital corridor. Orderlies with clipboards tap-tapped the floor as they passed me. Why was I there? With difficulty, I struggled to a sitting position. I seemed to be wrapped in bandages, like a mummy.

'Poor thing,' said a voice in French. 'She ate a bad oyster. We had to amputate the arm at the elbow.'

I looked around, to see who the voice was talking about. Then – wanting to be sure – I looked down at my body. There were so many bandages, twisting this way and that like tapers, that I couldn't really see myself. Was that my thigh? Was that my ankle? As is often the case in dreams, I could feel nothing. Then an orderly came and wheeled the trolley, slowly at first, and then faster, until we came to a mirrored door. I looked up. The orderly wore a surgical

247

gown; he had brown hair under his cap and a scrubbed, boyish face. He didn't look identical to Jonah Trace, and yet I knew that he *was* Jonah Trace, without doubt.

'Poor, poor thing,' he said again in English.

Slowly I redirected my gaze, until finally I could see myself in the reflective door. I looked utterly ravaged by disease, my face hollow, my eyes dull. Where skin was visible beneath the bandages, I saw that it was red-raw with infection. And my left arm was, indeed, gone.

I woke up with a scream.

Bel was there, perched on the camp bed in her room where I always slept, leaning over me, peering into my face. Her bedside light was on. She had a tumbler of brandy in one hand and a thermometer in the other.

'Sushi,' I said.

'Jesus, Nora honey. You scared the life out of me.'

'Just a dream,' I said. 'Shouldn't eat sushi.'

She took my temperature, shaking the digital thermometer vigorously as though it contained mercury. I looked around for something familiar, something comforting. Bel's copy of the *Jacaranda* script lay on the floor between the camp bed and the four-poster; next to it, face-down, forlorn – as if to highlight its lesser importance – was my copy of *A Doll's House*.

Bel scrutinised the thermometer. 'Normal,' she said.

She offered to read me a story, but I told her I was fine. Eventually, she climbed back into bed and fell asleep almost at once. I lay awake, listening to Bel's breathing, and the nocturnal grumblings of the house, my mind a kaleidoscope of flowers and oysters and sushi, and unanswered questions and unfinished thoughts.

I went home the following day. Evie was due back next week, and I wanted to buy food, washing-up liquid, get the flat in welcoming shape. Bel, I could see, was desperate to read the *Jacaranda* screenplay, and although I would have liked to be involved – I wanted to read the script too, very much – she did not ask me for my input.

I sat on our balcony in the spring sun, going through *A Doll's House*, making notes as I went along, as I knew Phyllis Lane had done. I wondered if Bel was doing the same, and thought she probably wasn't.

My phone vibrated and I felt a stomach-dropping sickness, anticipating perhaps a message from an unknown number. The text *was* from an unknown number, and for a moment I didn't quite understand it.

Hey, wife. Would you like to go swimming this afternoon?
I'm heading to the leisure centre at 2 p.m.

Then I realised it was from Megan Lattismore, who was playing my husband Torvald. I didn't know Megan swam;

I'd thought she was more of a track-and-field girl. I realised, as I got to the pool – the same one that we used at school – that I'd missed swimming regularly in my free time. It wasn't something Bel was especially into.

Megan and I shared a lane, and although she was taller than me, I was faster, so we were pretty well matched. The chlorinated water felt good on my skin as I alternated front and back crawl. My goggles dug into my nose and I stopped to adjust them.

'You're an amazing swimmer,' said Megan, stopping also.

'You aren't bad either,' I said.

Megan said she was training for a triathlon. She was what you might call a good all-rounder: the kind of person anyone would be glad to have on any kind of team. As we to'd and fro'd like synchronised sea lions, I tried not to look at the gallery, where Sarah Cousins had accused me of being a little liar. That memory still burned uncomfortably bright.

Megan and I swam seventy-six lengths. Afterwards, we went for coffee and post-training brownies. We discussed the play and I quickly realised that Megan Lattismore had no actorly ambitions beyond the Agatha Seaford Academy.

'Plays,' she said, emptying four packets of sugar in little mounds around her saucer in a kind of strange, subconscious ritual. 'They look good on your UCAS application.'

Her parents, she said, were very hot on things looking good on UCAS application. I remembered that her father was a school governor – although not, I thought, the one who'd been at the meeting with Caroline Braine in January. For a while I dwelt again on the Trace Incident, as I tended to do when I wasn't with Bel and distracted by Bel-ish things like *Jacaranda*.

As though reading my mind, Megan surprised me by saying: 'He brought you here, didn't he?'

'Who?'

'Mr Trace.'

I stared at her. I remembered the way he had patted her arm, and the way he had looked down her shirt. It was that look – sleepy and lidded and secret – that told me everything I needed to know about his psychology. I wondered how she knew. But then, it wasn't exactly a secret. I'd told a few people. Lori, for example. Although I might have told Lori that it was Nero we went to, or Eat or Pret. To my horror, I found that I could no longer easily recall which cookie-cutter coffee shop our former art assistant had chosen.

'Yes,' I said, at last. 'When he asked me out.'

I opened a packet of sugar and poured it into a sacrificial heap, adding to the mounds around Megan's saucer.

'What exactly did he say?' she said.

Megan was a frank kind of person, from what I could see. Was this a test of some kind? Or did she just want to hear the story in my own words?

'Just that he really liked me, and he wanted to get to know me better,' I said.

'And what did you say?'

'I told him he must be totally crazy.'

Megan Lattismore had a very oval, symmetrical face. With her flaxen hair and forget-me-not eyes, she looked like she had some Scandinavian blood. Her low, boyish voice and perpetual air of confidence made her a good choice for the role of Torvald, I decided. I willed a pathway into her thoughts, as she looked at me over the top of her cup. Did she believe me? The pause that followed was long, and it seemed as though she were trying to decide what to say.

Then:

'What a loser,' she said drily.

She changed the subject.

9

A couple of nights later, I was woken by my phone.

Darian's name flashed on the screen. It was twenty to four in the morning.

'Nora, I'm sorry if I woke you.'

'What's up?' I said.

'It's Bel. She's . . . I need you to come and help me. I'm sorry. I just . . . I can't do this by myself. Can you get in a taxi? I'll pay you back.'

So much for turning over new leaves, I thought, as I hunted for my keys. Now that Bel was sure that she had – definitely maybe had – the part of Clementine, she was clearly relaxing back into her old ways. And at four in the morning, she could be anywhere. She had a fondness for breaking into high-security buildings at night; she was a nimble, athletic climber and unafraid of guard dogs or alarm systems. She might be stuck behind a set of railings, or in somebody's walled back garden. There was a real chance that she'd been arrested; I knew that Cody, or Darian, had gone to fetch her from the police station once or twice in the past, where each time she'd been let off with a caution and warned against further disorderly behaviour. Or else she was stranded somewhere and needed to be collected. A party outside London. A date that had not ended well.

The address he'd given me was a street not too far from where they lived. As I got out of the cab, I looked for a house with all its lights on and that unmistakable aura of a party that is down to its dregs and embers. I looked for police cars. I listened for music and screams. And I heard nothing. The street lamps were wide-spaced and gave out a foggy orange light; for a strange moment, it felt like I'd been transported back a hundred years. I realised I was just by the park nearest their house, where Bel went jogging. Then quick steps echoed on the pavement. There he was, in a white shirt and a black suit. He must have been out playing music somewhere.

'Thank you for coming,' Darian said, as though I'd been invited to a party.

The park was empty. There were few lampposts and not much moon. We walked for ten or fifteen minutes, not saying much.

'Is she all right?' I said.

'She's climbed up a tree and she won't come down, and I can't persuade her.'

'How did you know she was here?'

'She was out with Azia; they had some kind of disagreement. Bel ran away. Azia called me, but she's gone now; I told her to go home. I can't leave Bel there. I'm worried she'll pass out and fall. A couple of times she threatened to jump. I figured it was you or the Fire Brigade.'

From up high in the leaves came the sound of hiccuppy crying.

'Bel? Bel, it's me. I've brought someone to see you,' said Darian. He nodded at me.

'Bel, are you there?' I called up.

'I'm keen to get out of here before a warden or someone catches us,' said Darian to me.

'Bel, darling, it's Nora. Will you come down?'

Another, more muted sob.

I came closer to the trunk of the tree and looked up into the knotty tangle of branches. It was hard to see; I saw just the heel of a boot at first, then, using the beam of my phone, I saw her heart-shaped face and cotton-wool glow of hair. I could see that there was a kind of novelty in my arrival: she hadn't been expecting me.

'D'you know, what I really fancy,' I said, 'is a Dutch breakfast. Wouldn't that be so perfect, right about now?'

This was a smart calculation: Bel liked few things more than breakfast.

'Heartless, patronising bitch,' said Bel.

'Who?'

'Azia. Sanctimonious, lecturing, officious . . . *cheap*.'

Oh: that was it. Azia had refused to pay for something. Bel was a genius at getting people to pay for things. No doubt she'd demanded something – caviar and blinis, a second bottle of champagne – that Azia had been unwilling to fund.

'I'm sorry to hear that,' I said.

There was no reply.

Cautiously, I put my hand up to the nearest low-hanging branch, trying to work out which route Bel had taken up the tree. But I'm a swimmer, not a climber; it didn't look easy. Finally I found something I thought I could use as a foothold.

'Nora,' said Darian. 'You don't have to . . .'

'I think I'd better,' I said. Noble Nora.

'Jesus, you're braver than I am. Here.'

He had an iPhone; it lit the way better than my Nokia. The low-hanging branch was up and to my right; I grabbed hold of it with both arms, and swung my legs up higher to a higher-up nub. Then I reached out for another branch, missed it, swayed and reached up again.

'Careful,' said Darian.

I had made it now to the first fork, and I felt safer in the cradle of branches. I took out the phone once more.

'Bel, darling,' I said. 'Are you going to make a girl come all the way up there? I do hate to mess up my hair.'

My American accent was improving, though it wasn't as good as hers.

The hiccuppy sob morphed briefly into a damp chuckle.

'Dutch breakfast,' I resumed. 'Ham, boiled eggs, croissants, Emmental . . .'

'Gouda,' came the voice from above. I knew that she wouldn't be able to resist correcting me. And I suspected that she wouldn't be able to resist the thought of a Dutch breakfast, which had been a pet obsession of hers since one of her artist friends had returned from Rotterdam.

'We can go home past the twenty-four-hour Tesco,' I said soothingly.

As I spoke, I scaled another rung of the tree. My size, I realised, was actually more help than hindrance, but I had no instinct for what I was doing and had to rely on logic alone. The problem was that I'd have to go all the way up to get her. She was very unlikely to meet me halfway. I found that my eyes were adjusting a little to the leafy dark. The branches sprang out like spokes from the spine of the tree; the leaves had a sharp tang that must have been chlorophyll.

Whatever the crisis had been, it was over by the time I got to where Bel was nesting. She'd stayed up only to prolong the drama. She'd stayed up because Darian had not been able to fetch her. She was, I saw, looking at something on her phone, and seemed almost comfortable. There was a strong smell of alcohol. Darian was right: if she'd passed out and fallen, it wouldn't have been pleasant.

'Breakfast in bed,' I said. 'And maybe a story. How would that be? Would you like that? Here. Give me your hand. Got everything?'

I watched her thinking about her choices. Was the scene over, or just beginning?

'Everyone'sh against me,' she said. 'They think I can't be trusted. Bastards, the lot of 'em. Darian too.'

'Of course you can be trusted,' I said.

'If that's true, then how-comesh he can't just leave me up here in peace. Huh?'

'You matter to him,' I said. 'He doesn't want you to fall.'

'I am safe as *houses* in thish tree,' she said, shaking her curls. 'I am a Child of Trees. I know them, and they know me.' Then a strange expression masked her features, as though a new thought had occurred to her. 'How-comesh he called *you*?' she said.

I pointed out that there weren't many other people available to call. But she was looking at me with deep suspicion, as Oscar might once have done.

'You,' she said. 'He called *you*. In the middle of the night. Are you having an affair with my brother?'

'No,' I said. 'Definitely not. I mean, he's a lovely person. But no. I promise. There's nothing going on between us.'

'I've seen the way you look at each other.'

I hissed a helpless, exasperated sigh. 'Bel . . . we don't . . .'

And even if we did, I found myself thinking, would it matter? But this – the tree, the fight-over-nothing with Azia, everything – was Bel's universe, where she decided what was real and where she decided what was true, and what was right and wrong.

'Good. You'd better not be lying, Nora. Because he's not the Art Man. He'sh my *brother*.'

For a long time, I was quite silent and still. Various options turned in my head like machinery. I could climb down leaving her to her own devices. I could take umbrage at her accusation, openly. But I did neither of those things. Inside, though, an old cold feeling reached for my heart with an ice-glove hand. She was Bel, and she was my friend. That was true. But at that moment, she reminded me very much of Old Evie in her drinking days. Irrational, furious, unpredictable, terrifying. And I did not like the way she spoke to me.

After five minutes or so, very neutrally, I suggested again that we should go down to the ground. I reminded her of the breakfast that we could make, and how pleased the cat would be to see her.

'OK, honey,' she said.

She did not apologise. With a hiccup and a slither, she descended, already cheered, as I knew she would be, by the thought of breakfast. I followed more cautiously.

'What the hell were you doing?' Darian said to Bel, when we were both safely down. 'Dad isn't going to be pleased. You can't go around doing stuff like this.'

'Don't tell him,' said Bel, lower lip shaking. 'You'll ruin everything.'

Breakfast was made (with Edam; there was no Gouda). I read Bel a fairy tale. And then Bel went to sleep, with crumbled bark under her fingernails. Darian made tea for us both and we sat in silence on the wicker sofa. He had his phone on his knee and kept starting messages and then deleting them. I wondered who they were addressed to.

'Cody went abroad yesterday,' he said. 'That's why she did this – she knew there was no one to babysit. You know, don't you, why he's always around? My dad pays him a retainer. To keep her out of trouble. Jesus, Nora. If she'd fallen out of that tree, you know whose fault it would have been? Mine.' He closed his eyes. 'I'm so incredibly tired,' he said.

'She said there might be something going on between us,' I said, almost conversationally.

'Did she? Sorry. She's kind of tricky about things like that . . . there was an incident, once.'

'What happened?'

He raised an eyebrow and smiled a non-smile, reminding me of Sarah Cousins. 'I was sort of going out with a girl for a while, called Emily. Bel tried to strangle her with one of my ties.'

He sat so still, for such a long time, that I thought he might have gone to sleep. Interesting that he remembered Bel's weapon as a tie. A scarf, Azia had said. Funny: the little things we change with the telling of our tales.

'Darian,' I said. 'Would you mind if I went home?'

The tube platform was almost deserted; there was only a man in paint-marked overalls, and some partygoers, rather the worse for wear. I made my way to a bench and sat down, waiting for the train. It was just past six. A mouse ran along the track, a whisper of fur, impervious to the oncoming trains. Away to the left and right, the tunnel led into the unknown.

I thought about the Ingram family. The grey Gothic house, built like a small castle, so solid and yet somehow so vulnerable. The pond, the black-and-white tiles, the framed posters of past glories. The cream-coloured jar on the windowsill. Nobody knew that I knew this, but even if that jar had once contained ashes, it was empty now. I'd been sitting alone in the kitchen one afternoon – Bel was in the bath, I think – and the cat, waddling fat-footed along the sill, had knocked it over. The jar toppled and I scrambled at once to catch it before it fell to the floor. It was on its side and I panicked, thinking perhaps that it wouldn't be sealed and the remains (*cremains*, they were called) would scatter blackly on the tiles. The lid did indeed roll off, and as I scooped lid and jar back together in a single, frantic motion I saw that the inside was as clean as a polished shell. I thought about the toast they drank to 'Mama', each time I was there for dinner. I was sure it was heartfelt enough. Why wouldn't it be? But the jar was a stage-prop, no more.

I thought about Anton, with his exciting, high-stakes film projects and the bargains he made with Bel, and how he paid Cody to watch out for her. I thought about Darian and his mathematical music that combined process and beauty in ways that intrigued me. The dark look in his eyes when Bel was preparing to misbehave. The way he had warned me: *Bel's all about what she can get.*

My train came, and I let it pass. Another mouse came scurrying by. I thought about *A Doll's House*. It was actually on at the moment in London, and I thought I'd ask Evie if we could go. I was sure she'd agree. I wanted to see another Nora, hear the way she inflected each line and how she moved on the stage. Not to steal her performance, but to be inspired.

I thought of Evie, preparing to walk into the Thames. Evie, crying in the octagonal studio, wanting to understand. The needles and thread she'd needed to stitch herself back together, which she had done, I was sure, for my sake.

And I thought of my father, who woke up one morning, ate his boiled egg and drank his coffee, chatted to me and Evie, cycled away to the library (so he said) and gave us no clue – not one – that he wouldn't be coming home.

We are shaped by decisions. Ours, and other people's.

For a long time I sat on the tube platform, watching the trains come and go, the people get on and off, dispersing into the day. I thought for such a long time that in the end someone approached me to ask if there was anything the matter.

'Thank you, no,' I told them. 'Everything's great.'

I climbed onto the next train, folding my hands into my lap the way Sarah Cousins had once done in the headmistress's office. OtherNora watched me in the reflective window; for the first time I decided that my irregular-shaped birthmark was really quite special, quite different, quite unique. There couldn't be many young aspiring actresses out there who looked like me.

I can't be sure, now. I don't know whether it was because of what Bel said to me in the tree or for other, more complicated reasons. The look on the little boy's face in the hospital ward when I stood on the makeshift stage. The fact that I am, and have always been, a liar. Why I do what I do is not always clear to me. Even when I try – as a historian or archaeologist would – to understand.

But I do think that moment, as the train pulled away, was the moment when I decided to do what I did.

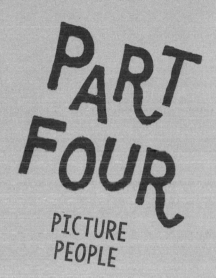

PART FOUR

PICTURE PEOPLE

1

Evie came home a few days before the start of the summer term, full of tales of on-set squabbles and costume dramas, her suitcase rattling with sweets, salted nuts, decorated pottery and embroidered blouses, as though she'd swept clean an entire rack at the airport shops. Two months in a trailer had softened her edges: she seemed less gaunt, more animated. I was glad for her.

'But I missed you, I missed you, I *missed you*,' she said.

I had missed her too, and I told her so. We celebrated at once with manicures. We chose a loud coral colour that suited neither of us, but we didn't care. In the afternoon we saw three exhibitions, talking sometimes and at other times maintaining our typical peaceful silence. That evening we ordered Chinese: smoked shredded chicken and seaweed and hot and sour soup. All the things we loved.

We talked about Nana.

'I dreamed about her, quite a lot,' said Evie. 'Speaking in Bible verses, as ever. I dreamed about Felix too. Just once. It was strange. We were in the Tuileries Gardens, flying the red-and-white kite, only it was shaped like an elephant ... He was in the distance, running towards me, and the kite was flap-flapping above him in the sky like a giant elephant bird.'

Sadness turned her eyes a darker shade of blue for a little while. I reached for her hand across the table, moving a plate of dumplings out of the way.

'So, *A Doll's House*,' she said. 'Who's doing the costumes?'

'I don't know,' I said. 'Some of the girls, I guess.'

'Want help?'

'Sure,' I said. 'Thank you.'

Previously, I think, I'd have felt sufficiently embarrassed by Evie – her outfits, her piercings, her swearing – to want her nowhere near my school. But now I found I didn't mind. I positively liked the idea of her helping with the costumes. Under her expert supervision, they could only be improved. I asked her if she'd ever seen *Jacaranda*, and she said of course; it was one of the great love stories of our time, wasn't it? She'd gone to see it with Petra, when it first came out at the cinema.

'The book's bloody wonderful too. Two boxes of Kleenex I used, the first time I read it,' she said.

I nodded. I also loved the book.

'There's a girl I know at school called Bel,' I said. 'Her dad is doing a new adaptation. And her mum was Phyllis Lane. Did I ever tell you that?'

Evie was impressed.

'And Bel's going to play the part of the daughter in the new film,' I went on.

'Is she any good?' asked Evie. 'Or is this Planet Nepotism?'

I smiled. 'No, she's really good. Really talented.'

Evie's thoughts turned to the costumes, as I knew they would, and we ordered some more green tea.

At the start of the new term, the cast of *A Doll's House* assembled after school in the theatre.

Mrs Tomaski greeted us in a rich baritone. 'Today, girls, is about getting to know each other. We shall play confidence-building games, and share the innermost secrets of our souls.'

I caught Megan's eye, and smiled. The games were not so bad. Mrs Tomaski had us hurling a beach ball at each other like demented toddlers, calling out the names of our favourite chocolate bars. (I didn't have one, but feigned a preference for Terry's Chocolate Orange.) Then we had to pair up and fall backwards into each other's arms, to exercise our ability to trust. I pretended to be Bel. She would be too cool for such games, I was sure, but she'd throw herself into them nonetheless, if they were for the good of the play. So I jumped for the beach ball and threw it with glee. I toppled into Megan Lattismore's cleavage with a girlish giggle.

After the festivities were over, we sat on cushions on the floor and did a read-through of Act One. At once, I felt perfectly at home. After *The Belle of the Ball*, and weeks of reading aloud to Bel, I felt that I knew every intricacy of my voice, and exactly how to bend and mould it to fit Ibsen's words. The lines I had already totally by heart. For the negative person – and indeed, for the habitual liar – acting truly is a gift. I could tell that there were certain girls who could not see why I had been given the part of Nora. It was up to me to prove them wrong.

Mrs Tomaski distributed printouts of the rehearsal schedule – twice, then thrice-weekly over the next six weeks, a technical and a dress rehearsal over a weekend, and then two performances near the end of June. Her trailer door, she said, was always open; if we had any doubts, any difficulties, anything at all, we were always welcome to come and find her.

'My dears, my dears,' she said. '*This* is going to be *quite* an experience.'

Now I was no longer just Nora, but Ibsen's Nora too. And in this Nora, I found various similarities to myself. This Nora was, like me, not afraid to lie: she took out a loan, forging her dying father's signature in the process, risking her honour, in order to help her unknowing husband. But she had more principles than I did, and more spirit. In my own life, I hated to dance. I thought it was the most embarrassing and undignified thing. But a few weeks into rehearsals, we practised a scene in which I had to dance the tarantella, a quick Italian dance, and as I circled the stage, wild-limbed and free-footed, I felt a rush of intoxication, the *being someone else* and *doing something different* that I loved so much. At the end of the play, when her secrets are known, Nora decides that what she really needs to do is be alone, to learn what she has to learn about life on her own. In this, I felt Nora was braver, much braver, than I was. I loved Ibsen's Nora, not because we were the same, but because of the person she allowed me to pretend to be. (Interestingly, I realised that Clementine, at the end of *Jacaranda*, also decides that she must be alone, rejecting the claustrophobic love of her parents and the long shadows of her childhood home.)

In the Phyllis Lane biography that I had read many times, it says:

Those who have acted with Lane over the years have much to say about her inimitable style. Dame Claudia Savernake, her co-star in the acclaimed BBC1 series Gilded Birds, *said: 'She occupied a part absolutely, like a soul travelling from body to body. It wasn't a question, with Phyllis, of trying on a hat or a pair of boots: she became the person she played; she knew their darkest secrets and the names of their great-uncles. And then, at the end of the show, or when filming wrapped, she'd have a real moment of sadness, as though that person had died. She'd fill a little box with trinkets from the production – a set of false eyelashes, a programme, whatever was most fitting – and store it with all the rest, under her bed. I used to think it was horribly morbid, but I also believe that the total dedication to the roles she played was what made Phyllis one of the real greats of British cinema.'*

I just loved that, about the boxes. I wondered if they were still there, under Bel's parents' bed. One day, I would have to look. Rereading the biography, I found more and more to inspire me. I began to copy little tricks of Phyllis Lane's. As well as keeping a notebook, as she had done, I drank lots of water and hummed little scales to open my throat, and did backbends in the mornings to mobilise my spine. After a while, I felt as though part of me was as much Phyllis as it was Ibsen's Nora.

At the end of the biography, there was a transcript of a radio interview with Phyllis Lane. Asked for some piece of life advice, she responded: 'Always carry a pedestal.'

The interviewer asked her what she meant by this.

'It's a long-standing motto of mine,' said Phyllis. 'I've been thinking it as long as I can remember. I've taught it to my children. What it means, I suppose, is – honour those who help and support you. Hold them high in your regard. A pedestal is a wonderful thing.'

So that was why Bel was always promising pedestals. I'd wondered for the longest time. Funny, though: I never really thought that Bel meant it. Which might have been unfair of me. But she was so self-centred, so self-serving so much of the time, that I never really thought Bel reserved pedestals for anyone but herself.

2

On the first Thursday of the summer term, when I came down to the studio for Life Class, I felt hands around my eyes, heard a velvety 'Guess who?' in my ear, and swung round to a puppyish hug. Bel and I had not seen each other since the night of the Tree and the Dutch Breakfast.

Ever-loyal Nora, I hugged her back.

'How's tricks, sugar?' she said.

She looked well, and smelled of shampoo and cocoa butter. The beetroot drink must have been back on the menu, and the jogging too. She was finishing the self-directed assignment that formed a substantial part of the course. For the first time, I saw all three paintings together.

'Oh, Bel, I never realised,' I said.

'Pretty cool, huh?' she said. 'So much work. But worth it.'

The pictures were three scenes from *Jacaranda*. The man and woman on the bridge, their hands not quite touching, were Matthew and Audra, as they struggled to reconcile their love for each other with what had happened. The young girl in front of the Georgian house was, of course, Clementine – played presumably by Phyllis, although on closer inspection she might easily have been Bel herself. And the

273

purplish-flowering tree was the jacaranda tree that grew beside the house.

'They're wonderful,' I said. 'I'm sure the moderators will think so.'

'I need to write a three-thousand-word essay to go with the pieces,' said Bel idly. 'I thought it would be easy, but . . . I don't know if you have any time, what with your play and all. Whaddya say, darling?' She smiled at me, at her most beguiling.

I paused for a moment, as though considering. I wondered if she even remembered what she'd said to me, up in the tree. If she did, she might have expected me to be feeling a little cooler towards her, surely, although her manner didn't suggest it. I thought about what to say, and how to appear.

'I do, of course, require a pedestal,' I said at last. 'Of rose gold with chocolate sprinkles.'

'Nora,' Bel said, 'you can have any goddamn pedestal you like.'

And so I helped her with her essay, and with other bits and pieces of work and revision besides. I sat at the kitchen table at the Rosewood Avenue house, helping Bel to draw up an exam timetable to stick on the fridge. And, by and by, as I had known she would, Bel asked me to help her learn the part of Clementine.

I like to think that my manner towards her, all this time, didn't change.

'Do you think they're auditioning anyone else for this role?' I asked her one afternoon, as we sat at the table with cans of Diet Coke and her Early Modern History files.

She crossed herself dramatically. 'Lord, I hope not. I *think* it's mine. I still need to meet the director, mind. He's got a reputation as a bit of a diva. His way or the highway, if you know what I mean. Then again, I'm sure I'll be able to charm him.' She pursed her lips, like a Burlesque dancer, mid-song.

About the need to pass her exams too, she said nothing, but I knew she was thinking about it. Slightly distractedly, she shuffled through the rainbow-coloured Ryman notebooks we were using for her revision, opening and closing them at random.

'Shall we have some tea?' I said, knowing that she would jump up, not so much from hostess-like duty as the need for a break. She went over to the range and put the kettle on; as she did so, I quietly slipped her *Jacaranda* script into my rucksack. We were going to see Darian play with a jazz trio that evening in Brixton. To get it copied in the morning wouldn't take long at all, and I'd be able to return it to the chaos of her bedroom later in the day.

With any luck, she'd never notice it was missing.

One evening, not too long after that, Darian and I were in the conservatory playing Scrabble. I'd discovered that he loved the game. Bel had no patience with it, and neither did Evie or Nana; since the death of my father I'd been longing for someone who shared my fondness for words. Anagrams, crosswords, word-puzzles of all kinds, in English and French, were my father's great obsession, and it had pleased him to pass this obsession on to me.

At first, I'd been worried that Bel would object to us playing together, after her outburst in the tree. But she didn't seem to mind. Darian was a strong opponent, able to play as many as three seven-letter words in a single game. Often, our combined score was as high as eight hundred.

I don't remember who was winning, but I do remember that it was my turn. Just as I was moving my tiles into position, we heard Bel's voice ringing out from the sitting room. She was reading, or reciting, Clementine's long speech at the end of *Jacaranda*. I knew it very well. Word for word, in fact. I was struck by how cleverly she'd taken her mother's famous performance and melded it with her own.

A voice called out, '*Brava*, child. Better than I ever imagined you would be.'

Unmoved, Darian took down my score and passed me the green tile bag. 'Well,' he said. 'I guess she might be getting the part after all.'

'Definitely?'

'Hmm,' he said, shuffling his tiles with professional speed. 'Knowing Dad, he'll keep the game going for a while yet. See if she passes all her exams. Then decide.'

I said, 'I'm so happy for her. She deserves it.'

'I don't know if she deserves anything,' said Darian. 'I love my sister, but she's a total liability.'

We looked at each other with a grown-up kind of understanding.

In the end it was Bel, not Evie, who came with me to *A Doll's House*, after all. Evie bought the tickets, but at the last minute was called into a meeting about a possible job, so I invited Bel. It felt like the right thing to do. At a loose end after too much revision, Azia asked to join us. I didn't know whether Bel had forgiven Azia after the Tree Episode, or indeed whether Azia had forgiven Bel. Neither of them mentioned it.

We met at the box office of the National Theatre one Friday night in May. I loved the National Theatre, a venue I'd never known before I met Bel. This magnificent modern institution, with its sumptuous view of the River Thames, was the place I thought I could happily visit every week for the rest of my life. I'd seen the sign at the side marked STAGE DOOR, and spent happy hours thinking about the greats of the stage who, having made their exits and entrances and curtain calls, had come out into the night, their faces clear of makeup, their attention already turning to the next performance. John Gielgud. Laurence Olivier. Maggie Smith. Judi Dench. Ian Holm. Simon Russell Beale. In my mind's eye I saw them all, and sometimes, when I dared, I imagined myself in their shoes. I'd always thought that you needed to come from a background of exceptional privilege in order to act, but deep reading on the subject was showing me that this was not the case. What you needed was talent, and desire. And to a greater or lesser extent, to be in the right place at the right time. Luck played a part of its own, but so did hard work, and hard work I was never afraid of.

'Stop,' said Bel, midway across the Hungerford Bridge. 'We must make wishes. I always make wishes off bridges. D'you have any coins?'

I checked the pockets of my jacket. 'This do?' I said, offering her a twenty-pence piece.

'Sure,' she said.

I noticed that she didn't check beneath her as she hurled the coin over the side of the bridge, to make sure that there were no boats passing. I was sure I knew what she was wishing for.

'What happens now?' I said. 'With the movie?'

'Now Papa sort of shepherds it along,' she told me; I wasn't sure if she fully understood what this meant, but it sounded believable. 'In Cannes. The *Marché du Film*. The most glamorous thing ever, Norie-love. You oughta see it.'

'Will you be going out there too?' I asked her.

'It depends, I guess. If there's any meetings Papa wants me to go to.'

'Maybe you should ask your dad,' I said. 'If the director is going to be there, wouldn't it be a good idea to show him you're willing to travel to meet him? Make it clear how much you want the part.'

'Maybe you're right.'

She tucked a silky arm through mine as we crossed the rest of the bridge. At the top of the stairs there was a man with a moustache playing the violin, sitting on sheets of newspaper, with a bowler hat in front of him. Feeling for more coins in my pocket, I threw what I had into his hat.

'I always get what I want, you know,' Bel said. 'Always. But it never hurts to wish for things, all the same.'

Azia was waiting for us at the box office. Late nights had pencilled delicate lines across her forehead; although I had no doubt her grades would be stellar, I knew it was in her nature to worry about her performance in the coming exams.

'Just the distraction I needed,' she said. I saw that she had a copy of the play in her bag.

'Drinkies,' said Bel.

A man in black tie and a top hat was playing the piano in the central concourse where the theatregoers wandered to and fro. Approaching him, Bel gave a flowery bow and asked if he took requests. The pianist nodded as he played. 'Anything for you, sweetheart,' he said.

'Sinatra!' said Bel, and he segued cleverly into *My Way*.

'This way,' said Azia, holding Bel's elbow gently and steering her towards the bar. Bel made as if to come with us, and then as we reached the bar she doubled back, slipped onto the raised platform where the piano stood, whipped the hat from the man's head and performed two verses of the song. He played along amiably enough; presumably this was all part of an evening's work. A handful of people applauded at the end, and Bel gave another bow before stepping down and returning the hat. The high colour in her cheeks told me she'd now had her fix, for the time being.

We had bought one programme to share; I read it all while Azia and Bel talked. The actress playing Nora was called Hannah Corbett. Hungry with curiosity, I stared at the black-and-white photographs of rehearsals. They looked so calm and steely and professional, these actors, clad plainly in T-shirts and comfortable trousers as they worked. Camouflage clothes, like Old Nora wore. Hannah Corbett had dark hair and a round, open face. I looked forward to seeing her Nora. It would be different to mine, I was sure, and no doubt better, since she was a trained actress.

'I should do more theatre,' Bel said. She exaggerated the pronunciation: *thee-yetter*.

'What happened to your agent?' asked Azia.

'Oh, I couldn't stand him,' said Bel.

'You fired him?'

'He fired himself, after *Teen Spirits*,' said Bel, putting her feet up on the seat in front. A white-haired man twisted round and frowned. She took them down again. I sank back into my seat, absorbing the calm hum of anticipation. A recording played, asking for mobile phones to be switched off, and we all dutifully did so. I heard a woman further along our row say to her companion, 'At the National, curtain-up is always on time,' and indeed, at seven thirty precisely, the lights went down and silence swelled to fill the auditorium in a way that I found peculiarly thrilling.

Bel's fingers found mine in the darkness.

We said our goodbyes at the foot of Embankment Bridge. Azia had money for a taxi, and Bel wanted her to drop her somewhere along the way home, although I knew most likely Azia would end up paying for Bel to travel all the way back to Rosewood Avenue in the safety of the cab. I said I would walk. There's a certain way I get at the end of a really good book, or film, or – now I'd seen a few of them – a stage play, and it was like this: I was filled with a *wanting* . . . a wanting to go out and do something, something wonderful and watchable and wish-fulfilling. And I wanted to be alone with that wanting.

The man with the violin was gone from the top of the stairs; the bridge was neither full nor empty, the moon somewhere in-between as well. As Bel and I had done a few hours previously, I stopped in the middle of the bridge. For a while I imagined it was not the Thames that I saw, but the Seine: more slender, more feminine, lit by different lights, edged by different buildings, filled with different boats. Notre-Dame not far away. Our little apartment tucked away under shingled rooftop. Evie behind a bar, speaking her rather good, though strongly accented, French to the locals who came in for beers and *petits rouges*. Me at nursery school. And my father, working at his slanting desk. In my memories, he appeared like one of his pencil sketches. I wished, not for the first time, that I could remember his face.

Where would we be, we three, I wondered, if he were still alive? Would Evie make costumes? Would the Trace Incident have occurred? And would I, Nora, ever have become interested in acting?

I had one coin left, and it was only a 2p piece, but better than nothing. A slight wind licked at my hair as I raised my arm and cast the coin over the rail. A metallic twinkle, fleeter than an eye blink, and then it was gone.

3

'Just smell the air, darling,' said Bel.

I sniffed. Smoke and saltwater, tomatoes and wine, and the heat of the day still weighing down the breeze. Bel and I were walking down a narrow, touristy street, where the shops were a throng of lavender bags and baskets, bread and honey and shoes. It was the first time I'd been back to France in ten years; this was a fact that I found very odd. Of course, I didn't know the south at all, and because I was with Bel the people we had met so far had assumed that I spoke no French. I found myself unsure of what language to use, and when I did speak French, it came out halting and hesitant.

'Oh, Cannes, I've missed you,' said Bel. 'Look all around you, Nora.'

Dutifully, I looked. We had come out onto the Boulevard de la Croisette, the main road that ran along the waterfront. The harbour was stacked with kitted-out yachts; the buildings of the old town glowed apricot in the evening light. In front of us, the great Palais des Festivals loomed geometric against the sky, with a red-carpet moat. It was here that films were screened and awards given; it was here that crowds waited to see the stars appear.

'Picture people,' sighed Bel.

I could feel a kind of relaxed interest in us as we wandered from place to place. Who were we? Or, more precisely, who was Bel? Her aura, as ever, was starry and self-contained; it was as though she were already famous. I saw a woman with a backpack stare at Bel's face and then down at her camera, trying to decide whether she ought to take a photograph. The smart-casual men with week-old stubble and festival passes slung around their necks took notice of Bel as she passed their café tables. No kimono today; it was late May, and the day had been hot; she was wearing a white sundress with a pattern of green leaves. I imagined that it had belonged to Phyllis Lane. I knew that Bel knew that people were looking at her, and how much it pleased her. I could see her performing, subtly: holding her arms aloft as though to balance along an invisible walkway, letting her clear laugh carry over the cobblestones.

'Mama came here for the first time the year that *Jacaranda* was in competition for the Palme d'Or. That's the prize for best film, you know. She stayed in the Hotel du Cap. We should go there, some time.'

Now Bel was looking around her in that focused yet vague way that she had, and I knew she was wondering where the next piece of entertainment would be found. I pre-empted her.

'Drinkies?' I said, in her language.

She smiled delightedly. 'I know just the place.'

Leading me by the hand, she danced along the main road, weaving in and out of tourists and lampposts, past canopied restaurants and shops full of designer goods, until we came to the grass-covered terraces of an enormous hotel called the Grand. There was an outdoor bar and a plethora of glass-topped tables and cushioned chairs; flinging herself into one, Bel gave me twenty euros and asked me to get her a gin and tonic.

'Cheers,' she said, when I returned with our drinks. 'Well, Nora, here's to you.'

'Why me?' I said, setting the bottles of tonic water neatly beside an ashtray.

My smile matched hers as we clinked glasses; I thought we looked older than seventeen and eighteen, sitting there in our dresses on the manicured terrace. No one else from Lady Agatha's was attending the closing of the Cannes Film Festival; of that I was sure. A year ago, six months ago – three months, even   I would never have been able to imagine myself somewhere like this.

'Because you're the real reason we're here.'

'Why?' I said again.

'You speak perfect French, for a start,' Bel said. 'You're some kind of academic genius . . .'

'Not really,' I said.

'Come on. We both know how smart you are. It's no use pretending. But better still, you're *responsible*. No way would Daddy have wanted me here, had it not been for

Knowledgeable Nora, to keep me on the Straight and Narrow. I assure-ya, Nora.'

She finished her drink.

'Another,' she said. 'Oh, look, you need one too.'

Waiting again at the bar, I watched a rich-looking man buying a whole bottle of vodka. It made me think of Old Evie. My mother was delighted that someone had invited me to Cannes for the weekend – for Anton had bought my ticket as well as Bel's, and paid for everything from taxis to tiramisù. Evie had given me a hundred euros, which made a handsome belated birthday present, although I knew she didn't expect me to spend it all. She'd spoken to Anton on the phone and found him charming, and had driven me and Bel to the airport herself. What she made of Bel I didn't know; I expected she'd tell me when I returned.

I thought back to dinner at the Ingrams' house, not long after Bel and I and Azia had gone to the theatre; all of us at the table – Darian, me, Bel and Anton – while the cat watched from the chair and the empty ash-jar watched from the windowsill.

'Dadd-ee,' said Bel. 'Can I come out to Cannes for the end of the festival?'

'You've got exams,' said Darian.

'It's half term right after,' she said. 'Plenty of time to keep working when I get home.'

Anton got up to carve second helpings from a roast chicken.

Bel said to his back: 'I deserve a break. But more importantly, I do need to meet Gabriel Glass. Don't I? And he's going to be there. It said so in *Screen Daily*.'

Coming back to the table with an oval platter, from which we helped ourselves, Anton said: 'It is an idea. You should meet Gabe. If not now, then soon.'

'Well, then,' said Bel. 'It's meant to be. Ooh. I can wear some of Mama's Riviera dresses.'

'And there's room in the apartment,' said Anton. 'The problem is . . . if you come out to meet him, you'll have to be on best behaviour. Your mother was always exemplary about meetings. A true professional. It's her attitude I'd like you to inhabit, not just her dresses. No nonsense, Annabel. No drama.'

Bel looked appalled. 'As if I would!'

'What if you get lost again?' said Darian. 'Like last time. You can't speak a word of French.'

'True,' said Anton. 'On balance, maybe it's best if you don't fly out, Annabel.'

Bel began to protest. With an awkward movement of my arm, I knocked over the salt cellar. I think they'd forgotten I was even there, because they all looked at me as I rescued the grains of salt from the table. I looked up, apologetic. I caught Bel's eye. We had rehearsed this, the two of us.

'What if *Nora* comes too?' said Bel. 'She can help with everything. Revision, French-ism . . . best behaviour.'

This last she said in a dainty, childish whisper.

Anton and Darian looked at each other.

'Nora,' said Anton. 'Would you . . . would you like to go too?'

You shall go to the ball, said the fairy godmother.

'Can I help you?' asked the barman in English, interrupting my thoughts.

I ordered in French; my fluency was back and he shot me a look of gratitude, as if to say: here's someone, perhaps, who really belongs here. But, as you know, I do not belong anywhere. From what I'd read about successful actors, it seemed many of them felt the same way. *Stay true to yourself*, Nana would say. But in order to do that, one needs to know the self to which to be true. Easy for Nana: from the West Coast of Scotland to the waterfalls and plains of South America, she never varied her Bible-verse stance on life as she buried her husbands and ferried her beloved dogs and murder mystery novels from city to city. Nana belonged everywhere, because Nana knew who she was. I looked over my shoulder at Bel, who was being chatted up by two men in pastel-coloured linen jackets. Bel also belonged everywhere, I felt, because she belonged to herself.

When I got back to our table, Bel said: 'Let's go on from here to a bar on the beach. And there's a party a bit later, so these guys say.'

The pastel-jacket men had gone back to their own crowd;

one of them turned a little and smiled. His blond hair reminded me of Darian.

'That one's Claude and that one's Eric,' said Bel. 'What do you think? Or shall we just have dinner?'

It was a fact well known about Bel that if she drank on an empty stomach, things generally proceeded downhill at considerable speed.

'Might be a good idea,' I said, in a tone of voice that implied that I did not mean it.

'Do you have any money?'

'Not much.'

'Are you hungry?'

I shrugged. 'Not really. But if you want to, we should eat. Don't forget you've got lunch tomorrow with the director.'

A lunch meeting had been set up between Anton, Bel and Gabriel Glass for the following day.

'Not until one o'clock,' Bel said. 'It's early yet. I feel like more drinkies. And a party or two. If we don't like it we can always come back here. It's jumping until the small hours. They drink rosé by the magnum. Everyone in Cannes does. Nora, I do believe you've already drunk *two* gin and tonics. The air must agree with you!'

I laughed loudly at this.

'I think we'll let Eric and Claude buy the next round,' said Bel. 'I haven't told them our names yet, by the way.'

'Maybe we should make up some new ones,' I said.

'Yes,' said Bel. 'I think we should.'

'OK,' I said, anagramming at speed in my head. 'I shall be Ronia Sabot. And you . . .' I wrote out her name on a cardboard beer mat, using both hands to amuse her, and then gracefully rearranged the letters. 'Lianna Bergman,' I said. 'A possible descendant of Ingrid, don't you think?'

'I love, love, love it,' said Bel. She raised her glass. 'Lianna and Ronia,' she said. 'May our shadows never grow less.'

Given the quantities of gin and tonics that were imbibed that night, I ought not to remember what we did and where we went. I shouldn't be able to recall the thudding techno music that we (even I) danced to, standing on tables at the bar on the beach, or the half hour that Bel disappeared for with Eric, or perhaps Claude, while I searched up and down the sands for her in vain. I shouldn't remember the names of the people we spoke to, or the street corner where we hailed the cab that took us up to a party in a villa in the hills above Cannes, where Bel eventually forgot that she was Lianna Bergman and told everyone that she was the daughter of Anton Ingram and Phyllis Lane, which took place just before she was sick in the outdoor hot tub. I should not be able to recall with word-perfect accuracy everything I said, to everyone I spoke to, but I do. I was Ronia Sabot, a drama school graduate with an intriguing future ahead of me; I was Ronia Sabot, apprentice chef; I was Ronia Sabot, sculptress.

I shouldn't remember saying to Bel, at the top of a very

white staircase: 'We really ought to be thinking about going home.'

But Bel was wearing a coat of armour that she'd prised from the wall and was halfway through what she claimed was a re-enactment of the Battle of Hastings with three minor characters from the new *Star Wars* film.

'Can't leave now,' came the voice from behind the visor. 'Party's just getting started.'

'It's already three,' I protested.

She did not hear me, fully immersed in her new role, shrieking with delight as she gesticulated with her sword. I hoped it wasn't a real one. It was so hard to tell what was a prop and what wasn't, nowadays. I slipped down the stairs and across the gleaming hall to the door. Balmy night air, rich with honeysuckle, greeted me as I came out. A uniformed doorman with an earpiece stood motionless on the step, hands clasped behind him. Why he was there, I didn't know; either to protect the house, or one of the guests. In French, I asked him to call me a taxi.

Anton had rented, or perhaps been lent, a magnificent apartment that overlooked the Boulevard de la Croisette. I turned the key quietly in the front door and walked up the stone stairs. When I entered the apartment, all was quiet; faint snores came from Anton's bedroom. He would go out early the next morning for meetings, I knew; Bel was expected to join him and Gabriel Glass at one o'clock at Giuliana, an expensive-looking Italian restaurant near the

Palais. Firmly, I'd said that I would be happy to amuse myself elsewhere. My feet bare, shoes in my hand, I went to the fridge and took out two Petit Filou yogurts. I ate these on the balcony, watching the beach parties disperse as the sound systems shut down. Now and again there came a screech of car tyres, as though some drunken reveller had strayed unwarrantedly far into the road. I wondered if Bel was all right.

'If only she'd agreed to come home with me,' I said aloud, to myself.

Going to brush my teeth, I watched myself thoughtfully in the mirror. I did not look especially the worse for wear. This wasn't surprising. I might have appeared to be drinking gin and tonics all night, but in point of fact my glasses had contained nothing but sparkling water. This is one of the oldest tricks in the book, and I was glad that I knew it.

Sober as a judge, I slept; I kept my phone on my pillow, so that Bel could call or text if she needed to. She had her own key. But I did not really expect her to return. It would be very, very unusual if she did.

Four or five hours later, the whoosh of the coffee machine told me that Anton was awake. I heard the shower, the sound of his phone; I heard him holding the kind of executive conversation that I'd gotten very used to during my time at the house in Rosewood Avenue, something along the lines of: 'Close it. Close it. Take the money and run.'

The door to the flat clanged shut, and clanged open ten minutes later and then shut again. He'd gone out for bread, I was sure, to leave for me and Bel, before heading out for the day. It was nine o'clock, and the sky promised heat and excitement.

I went out in my T-shirt and pyjama bottoms to the marble-floored kitchen and dining area. A cream sofa lined one wall; you could lie on it and look through the glass doors to the balcony and the sea beyond. It was a balcony that put Evie's and my veranda to shame. There was a white dining table with silver-backed chairs; a marble island with high stools; a fridge full of Evian and prosecco. I ate another yogurt, and then, after some thought, toasted a bit of baguette, which I had with butter and honey. Then I washed up my plate and put it away. I didn't want to look as though I'd had a leisurely breakfast. By this time, I would, of course, have realised that Bel had not come back, if I hadn't known already. I checked her room, to be triple-sure that this was the case, and indeed it was.

'Now, Responsible Nora,' I said. 'What would you do first?'

I texted Bel: *Honey, are you OK? Where are you? Want me to come and get you?*

I wasn't sure that my phone would work abroad. After some fiddling with the settings, I managed to activate delivery reports. Bel's phone, I could see, was not switched on. This wasn't surprising: her phone had very poor battery life and she wasn't particularly good at remembering to charge it. What next? Although Responsible Nora was, of course, a trifle concerned about Bel, I did not think it would be inappropriate to go out for a time. It was a beautiful morning.

I sent another message, as Responsible Nora would: *Don't forget, darling. Giuliana at 1 p.m.*

Then, gathering a beach towel, a book and my sports bikini, and practising in my head certain lines that I thought might come in handy a little later on, I went down to the beach for a swim.

4

Slightly out of breath, I pushed through the glass doors of the restaurant. It was five past one. Anton was sitting alone at a corner table laid with a peach-coloured cloth; arranged in front of him were his phone, sunglasses and notebook, like a Cannes survival kit. Ten days in the south of France had tanned his skin. He was wearing a navy shirt, a cream jacket, jeans. I could not see Gabriel Glass, and that was good, because the conversation that Anton and I were about to have was one best not shared with anyone else.

Anton was studying a wine list and looking up from time to time. When he saw me, I witnessed the unfolding of different emotions in quick succession. Recognition, then surprise, then suspicion and possibly dread, and possibly also disappointment. I hated to be the bearer of bad news. Daintily, I wove a path through the maze of tables, apologising to my left and right, although I was in nobody's way. Meeting Anton's gaze, I smiled, keeping on my face that same subtle mask of apology.

I knew exactly how I wanted the scene to be played.

He stood up as I approached, but didn't kiss me hello.

'Is everything all right, Nora?' he said.

A waiter appeared at my side, drawing out a chair for me. I shook my head, telling him in French that I wouldn't be staying. He nodded deferentially and withdrew.

Then, to Anton, I said: 'I'm afraid Bel's still out. She hasn't come home.'

He glanced over to the door, and then back at me. I always think it is a tremendous cliché when people in books are described as sighing, or exhaling loudly, or breathing out through their noses, but that is exactly what Bel's father did. He exhaled loudly and long, looked at his watch, half closed his eyes and then opened them again.

'For heaven's sake,' he said, not loudly and not particularly emotionally. 'Do have a seat, Nora, please.'

I sat down on the edge of the chair. 'I'm so sorry,' I said. 'It's my fault.'

He nodded: *go on*, and poured me a glass of water.

'We went out to the Grand, and then on to another bar,' I explained. 'Bel was – she was celebrating a bit. You know. Enjoying being out in Cannes, and relaxing after her first exams. I mean, she's been working so hard . . . I think she felt as though she deserved a bit of time off.'

'Letting her hair down, shall we say,' said Anton dryly.

'Yes,' I said. 'She had a few drinks. I – I wasn't watching very closely, so I'm not sure how many. I don't know . . . Certainly more than me. I don't really drink. It got later and later, and I felt it was time to go home. It can be a bit boring, you know, if everyone else is drinking . . . and

I was really tired. Bel said she'd stay out an extra half hour, maybe an hour, and then come back. She *promised*. I made sure she had her phone and enough money for a taxi, and then I . . . I just couldn't stay awake any longer. I had to leave. I wish I'd been able to persuade her to come back with me.'

'What time was this?' asked Anton.

'About a quarter to four,' I replied. I didn't think this was a test, but I couldn't be sure. It hadn't sounded as though he had woken up when I turned the key in the door, but there was the slimmest chance that he was trying to catch me out with the question, so I thought it was best to be truthful.

'And where is Bel now?' he said.

I shook my head.

'I just don't know. I . . . When I woke up this morning she hadn't come back. Her phone isn't on. I rang and rang . . . I wanted to go back to the place where we were, but it was a big house up in the hills and I didn't know the address. I thought about calling you, but I didn't want to worry you, or interrupt your meetings, and I'd reminded her about lunch today at one o'clock, so I thought, you know, that she might even come straight here. But I waited at the flat most of the morning, in case she didn't have her phone or her key. And then I realised it was nearly one o'clock so I sort of ran down here. To tell you.'

At this, I looked ruefully down at my slight dishevelment.

My hair was a tangle over one shoulder; I wore flip-flops and a denim skirt and a T-shirt of Bel's that said *Desperately Seeking Susan*. In spite of this, I'd taken some care with my makeup. My skin was bright and dewy and made it clear that I had no hangover to speak of, and the biro marks on my hands indicated that I might well have spent the morning hard at work on some kind of academic assignment.

'It really is my fault,' I said again.

'Don't be silly, Nora,' he said. 'You can hardly keep her under lock and key, and no one was expecting you to.'

A different waiter came with a tall orange drink.

'Will you have a Campari and soda?' said Anton.

'No, thank you,' I said. 'I should go back, just in case . . . I'm quite worried about her.'

'Was she in any discernible danger?'

'None.'

'Then don't be worried,' he said. 'She's a big girl. She'll come back when she wakes up and remembers where she is. If I had a penny for every time Annabel did something worrisome, I wouldn't have to work so hard to raise financing. Trust me.' He broke a bread roll and buttered one half absent-mindedly, and then laid it by his plate. 'Mind you,' he said, picking up the bread again, 'I'm not entirely thrilled by her behaviour.'

This, I felt, was an understatement, quite typical of Anton and the way he spoke. It might not have been Bel's only opportunity to meet Gabriel Glass, but it was a good one.

And not turning up for a scheduled meeting was one of the worst things you could do in the business. Everyone knew that.

'Ah,' said Anton. 'Here he is.'

A slight, dark man of about forty with a mass of corkscrew curls was shaking his hand and then embracing him in the European style. The man turned to me and smiled, his eyes hidden by aviator shades, and said to Anton: 'And this must be your lovely daughter.'

'In point of fact, this is my lovely, or my not-always-so-lovely daughter's lovely friend, Nora.'

I stood up. 'Nice to meet you,' I said. 'I'm a big admirer of your work.'

He looked pleased and a little surprised.

'I'm afraid Bel is indisposed,' said Anton. 'Nora, you are going to stay for lunch, aren't you?'

'Oh, I shouldn't,' I said.

'Do stay,' said Gabriel Glass, sitting down and removing his sunglasses. 'I can't possibly talk to Anton for an hour on my own.'

He had a strong, complex accent – there was a bit of German in there, I thought, and a bit of something Nordic, perhaps, although I am no expert. He asked for some fried zucchini and a glass of Pinot Noir. A long conversation ensued about wine. We ordered: asparagus, squid, pasta. I kept my choices very plain, as befitted a guest who shouldn't, in fact, even be there.

'Nora,' said Gabriel Glass. 'I'm dying to know which of my films you particularly admire.'

I saw Anton looking on with interest, wondering, I was sure, what I was going to say. I won't report the speech I then gave, covering more or less every film that Gabriel Glass had either written or both written and directed over the past decade, but I can assure you that it was very pretty indeed. The thoughts and opinions I shared were very much my own too; I had cribbed from no critic, but instead watched his films and decided what I, a well-read, considerate seventeen-year-old girl, felt about each one. The story, the characters, the moods and the music. Anton was smiling at me as I spoke, and I realised something: he was relaxed now, but he hadn't been relaxed at all when I first walked into Giuliana's. Our starters came and Gabriel said how refreshing it was to meet a teenager who was so incredibly film-literate.

'Did you watch my films with Annabel?' he asked.

I hesitated. 'No,' I said. 'I'd seen them all a while ago.'

'And do you want to work in film yourself?'

At this I looked bashful and a shade unsure of myself.

'You're acting in a play at the moment, aren't you?' said Anton. '*A Doll's House*, I think you said.'

The conversation moved on to theatre. By the time our plates were cleared I knew one thing absolutely: both my dining companions were very impressed with my knowledge of the dramatic arts. There was laughter and refilling of glasses; I was careful not to dominate discussions at any point, just to supply intelligent Norian thoughts when invited to do so. And it was working.

Oh, it really was working.

All around the restaurant thrummed with activity: knives scraped and glasses clinked and peals of hysteria rippled from wall to wall. At one point, Anton said, 'Don't look now, Nora, but Brad Pitt has just come in,' and I giggled with appropriate delight at this piece of news, although it didn't interest me in the slightest. I wondered when Anton and Gabriel would start to discuss *Jacaranda*. I felt that I shouldn't bring it up myself, although I wanted to desperately.

Finally, Gabriel said, 'So. Where are we with the cast?'

'Dennis Havelock only wants to do one film this year,' said Anton, 'and it's this one. Miriam Campbell will play Audra.'

'Is she a big enough name?'

'I think so. I think she's right for the part.'

They talked then about a certain casting agent whose services they wanted to use. I could hear from the shift in their tones of voice that they did not necessarily agree on casting matters. It surely made it all the more important that Bel should have been there to meet Gabriel. The waiter murmured contritely that our main courses were on the way; I suspected that the arrival of Brad Pitt had slowed down our orders.

'I was very much looking forward to meeting Annabel today,' said Gabriel. 'It's a shame she couldn't make it.'

'Perhaps she and I could meet you this evening?' said Anton.

'I'm taking a flight at six, unfortunately,' Gabriel replied.

'Pity.'

'Her showreel was most instructive,' said Gabriel. 'I do see why you suggest her to play Clementine. And of course, the fact that your wife also played the part . . . well, it's a touching side note.' In his tone of voice, I could hear that he was not totally convinced.

Some technical chat ensued about money and locations. I excused myself and went to find the bathrooms. The ladies' room was peach-coloured, like the tablecloths, and as opulent as I'd come to expect of all things Cannes. OtherNora stared back at me from the mirror, eyes alight, as I washed my hands.

Am I doing enough? I said to OtherNora.

But she didn't reply.

I tied my hair back, thought better of it and fanned it over my shoulders. I imagined Gabriel Glass, during my absence from the table, saying: 'What a delightful girl. So intelligent,' and Anton agreeing: 'Yes, she's really quite something.'

Walking back towards the dining room, I smoothed the wrinkles in my skirt and rehearsed a couple of throwaway phrases that would, very subtly, recall Clementine's famous last speech in *Jacaranda*. When I got to the table, I saw that the main courses – china bowls piled high with *linguine alle vongole* – had arrived.

And so had Bel.

She was wearing another white dress. This one had panels of French lace at the sides and a pleated skirt; the cap sleeves allowed her arms to float like swan's wings, and a row of brightly-coloured wooden bangles sailed from elbow to wrist each time she made a gesture. She was sitting in my chair, next to Gabriel, and I saw that another one had been brought to the table between her and Anton, presumably for me. She was talking with her mouth full of bread. Her eyes shone, and her hair, which she must have washed and conditioned, was a cluster of burnished buttercups. None of them had seen me yet. Without even meaning to, I reached behind my head and tied up my hair again. It just couldn't compete.

Gabriel gave a burst of laughter at something Bel said. 'That's hilarious,' he said.

'Oh, that's nothing,' she replied. Then she saw me. 'Honey!' she said.

'Hey, darling,' I said.

Anton caught my eye, as though to ask me not to betray any of my concerns about Bel's wellbeing.

'I've had *quite* a time getting here, I can tell you,' said Bel.

She went on to recount a tale that was, frankly, Norian in its sheer outrageousness. A trip for a last-minute manicure, the theft of her handbag, a kind man who apprehended the thief, getting lost in the backstreets of Cannes, and hitching a lift with a butcher on the back of a moped in order to get to Giuliana by one forty-five.

'Unforgivably late, I know,' she said, in her Britishest, most Clementine accent. 'I just can't apologise enough.'

But I could see from the look of wonder and admiration on Gabriel Glass's face that no apology was necessary.

'So,' said Evie. 'How was it?'

Back home, looking out at our balcony, I decided that the world had shrunk immeasurably. It was, appropriately, raining. My head ached from the air conditioning on the plane; my feet were sore from walking in flip-flops, and I felt the empty kind of ache that a Christmas stocking must feel when it holds no further delights.

I told her all about the red-carpet event we'd gone to on the Saturday night, the party in the hills, the apparition of Brad Pitt, the boat trip on Sunday to the island of Sainte Marguerite, where it was said that the Man in the Iron Mask had been kept prisoner.

'How was the food?' Evie wanted to know.

'Bland, overpriced,' I told her. 'We had lunch in an Italian restaurant that was pretty good. And it was fun to speak French.'

'What about the movie your friend's dad is making?' she said. 'Is your friend still going to be in it?'

'She sure is,' I said, thinking of the way Gabriel Glass had held Bel's hand to his lips and kissed it when he said goodbye. It seemed that no one was immune to Bel, but no one. It didn't matter what I'd had to say about his work; it didn't matter how smart I was, or how capable. There was nobody like Bel. Even though she'd thrown up all the way home on the aeroplane, her skin robbed of its ambrosial glow; even though she'd slept with her head in my lap all the way back from the airport, she'd done what she'd needed to do. And she'd done it brilliantly.

'Exciting,' said Evie, reaching for her sewing box, a tin that had once held Danish Butter Cookies.

We watched an episode of something corsetty, and Evie talked about vampires, and we ate dinner in tranquil silence. When I went to bed, my dreams were full of tables covered in peach-coloured cloths, over which flowers crawled like spiders and light bulb letters glowed bright in the sky above the port of Cannes, like the title of some hot-ticket show: *Picture People.*

5

Bel was now on study leave. She did not have many more exams to do. I knew, from the way she'd been revising, and from what she said about each exam, that they had gone well enough. Buoyed by her meeting with Gabriel Glass, she was calmer and more organised about the exam period than I'd ever thought she could be: checking the timetable we'd pinned up in the kitchen, making sure she read through her files and notes the evening before. I noticed she didn't call me every day, the way she had once done.

On Sunday afternoon, the day before we were due back at school, with Bel away somewhere for the weekend, I texted Darian and asked if I could come over to collect a forgotten notebook. He agreed at once. It was the first time I'd ever been to the Rosewood Avenue house without Bel. Darian made tea with the old-fashioned pot that Anton also liked to use. We carried our cups into the conservatory. The cat lolled like a reclining queen on a corduroy cushion.

'Where *is* Bel?' I asked, stroking the cat's head.

'She's gone to some house party. Thurston's mate's country estate. Not my scene.'

It was funny, I thought, how the word *estate* meant something so different to the Ingram family.

The *Jacaranda* script lay open on the glass-topped table. I thought back to a night – how long ago? Two weeks, ten days? – when, as usual, I'd been over at the Ingrams' house, reading through the screenplay with Bel at the kitchen table. We'd reached a very well-known scene; YouTube was awash with clips of Phyllis Lane saying these lines.

'They say it takes a gardener of extraordinary abilities to coax life from a jacaranda tree on English soil. To raise it from a seedling and watch it grow; to ward off the bitter winter frost, to gift it with heat and light. There are few who can do it. All these years, I've come to believe that love – real love – is like that jacaranda tree. Even now, I don't think any different.'

Try as she might, Bel just couldn't quite get the hang of it. She said the words too fast, not giving them enough weight.

'It's bloody impossible,' she said, throwing the script across the room. I went over to pick it up.

'You try it and see,' said Bel.

I read the lines aloud, faltering a little – on purpose – at first, and then faltering less as I carried on, because there was something about Gabriel's *Jacaranda* screenplay that was so heady and delightful that it made you want to keep reading it.

Bel was pleased. 'It's glorious to hear this in your voice,' she said. 'Read *more.*'

So I did, and after a while I could sense, without seeing, that Darian and Anton had come into the kitchen and were listening to me as I read.

'Clever little Nora,' said Bel. 'That's helped me no end.'

The script still lay open on the same scene. Bel had scribbled some notes in the margin, I saw.

Following my gaze, Darian said: 'You know every word, don't you?'

He was right, of course. I did. In all likeliness, I'd known them – deep down, at blood level – long before Bel had even tentatively mouthed the opening lines of Clementine's first scene.

Darian said: 'You know, I don't think Dad ever actually intended to give her a part in the film.'

'You think so?'

'He was just using it as a carrot. With Bel, it's better to use carrots than sticks, as we all know. He offered, knowing she'd pull her socks up, but knowing that she'd probably mess up at some point, and then he could withdraw his offer. This is what they do, Bel and Dad. But – I don't know – maybe because you were there to help her, with her work, her lines . . . it's somehow made all the difference. I've never seen Bel like this before. So intent, so focused . . . I mean, still crazy. She'll always be crazy. But I reckon maybe Dad's decided to give it a go after all. I thought it would all end in tears.'

'I guess you were wrong,' I said.

'Well,' he said. 'They haven't started shooting yet.' He was clasping his hands inside-out, stretching out his arms, in a way that I knew meant he wanted to go and play the piano. The cat slithered off the sofa, stretched like an uncoiling spring, and followed him as he wandered into the sitting room.

I went upstairs alone.

Bel's room was no messier than usual. If anything, there was evidence of some organisation: on her desk, which had once been merely a kind of drinks cabinet, her revision files were stacked by subject. There was a jar full of pens and highlighters, all with lids on. My eye fell on a pile of reading matter. Interesting: Bel was also reading the biography of Phyllis Lane. Rereading, perhaps. There, on the floor by the bed was my notebook. Just where I'd left it.

Not long afterwards, Darian found me standing by the fridge, where Bel's exam timetable was neatly stuck, along with a variety of recipes, lists and clippings from *Screen International*.

'All right?' he said.

'Just looking at this photograph,' I said, indicating a picture I'd never seen before stuck to the freezer door.

'Oh, yes,' he said. 'Bel found it in the pocket of one of Mum's dressing gowns.'

There was Phyllis Ingram, or Phyllis Lane, in a voluminous candy-stripe skirt, her skin bleached by the exposure, a hand shading her eyes. Bel, aged maybe seven or eight, ragged-haired, snaggle-toothed, was bunched against the candy stripes, grinning. Darian was a little to the side, holding a plastic truck. All three were standing on a stretch of white-gold sand, against an inviting sea.

'Where are you?' I said.

'I don't know,' he said. 'It's ridiculous that I don't know. But I find one beach looks an awful lot like another.'

He offered to play me a piano piece by Debussy that he'd been rehearsing. As we left the kitchen, I cast a look back over my shoulder, to where the photograph was stuck to the fridge with a Monet magnet, amid all the other things that were stuck there, and gave myself a little inward nod of satisfaction.

I'd never thought much about Bel's abilities to tune in to other people. I didn't think she had a particular talent for it. Not the way I did. But perhaps Bel was able to pick up more subtle vibrations than I'd thought, because a week later, she did something that surprised me.

It was a breezy, blossomy evening. Bel, Azia and I were walking on Hampstead Heath. We'd been hanging out at Thurston's house – his mother had moved into a sumptuous, yellow-brick mansion, complete with butler and chef – and Bel had decided that we ought to go to the ponds on the heath for a swim before going home. She needed to clear her mind before her final week of exams, she said. The heath was seeded with happy couples, children on scooters, picnicking parties. The performances of *A Doll's House* were approaching, and I asked Azia and Bel whether they wanted to reserve tickets.

'Of course,' said Azia, changing nimbly behind a towel.

'I don't know if it'll be any good,' I said.

'Now, Nora, everyone has to start somewhere,' said Bel. 'I'm coming too. Wild horses, and all that.'

I could have guessed that she'd be a terrible swimmer, and she was: she had no coordination of arms and legs to speak of, and no style. Even her breaststroke was closer to an unformed doggy-paddle, but she didn't seem to notice, or mind. Most of the time, she floated on her front or back, while Azia did ten diligent back-and-forth lengths and I did twenty-five. Then, since Bel and Azia were keener on talking than swimming, I swam back to join them in the shallows.

'Are you nervous about the play?' Azia asked me.

'Very,' I said.

'Don't be,' she replied. 'You're good. You're really good.'

'Just fancy,' said Bel. 'Ten years from now, me and Azia might be waiting outside your dressing-room door, in the hope that you'll come out and give us your autograph. And you'll be far too grand to remember us.'

'That'll never happen,' I said.

'It might.'

She looked wistful, then chuckled to herself softly, one foot extending out of the water as she floated on her back. And then suddenly she plunged towards me, seizing me heavily around the shoulders and pushing me down, right down, under the green-gold water of the Hampstead pond. She was, I realised, much stronger than I was.

She relaxed; my head broke the surface. I coughed, shoved her off me and breathed deeply. Bel laughed and wound her arms again round my neck.

'Chill out, Bel,' said Azia.

'What was that for?' I said.

'Oh, I was just thinking,' said Bel.

'Thinking what?'

I could freeze, for ever, my frame of this moment. It's like a French Impressionist's painting. Three girls, one with ringlets and birthmark, one elegant and dark-haired, one blonde and buoyant and beautiful, cutting a triangle of wavelets into the great green pond. Looking at this picture, you'd see only the tranquillity of the June-evening sunshine.

She kept her hands on my shoulders, pressing, not-pressing, like a promise.

'Well,' she said, 'I was thinking that if you ever let me down . . . people have, you know. If you ever betrayed me, Nora darling . . . well, I'd drown you.'

The fingers pressed. She was back to her American South.

'I'd drown you and drown you . . .'

I'll huff and I'll puff and I'll blow your house down, said the wolf to the three little pigs.

'. . . until you were dead.'

Her laugh pealed across the surface of the pond.

6

June the fifteenth was a Thursday, just as that first Life Class with Jonah Trace at the helm had been, although it seemed a lifetime ago. It was two days before the technical rehearsal of *A Doll's House*, and three days before the dress rehearsal. There was a kind of blooming excitement about the summer holidays, although since Evie and I seldom went anywhere but Scotland, I generally regarded the holidays as a stretch of numberless days and numbing dullness. This particular Thursday was also the date of Bel's final exam. English Literature: Poetry and Drama, if I remember correctly. Questions on Milton and Wilde. As ever, I'd texted to wish her good luck, the previous night.

Formal exams were held in the gym, above the Art and Design Studio. Although I'd been in the habit of going to find Bel in the queue outside, either at a quarter to ten, if the exam was in the morning, or a quarter to two, if in the afternoon, I was busy all day with costume fittings and didn't see her. As good as her word, Evie had taken a week off work to help out, and having my mother in residence backstage, her mouth full of pins, her busy LOVE HAT hands twisting and threading and making things look beautiful, was a diverting pleasure. She seemed to get on especially well with Megan Lattismore.

'Thank you, a hundred times, Nora, for the loan of your magnificent mother,' said Mrs Tomaski.

Megan texted me after the costume fittings. *Your mother is the coolest person I have ever met.*

Life Class was over now for the year. My nudes were rolled up in a cardboard tube at home, for me to keep or discard as I saw fit. I went through them in a moment of lazy curiosity, later that afternoon. Here were my sketches of the very first model – not Vanessa, the one before that – with the jar-like body and sandbag breasts. Then Vanessa, whom we'd drawn with both hands. I remembered the frustration of Jonah Trace, the flushed-faced humiliation when he realised that I was ambidextrous. Ah, the good old days. The time in which he and I were 'going out' was marked with little smiley-faces that he'd drawn at the bottom of my pictures. Even, in one place, a heart. Then, in January, the smiley-faces were gone, as Jonah was.

I was so absorbed in the drawings that I didn't notice for a while that my phone was vibrating. It had slipped down the side of my bed. Fishing it out, I saw Darian's name on the screen.

'You won't believe it,' he said. 'Or maybe you will.'

'What is it?' I said. 'What happened?'

'Bel didn't go to her last exam.'

'*No*,' I said.

'Yes. Dad is apoplectic.'

I sat up, catching a glimpse of myself in the mirror on my chest of drawers. Concern blossomed on my face.

'Why didn't she go?'

'She says there was a mistake on her exam timetable. She thought it was in the afternoon, when actually it was in the morning. She's an idiot. I should have checked – but she can't expect to have her hand held when it suits her, and then be treated like an adult the rest of the time. She can't have it both ways, can she?'

His voice, usually low and precise, was jagged with agitation. He didn't say so, but I knew he was worried that Anton would blame him, somehow, for Bel's failure to attend the exam.

'So what happens now?' I asked.

'I dunno. She'll get a lower grade, I suppose. Maybe she can re-sit. Best-case scenario. I don't know what the procedure is.'

'Neither do I,' I said.

'Dad should have been here,' said Darian. 'Instead, he's in Ireland on some film set, not even answering his bloody phone half the time. He makes all this fuss about Bel doing well, and then he goes off abroad and leaves me to pick up the pieces. Sorry, Nora. This isn't your problem, I know. I just . . . I'm so sick of them both. I can't tell you.'

'It's OK,' I said soothingly. 'Everything will be OK. I'm sure he'll still let her be in the movie.'

'Christ, Nora, do you really think I care? D'you know who I think would be much better in his stupid movie?'

'Who?' I said.

'You would,' said Darian. 'You know every word. I think you'd be amazing.'

Long after the end of our conversation, I remained on my bed, sorting and re-sorting my life drawings. First chronologically, then by size, then in the order of worst to best. Still Darian's words reverberated, like one of his beloved sound experiments.

You would. I think you'd be amazing.

Who?

You.

I went over to my desk and put the life drawings down. I reorganised my files, my diary, my notebooks. A sheet of paper strayed loose; I stared at it briefly and then took it into the kitchen, where I ripped it into confetti and tipped the pieces into a recycling bag.

If anyone were to ask me, then, what the worst thing was that I'd ever done to anyone, and if I didn't want to respond with the story of Rita Ellory, or the story of Jonah Trace, I might – if inclined, as I might one day be, to tell the truth – have told them what I am about to tell you. That stray sheet of paper, which I'd thrown away, was Bel's old exam timetable. The timetable she'd read on the fridge earlier that day, so diligently written out in her slanting writing – or so

316

it seemed – was, in fact, a superlatively good counterfeit. I had mimicked her writing, copying the old one exactly (save, of course, for the time of her final exam), and the afternoon that I went over and saw Darian I had stuck it to the Ingrams' fridge.

I have never claimed to be a nice person.

It was a couple of hours later.

Evie was on her way back from a meeting in north London. She called me, asking me to sort dinner. I was in the kitchen, cutting up a courgette for a rather uninspired dish of vegetable pasta, and rattling very fast through some key Norian scenes that I felt needed a little more work, when the buzzer rang. I wondered whether it was a delivery for Evie.

'Hello?' I said, into the intercom.

Silence.

'Is anyone there?' I said.

I could hear breathing – syncopated, uneven – over the evening traffic.

'Bel,' I said. 'Come up, darling. Eighth floor, second door from the end when you come out of the lift. Number eighty-seven.'

Despite my instructions, I had low expectations of Bel managing to find the right flat. I went out and waited at the entrance to the lift. I felt strangely unnerved at the idea of Bel being in our flat. It was too small for her; she'd take up too much psychic space in it, like a sunflower in a goldfish bowl. How did she even know where we lived? As the lift doors pinged open, I had a flashback to the end of *Aliens*, the second film in the *Alien* franchise, when the Alien queen, monstrous in her vengeful anger, emerges from an industrial lift. It was an absorbing vision and I struggled to be free of it.

Then, in a flash of silver kimono and white-gold hair, Bel fell into my arms.

'Oh, Nora,' she said.

She did not smell of alcohol, which was interesting and unusual. Her voice was subdued. She clung to my neck as though to save herself from drowning, and although she had clearly been crying for a long time, she was not crying now.

'Come in,' I said, leading her into our flat. OtherNora watched from the mirror as I closed the front door behind us. I offered Bel tea, juice, water, explaining that we did not have anything stronger in the flat, but she said that she didn't want anything.

'So this is where you live,' she said, looking at the framed costume prints above the sofa, the view over the Thames from the balcony.

'Very small,' I said.

'It's cool. Just how imagined it would be. A kind of fairyfolk dwelling.'

'I'm just making dinner,' I said. 'Are you hungry?'

She looked at the chopped-up vegetables without enthusiasm. 'I may never want to eat again,' she said. There was nowhere to sit in the kitchen, so she pulled herself onto the counter and perched there, kicking her legs like an ungainly, kimono-clad beetle.

'Don't be silly,' I said. I was sure there were still some Romanian goodies in one of the cupboards. Bel could never resist sweets. Rummaging through old plastic bags and multi-packs of juice, I unearthed a garish packet of something that promised additives and sugar.

'Here,' I said. 'You might like these.'

She tried one. 'They're disgusting.'

'How did you know where to find me?' I asked her.

'Cody knew,' she said. 'He's back. He's waiting outside.'

Of course: he'd dropped me home a couple of times. I wondered if Bel had ever been told the arrangement between Cody and her father. Now didn't seem like the time to enquire.

'Darian said he told you what happened,' she said.

'He told me you missed your exam,' I said.

'How could I have been so stupid?' she said, voice flat and dull.

'It could've happened to anyone,' I said. 'You, me, Darian, anyone.'

Bel shook a clump of sweets into her palm and ate a few, wincing at the sweet-sour taste. 'I just don't know what's going to happen now,' she said.

'Surely you can re-sit the exam.'

'Not that . . . with Dad. With *Jacaranda*. He is so mad at me, Nora. He said it was the final straw. I nearly missed the lunch with Gabriel and that was bad enough, he says, even though I never said we were out partying – and you wouldn't have said anything, would you, honey?'

'Of course not,' I said, hoping that Anton hadn't told Bel that he knew that she had, indeed, been out partying. 'I just told him we had a couple of drinks.'

'He says he needs to think about it all. He says he doesn't know if I can be trusted. Nora, if I can't play that part I think I will die.'

It seemed callous to continue deseeding a red pepper while she was talking. Wiping my hands on a tea towel, I sat down at the table and took her hands in mine. It was surprising how calm she seemed to be. Maybe she'd taken something, a tranquilliser of some kind; I think Cody kept them in his glove compartment.

'Don't say those things,' I said automatically. 'And look. If the worst comes to the worst, there'll be other . . .'

'No, there won't. There *won't* be other opportunities. Not like this one. This is the film I'm *meant* to make. Do you want to know something really bizarre, really hard to explain? I don't remember my mother. I look at pictures of her and I hear anecdotes about things we did together, the four of us, and I see videotapes and . . . Nora, it's like I'm looking at a group of people I don't even know. I was eight when she died; I ought to remember so much. But it's like it's all gone.'

Uncharitably, I found myself thinking that perhaps if she had taken fewer mood-altering chemicals over the years, her memories might have remained intact. But surely that was unfair: I could also sympathise with what she was saying. I understood about not remembering. I couldn't remember my father's face at all, and it caused me great sadness.

Getting up, Bel wandered around the kitchen, opening cupboards and drawers. I realised that the recycling bag was right there, in the corner next to the bin. What if she suddenly emptied it, looking for an egg box or a yogurt pot? Bel had been known to do stranger things. Rarely do I feel out of control, but that was a true moment of existential – and irrational – panic. Whatever happened, she mustn't see the ripped-up exam timetable. At least it *was* ripped up, but still . . .

She was talking, and I hadn't even been paying attention.

'Playing Clementine,' said Bel. 'When I found out Pupu wanted to make the movie, I just felt like it was my chance to *be* Mama for a while. Close to her. In her shoes. And by being her, maybe I'd remember her . . . or maybe it wouldn't matter whether I remembered her or not . . .'

She looked around her for more distractions. Then, to my relief, she wandered into the living room. My stage outfit was draped across the sofa, encased in a dry-cleaning bag. She swept it aside and threw herself across the cushions, wriggling around as her cat sometimes did. She still had her trainers on; I itched to ask her to take them off – Evie loved that sofa. Thinking of Evie reminded me that dinner was still unfinished. Taking a fine-blade knife, I made quick work of an onion and a clove of garlic; then I lit the gas (a bubble of Old-Norian fear burst with an insouciant *pop* as the flame jumped up) and heated oil in a pan. Through the hatch cut in the kitchen wall, I kept an eye on Bel as I cooked.

'Do you want the TV?' I said.

'Don't care.'

I turned it on for her; it was the news, which must, for Bel, have had all the oddness of science fiction. She lay on her back, one foot in the air, rotating her hands in front of her as though performing some kind of meaningful religious rite.

'I'm so sorry, sugar,' I said, adding more vegetables to the pan, and then tomato purée. 'But I think it's all going to be all right, you know. You've worked so hard these past months. I'm sure he'll overlook it. And you're perfect for Clementine. He knows that.'

'You really think so?'

'I'm sure of it.'

Her face popped up suddenly in the hatch. I thought that no one in the world had such an expressive face. It was as though it came with its own stage lighting.

'Nora,' she said. 'Maybe if you went to talk to him . . .'

'Oh, Bel, I don't know.'

'*Please.*'

Suddenly I was back on the carpeted stairs in Rosewood

Avenue, looking down on that same lit-up face as she asked me to be in her play.

'You don't understand how important it is,' she said.

But I did understand. I understood from her point of view, and I understood it from her father's too, which was something she had probably not considered. Another thing I understood: she hadn't even offered to make me a pedestal. That was how important it was. Beyond pedestals.

I was about to say something when the key crunched in the front door.

'Mum's home,' I said. 'Honey, do you think you could take your feet off the sofa?'

She jumped up rather huffily, just as Evie came in, her arms full of silky fabrics and her hair wound into an elaborate bun.

'Hello, Norie. Hello again, Bel,' she said. 'What's your costume doing on the floor, love?'

In the kitchen, *sotto voce*, I told her that Bel had arrived unannounced, needing counsel, and I didn't know if she was staying for dinner. Evie seemed relaxed, pouring herself a cranberry juice and offering to take over the pasta sauce.

'Is everything all right?' she said in French.

'I'll explain later,' I replied, keeping my voice low.

Evie went into her room with her bundles. In the living room, the TV warbled away; the news had been replaced by some kind of celebrity game show, and I imagined that Bel was now sprawled on the floor, watching in childlike silence. But something about the vibe of the flat made me look through the hatch, and I saw that she was no longer there. She might have been in the bathroom or gone into my room, I supposed. Then I saw movement on the balcony. Turning down the flame, and leaving the pasta water to simmer, I went out to find her.

She'd climbed onto one of our folding chairs and was holding onto the rail with one hand; the other was aloft in a kind of regal wave, although whether it was to the birds, the planes, or the angels, I didn't know.

'Jus' admirin' the view,' she said, and for the first time I heard how messy her syllables were, how indistinct.

'Honey,' I said, hoping Evie wasn't going to look out of the window. A suddenly-appearing gallop of Evie might be enough to prompt Bel to do something elaborate, uncall-ed-for, and fatal.

'Woah,' said Bel. 'It's quite a drop, huh? I wanna see if I can see Cody.'

Bending at the knees, still keeping hold of the rail, she leaned forwards. I was so paralysed by fear that I felt actual pain. And still I said nothing, and still she leaned. I didn't know whether to reach out a hand to pull her back, or say something hard and jarring, to jolt her. And another thing. Because these are the Chronicles of Nora, and because I've sworn to tell the truth, as much as I am able, I will confess that for a moment something inside me wondered what would happen if she fell . . .

It seemed like many minutes. Her sleeves shimmered like the fins of tropical fish; Big Ben tolled in the distance.

Then I said: 'I'll talk to your dad.'

'Really?' Securing herself with both hands, she twisted around to look at me.

'I don't know what help it will be, but I'm happy to try. Now, angel, my mother has a thing about heights, so please, be a good girl and climb down? She'll have conniptions if she sees you on that chair.'

Once Bel was back inside, I bolted the balcony door and even though the game show was a riot of noise, it was my shattered pulse that clattered loudest of all.

She did stay for dinner, and ended up eating two plates of rigatoni. We ate at the fold-out table in the living room. Bel went back into the kitchen once, to pick up her bag from the floor, but she was there for only a second and I knew she had not looked at the recycling in the corner. When, finally, she was gone, driven home by faithful Cody, Evie tactfully asked me nothing about her visit, presuming that it was Private Girl Stuff.

That night I had trouble going to sleep. When I did, the flowers were waiting in the darkness beneath the tightrope. I had no shoes, and through the skin of my feet my bones showed up, luminous and whitish-blue. The rope kept going slack for a moment, and then tautening again, and it took every ounce of balance that I had to stay upright. No matter how far I got, placing one foot after another, I could never escape those flowers. The air smelled smoky; there was a fine wind coming from somewhere, as if a door had been left open, a door leading into – or out of – the darkness.

The rope became two ropes, side by side, with rungs between them, like a ladder. And then the ropes became train tracks. The darkness domed above me. A screech of hot metal signalled danger in the tunnel ahead. I could hear them now, two trains, travelling at right angles, swift and unstoppable; I could feel the air crumple as they collided with a creak and groan and burst of oil and fire . . .

And then Evie was there, holding me by the shoulders.

'That sounded,' she said, 'like a Very Bad Dream.'

It was a while before I was able to speak.

Evie went to the kitchen and made hot chocolate. Returning with two mugs, she sat on my bed, her spider-legs bent underneath her. 'Was it Dad?' she said.

Slowly, I said, 'In a way.'

I never used to dream about him,' said Evie. 'Now I do, all the time. Ever since that night in Petra's studio.'

'Me too,' I said.

Silence followed this. If you haven't by this point already guessed, I shall say it now: Felix Tobias committed suicide. It wasn't anything that could have been accidental, either. He woke up one morning, behaved very much as normal, as I've told you before, and then left our flat just as he usually did, on his bicycle. But instead of going to the library, where he usually spent the early part of his day, he took a train to Rouen, and then a bus to the outskirts of a small village near the sea, where our run-down cottage stood. Whether he'd planned what he was going to do, or whether he decided once he was there, nobody can say. In the kitchen, there was an old gas oven. He did not leave a note. I cannot fill in further details. He was found the next morning by a neighbour.

Perhaps now you will wonder less why I made up so many different accounts of his death. The true one was impossible – unbearable – to tell.

'D'you think you'll be able to sleep?' said Evie.

'I think so.'

'Stage fright,' she diagnosed. 'That's what you've got.'

'I know. Stupid, though. I mean, it's just a school play,' I said.

'Not a big-budget movie, you mean? Like *Jacaranda*.'

'Right.'

She kissed me, and then said: 'You really like that girl, don't you?'

A strangely difficult question.

'*You* don't like her at all,' I said, deflecting it.

'It's not that I don't like her,' said Evie. 'It's that I don't trust her. You know who she reminds me of?'

'Who?'

'Me,' said my mother. 'In the dark days.'

7

Opening Night dawned crisp and swimming-pool-blue. Megan and I texted each other with girlish glee: *It's opening night*. What a phrase: it was almost holy. It conjured images of velvety skies, star-spangled; it was the beginning of the *Arabian Nights*, the first of a thousand and one stories, each more potent and magical than the last.

Evie'd been booked for a last-minute job out of London, well paid. She'd need to leave mid-week. She was distraught about this, but I told her not to worry: she'd seen both the dress and technical rehearsals, and, besides, it would put me off to have someone I loved so much watching me. This had a ring of truth to it that she bought immediately. A good-luck card from Nana sat on my bedside table; I wished that she were well enough to travel.

Azia asked for tickets for the Friday performance, saying she might bring Zubin with her. I wasn't sure about Darian. I'd not heard from him at all since he'd called me to tell me about Bel's exam.

That only left Bel.

I'd called her late on the Wednesday night. She sounded

sleepy and low, just as she'd been when she came round to my flat the previous week.

'Sugar,' I said, 'I have an idea. Has your dad come back from Ireland?'

'This morning,' she said.

'Well, how about this,' I said, keeping my tone tentative. 'How about if he comes with you to see the play, either tomorrow or Friday? It'll probably be desperately dull, I know, but . . . here's what I'm thinking: you could make your excuses for a few minutes, and it would give me a chance to speak to him just after? What do you think, darling?'

I waited while she considered the plan. I knew she'd want to improve on it – to make it her own – and that was fine, because it could certainly take improvement.

'Pretty good,' she said. 'But I think better if I don't come. I'll make an excuse at the last minute, before we leave. Then Papa can drop you home and you'll have a chance to talk properly.'

'D'you think he'd really come by himself?'

'Oh, but he loves amateur productions,' she said. 'And he adores you! He'll want to be supportive.'

'Does that mean you won't be coming at all?' I said.

'I wouldn't miss it for the *world*,' she said huskily. 'Just put me down for the second night. Isn't Azia coming then? I'll come with her.'

* * *

As I ate the breakfast – rye bread, honey and banana – that Phyllis Lane preferred on show days, I wondered what Anton Ingram would think of my performance. What he thought of the production – Mrs Tomaski's artistic touches, the other girls, the set and even Evie's excellent costumes – didn't matter. All that mattered was what he thought of me. It was of indescribable importance. But I couldn't allow my nerves to get the better of me. Again and again, I returned to Phyllis's breathing exercises, to her pencilled Buddhist mantras, to stay calm.

'Flowers,' said Evie, interrupting my reverie. 'They just came.'

It was a bouquet of yellow roses, wrapped with lilac ribbon and cellophane.

Phyllis Lane loved to be sent flowers on Opening Night, or the first day of filming. She liked tulips, agapanthuses, lilies. For years, ardent fans would send her jacaranda seeds, although it was well known that jacaranda trees are hard to grow in this country. Looking at the bouquet that Evie was now arranging with dexterity in a vase, all I could think of were the Chakra Flowers of Doom, and the way they waited in the dark pit under the tightrope. A thought came to me, fully formed and utterly horrifying. What if, when the lights went down, the flowers were there? It hadn't happened in rehearsals. Both the technical and the dress rehearsal had passed, as they say, without a hitch, although a superstitious thespian might say that it's good luck for a dress rehearsal to go badly. It would surely be just my luck if the flowers came back, and the unwieldy, all-enveloping darkness that yawned like a void, just as Anton Ingram was watching . . .

'You OK, Norie?' said Evie.

Slowly I breathed in through my nose – one, two, three, four – stretching the air like bread dough, and then out through my mouth. I did this twice, three times.

'Fine,' I said.

'In the language of flowers,' said my mother, 'yellow roses mean friendship. Must be from a friend of yours.'

But the roses were from Petra and Bill. I didn't have that many friends.

Sarah Cousins had kind, confidence-boosting words for all the cast members in her form. She was too fair to exclude me. At registration, she gave to each of us what she called 'a little care package' – nail polish, an emery board, fizzy bath salts – in a shiny gift bag. It was just the sort of gesture she was known for making.

'Good luck, Nora,' she said. 'I'm very interested to see your performance.'

Surely she must have known it is bad luck to say 'good luck' to an actor.

By mid-morning, my nerves were in full flow. My lines, once as cemented in my head as Nana's Bible verses were in hers, crackled and faded as I recited them in the toilets. I had to do something I'd not needed to do for weeks, which was to check my script. I told myself not to panic. It didn't help. I was in the far-end cubicle, where the overhead light was broken, with my feet tucked under me on the closed toilet seat. What did Phyllis Lane do in the thick of a panic attack? I couldn't remember. Footsteps echoed and pipes whistled as girls came and went, their voices shrill and excitable.

At last, I heard Phyllis's voice, soft and fuzzy, in my head.

'*I focus on the smallest possible thing,*' she'd said in an episode of *Inside the Actors Studio*. '*I see the universe in the petals of a rose. I look at a wall and find one brick, and focus on that, and then on a single speck of dust on the surface of that brick. Smaller and smaller, until it's practically just a molecule.*' (She'd sounded very like Bel, when she said this bit.)

There were no bricks in the grey toilet door. Only graffiti. Poor-quality slogans of love and the occasional subversive poem about drugs. Still, I obediently sank my gaze into the arrow that pierced a lopsided heart and waited for my own to beat more slowly. The bell rang for the end of break.

I reread the graffiti.

Chrissie ♥ *Josh 4EVA*
a friend with weed is a friend indeed
Nora Tobias tells lies

There it was, tucked down below the lock, small and scratchy. Not in black-and-white so much as purple felt tip. *Nora*

Tobias tells lies. I was known. How long had it been there? I wondered. A month? More? Who wrote it? Did everyone know? Would the entire audience tonight be replete with knowledge that I, Nora Tobias, was a manipulative little witch who had punished her art teacher out of spite and petty vengefulness? Would it be like *Carrie*? I wondered. Would a bucket of pig's blood (set up by Sarah Cousins, harbinger of justice) come tumbling down on my head as I took the stage for my opening scene?

'Nora? You in there?'

The voice belonged to Megan. Grudgingly, I slid open the lock; the door swung open. Megan's honey-coloured hair, usually up in a high ponytail, was brushed straight over her shoulders, and it tickled my neck as she bent down and hugged me.

'What's up, wife? You look like a pixie crossed with Gollum,' she said. 'I brought you a tampon and a tube of Werther's Originals, in case you need either of them. What's the matter? Is it nerves?'

I nodded at the writing on the door. She read it aloud. '*Nora Tobias* . . . but . . . did you just write that yourself?'

'I . . .'

Megan looked at the pen that I still held loosely in my hand. She licked her cuff and scrubbed at the letters until they began to disintegrate. 'All gone,' she said. 'Silly Nora.'

Saying nothing, I kept staring at the smudge where the writing had been. Had I written it myself? Was my guilt becoming such a burden that I was losing the ability to control my own actions? And what was my guilt about, precisely? Jonah, or Bel? Or simply everything?

'Look,' said Megan. 'Who doesn't tell lies? I've heard worse rumours about other people.'

'What have you heard about me?' I said, unable to keep a kind of childish whine out of my voice.

'I'll be honest,' said my co-star. 'I heard you made up a lot of different stories about your father. And you know what? How he died, or why, is none of anyone's business, and I've said so. I also heard . . .' She paused to examine her inky cuff. 'I also heard that you maybe had a little more involvement with Jonah Trace than the school officially knew.'

Perhaps the cubicle had the aspect of a confessional box in a church; I just don't know. But I found myself telling Megan the entire story of Jonah Trace, from the beginning, nothing withheld. Internet searches, science-fiction movies, the kiss on the common, the story I had made up for Sarah Cousins, everything.

'There,' I said. 'I don't know what you'll think of me.'

'I don't know you well enough to think anything,' said Megan thoughtfully. 'But I can tell you what I think of *him*. You know in Costa, when I asked you about him then? And what happened?'

I nodded.

'Well,' said Megan. 'What I didn't tell you was this. He

brought me there too. We sat at a corner table, near the loos. By the newspaper rack. Like he didn't want to be seen.'

'We sat at the same table,' I said, remembering.

'I've been trying to work out whether it was before you, or after you,' said Megan. 'I think it must have been just before.'

'And he asked you out?' I said.

'He did. All: I really like you and I want to get to know you better and all this crap. Just like you said. I said no, and he backed off, and it must have been you next. I never told anyone. I don't know why . . . I think . . . I was just so embarrassed. I thought it was my fault. Everyone thinks I'm so good at everything, so confident and stuff. I didn't know how to tell people. Even my parents. I thought perhaps they wouldn't believe me.'

Silence. Just our breathing in the cubicle, the sound of water in pipes. How often, I wondered, were true stories told and their tellers disbelieved?

'I should have said no too,' I said. 'But I wanted to punish him, I guess.'

She hugged me, and it was a proper, no nonsense hug. 'Glad someone did.'

'Sarah Cousins,' I said. 'I reckon she knows. They were mates, her and Mr Tracc.'

Megan said, 'She took your statement. I know how these things work. If she tries to involve herself any more than that – for whatever reason – she'll be in the wrong, and they'll come down on her like a ton of bricks. They messed up, hiring him. Trust me, Nora. If you ever need me to, I'll back you up.' She motioned me out of the cubicle. 'He shouldn't have been teaching in a school,' she said as we left.

'Break a leg, my children,' said Mrs Tomaski.

Lady Agatha's theatre, with its rickety seats, creaking lights and dusty curtains, was hardly the National Theatre. But as I sat backstage while a helper dabbed thick peach makeup under my eyes, my nerves fled, all at once, like a shoal of fish. I inhaled the adrenaline and hairspray, and heard the audience coming in, and I felt electric with anticipation. It was a feeling I associated with Bel's more hyper moods – when she danced along the garden wall or broke into some high-security building in the dead of night – and with Evie's old upswings, when everything in the world was beautiful and right and had a tune or two to go with it.

Up, I thought. This is what it's like to be up.

It was sensual, and I mean that in two ways. Firstly, that all of my senses were awakened: the plasticky smell of my lipstick, the hotness of the lights overhead, the sonorous way our voices carried from the stage to the seats as we performed. It was also a physical wanting, like the wanting I felt when I watched certain films, or read certain books. I wanted the audience to want me, and the more they wanted me the more I wanted to give back.

I forgot about the flowers and the darkness. I forgot about

Bel, and the house in Rosewood Avenue, filled with talent and sadness. I forgot about Cannes and Anton Ingram. I forgot about Jonah Trace. I forgot about Evie and Nana. I forgot about my father and I forgot about every iteration of every Nora that I had ever been, because now I was Ibsen's Nora, Nora Helmer, and no one else but that Nora.

And then the applause.

The cast in a row, hot with achievement, happy. We bowed, synchronised, Megan's hand warm in mine. The applause was cheery and sustained; some people were standing.

This is up, I thought again.

This is the highest possible point.

And what goes up comes down.

By the time I'd come backstage, weary, my throat dry from speaking and the heat of the lights, I was starting to feel it. No one can be brim-full of adrenaline for long; it has to run out of you some time. The praise I'd heard from the lips of Mrs Tomaski, from the other girls, held less and less meaning. Doubts surfaced like weeds: had I really done all right? What about the moment I nearly tripped on the hem of my skirt? Could the audience have been bored? What if someone couldn't hear me? Down and down I went, like Alice in her slow-moving freefall, as I moistened a sponge and wiped the foundation away, until I was nothing but empty and tired, though ready already for the next night, when I'd be able to come up again.

If that is not the basis of addiction, I don't know what is.

'There's someone to see you, Nora,' said Megan.

For a moment, I couldn't remember who in the audience might be coming backstage to see me. Then Anton Ingram, stooping a little, appeared through the archway. He had on a red-checked shirt and dark jeans, still with a bit of a tan and looking – to my eye – every inch the movie executive. I scanned the darkness beyond him for Darian, but Darian wasn't there.

Anton gave me a kiss on both cheeks, saying: '*Brava*, Nora. That was really quite something, you know.'

'Thank you,' I said.

He sat on a chair next to me, moving a pile of programmes and a box of hairgrips in order to do so. He smelled of that lavenderish fragrance again.

'I mean it,' he said. 'Was Bel's hospital drama really the first time you'd ever acted?'

'Yes.'

'Staggering,' said Anton. He wasn't one to exaggerate, I was pretty sure. Was he just trying to be kind?

'Bel instructed me to offer you a lift home,' he said. 'I feel I should offer you champagne somewhere, if you . . . ?'

And that is how I found myself sitting opposite Anton Ingram in a dark booth lit with an old-fashioned lamp with a green shade in a private members' club in Soho that I'd heard of, but never been to. Bel didn't care for members' clubs, she always said, but this was most likely because she was banned from most of them. Someone was playing the piano in a corner; muted discussions were taking place around us, and everywhere I looked I saw beautiful people. At a table nearby, a group of people – more conservatively dressed than Bel's crowd but with the same free-and-easy air about them – were singing *Happy Birthday* to a rotund young man with a dark goatee. It amused me to hear that his name was Frodo; I wondered if it was a nickname. Once again, I thought about how a few months ago I could never have imagined myself in such a place.

It was surprisingly easy to have a glass of champagne with Bel's father, and that was because he knew how to hold a conversation. We talked about Evie's work, and he said how well he thought the costumes had worked in *A Doll's House*. He told me how his late wife had also played Nora, when she was quite young, at a theatre in the north of England. He congratulated me again. We talked about Darian's music, and I said how much I liked to listen to Darian play.

'It seems that both my children have inherited our love of the arts,' he said. 'But Darian wants to immerse himself in music. He wouldn't care if he never got a penny for his talent. Bel's wants are different, I find. It's the thought of stardom that motivates her. The parties in the Cannes hills, the money . . . she finds it irresistible, and I understand that, of course. I mean, what teenage girl wouldn't?'

At this he gave me a look, as though to ask what I thought.

'I don't think the trappings would mean much to me,' I said, brow lowered in consideration. 'It's the research that I love so much. Reading scripts, looking at old performances, reading books about the actors . . . learning the lines, preparing myself, being that person, imagining the context, how they talk and think and feel . . . I guess I'm more like Darian. It's the immersive quality that appeals to me.'

He listened and nodded intelligently all the while, and then said: 'So you don't feel motivated by the thought of success?'

'Oh no,' I said. 'I do want to be successful. I do want that. Although, you know, I'm not like Bel. I don't really feel like I . . . belong in this world. I don't have the right background.'

'Don't be silly,' said Anton. 'The theatre is for everyone. Don't ever forget that.'

I sipped a little more champagne. The glass was very cold. I felt a drip-trickle of adrenaline again. The pianist was playing something I recognised: a song from *Cabaret* called *Maybe This Time*. Bel loved to perform it, drunk or sober, with great flourishes and a peal of falsetto at the end.

'About Bel,' I said, after a pause.

'Yes,' said her father promptly, as though he'd been waiting for this himself.

'I don't think it's fair to say it's just money and parties

that she cares about,' I said. 'I think there are people that make decisions about who they want to be and how they want to live, and there are people who are so . . . forceful and full of life and absolute talent that they almost don't have the same kind of ability to choose. Bel can't help the way she is. She doesn't study a part so much as . . . she just lets her talent kind of overflow into it. She's a proper, natural actress.'

'You think so?'

'Maybe I don't know that much about it,' I said, 'but I've seen her on stage a few times in different things. She's not just competent or convincing. She's . . . orchestras and fireworks. She doesn't just want to go to parties. I'm sure of it.'

He finished his champagne, pushed the glass aside and poured water into a tumbler from a bottle that stood on the table. 'How lucky she is to have you for a champion,' he remarked. 'Now, Nora, I'm going to tell you something that my children don't know. *Jacaranda* is a project I've wanted to do for a long time.'

Making a cat's cradle of my fingers, I listened.

'But raising the finance was very hard,' Anton went on. 'In the end, I put the house on the line. Which sometimes happens in film.'

At first, I didn't understand what he meant. Then it was clear. He'd mortgaged the Rosewood Avenue house, or put it up as collateral, or however these things worked. Well, it was a large, probably very expensive piece of property – Evie and I could have fitted all our things into the conservatory, more or less. I appreciated the huge financial risk that Anton had taken.

'What I cannot afford is for anything to go wrong on-set,' he said. 'Now, you may not think it would be much of a problem, say, if Annabel turns up late or forgets her lines or messes up a scene or causes a drama off-screen, but I'm afraid it will. If she had to be replaced a couple of weeks in, it would necessitate costly reshoots, the budget would spiral out of control . . . to say nothing of how embarrassing it would be, for her and for me. Then again, she and I did make a kind of deal. And apart from this recent debacle with her English exam, I realise that she has kept her side of the bargain. And oh, I know she can *act*. That's not really in doubt.'

I nodded sagely, just as he had done earlier on.

'So what I'm asking you, Nora, is this. You've spent more time with Annabel than anyone else has this year. You've been more or less inseparable. You've seen her in good moods and bad, and you've presumably seen many things that I haven't. I've spoken to Cody, and I've spoken to Darian, but I'd like very much to hear your take, because you seem like an exceptionally intelligent girl.'

We looked squarely at each other, as the pianist played on.

'Do you think Annabel is capable of playing Clementine?' said Anton Ingram. 'Don't worry. I won't say I've asked you, I assure you. I want you to think carefully before you answer.'

The pianist finished the song and began another. In my head I rehearsed lines, discarded them, rehearsed others. In the dim-lit room, while the pianist played on, the wheel of Bel's fortunes turned imperceptibly, with only my hand to steady it.

'Anton,' I said.

He leaned forward.

'I *want* to say that I don't think Bel would cause any trouble,' I began. 'I really, really want to . . . but I don't think, in all good conscience, that I can . . .'

It must have been close to midnight by the time he dropped me home. Checking my phone, I saw that I'd had three missed calls from Bel.

I sent her a text: *Did everything I could. See you tomorrow.*

For reasons I couldn't articulate, I felt indescribably sad.

8

Closing Night had such a different ring to it, I thought, all through the hymns and prayers at Chapel. It felt oddly like someone was going to die. Lori Dryden was asleep, her head on Sangeeta's shoulder. Out of habit, I looked for Bel. But Bel, of course, no longer came to school. She was officially a Leaver now. If she came to the play tonight – and there was no reason why she wouldn't – it would probably be the last time she ever set foot inside the Agatha Seaford Academy.

I tried to put the previous night out of my mind, but it was hard to do. Flashes of the conversation between me and Anton – cold champagne, tinkling piano – kept repeating and repeating, sending little flashes of fear and anticipation along my skin. The question was: what would he do with the opinion he'd sought from me? Would he decide against casting Bel? And if so, was there . . . was there the smallest chance that he'd think of casting me instead? Would he think it was appropriate? I had an idea that Anton would do what was right for *Jacaranda*. But he'd have to tell Bel eventually, if so. And then – what would happen to our friendship? This was so tricky to handle in my head – thorny and snarled – that I kept giving up and focusing on the performance that lay ahead of me, the upness that I longed to recreate and the applause that I wanted to go on and on into the night.

It kept coming back to me, all the same.

There were many things I could say to myself to justify my actions, and all through the day I said them. But even though I tried my best to persuade myself of three possible outcomes – one, that nothing would happen; two – that Bel would want what was best for the movie; three (a vague one, this) – that 'everything would be all right', I felt less and less sure that this would be the case.

By the time I stepped onto the stage I was bone-dead tired, with a head full of ladders and snakes. But even so, I think I raised the bar considerably for the second performance of *A Doll's House* that was also the last. I pushed myself that little bit further, reaching for greater emotional depths, trying to convey Nora's desperation, her conflicting desires, with both subtlety and power. I didn't even look for Bel and Azia and Zubin, to see if they were there, because I could not afford to take myself out of Nora Helmer. I assumed her, as though her skeleton were mine, and when the curtain fell I clung to Megan's hand and knew that this was a higher and finer *up* than there had ever been before.

Now I understood why Phyllis Lane mourned at the end of her productions. When it was all over, and Mrs

Tomaski was warbling praise and donations were clinking in buckets, I realised that my Nora was dead. I would never see her again. Evie'd left a pile of shoe boxes in the dressing room in order to collect small accessories and store them together. Taking one, I filled it with Nora's things. False eyelashes. Sheer tights. A stick of foundation. My scribbled-on script.

It wasn't until I came out, when the audience had mostly gone and they were sweeping the theatre floor, that I saw her, sitting at the back, her feet up on a seat, as usual.

'Darling, you were marvellous,' said Bel, in her most English-English accent.

She was wearing a red-and-gold kimono, one I'd never seen before, and a bowler hat.

'And Azia and Zubin? Did they like it too?' I asked, as she hugged me fiercely and I hugged her back.

'They thought it was too, too marvellous,' Bel told me, taking me by the arm and leading me away through the car park. 'They had to go, buzzing off home. Good little worker bees.'

'I saw your dad . . .' I began.

'I know.'

'I don't know . . . I hope . . .' It was hard to express myself, for once. 'I think he's going to think about everything. I did what I could.'

'I know you did, honey,' she said. 'So long, Lady Agatha

Shithead.' She turned and gave the gates a smart salute, turning it at the last minute into a raised middle finger. 'God, I'm glad I never have to come back to this place. What you got there?' said Bel. She was looking at my shoe box.

'Oh, nothing,' I said. 'Just rubbish.' I pushed it into the bin on the corner as we passed.

'Now we must have an after-party,' said Bel. 'Where would you like to go?' She reeled off various places: a house party in Shoreditch, a squat party in Brixton, a rave in Kings Cross. All had possibilities, by which she meant the music would be loud and the drinks free-flowing.

'Anywhere's fine with me,' I said. 'Whatever you want to do.'

I was actually quite hungry; what I really wanted was dinner somewhere cheap and near. But I didn't suggest it. I wished Azia had stayed. I wanted to hear her observations; I needed an objective dissection of the play. *Marvellous* was not enough. I wondered what Bel had really thought.

'Oh, I know,' said Bel, whistling shrilly for a cab. 'Giacomo's boat! He's having a do. Someone's birthday. We'll crash it. Perfect.'

I protested: 'But that's miles away.'

She was already instructing the driver, in the expansive, confident way that she had. I wondered where Cody was. Out doing her bidding elsewhere, perhaps. She lounged back, boots on the flip-down seat, as though she were at the cinema. From her pocket, she took a blister pack of pills and a hip flask. I watched her medicate herself, not asking what it was that she was taking. I'd see soon enough from the effects.

'Nora's a bit of a heartless cow at the end, don't you think?' she said. 'Just to waltz off and leave him.'

'I don't know,' I said. 'I think she's brave. She realises he values his reputation more than he values her – as a person, not as an idea . . .'

'Maybe it was just the way you played her.'

I looked at her sideways; she was grinning wickedly, showing her missing tooth. Her bubble-hair was growing out, clouding around her ears.

'Just kidding,' she said.

'Isn't Giacomo annoyed with you still?' I asked.

'Oh, all is forgiven. He never holds a grudge for long.'

From this I inferred that someone had paid him back for the damage to his property, though it wouldn't necessarily have been Bel. A Chaka Khan song flared on the radio – *Ain't Nobody* – and Bel tapped on the screen in front of us, asking the driver to turn up the volume. She sang along loudly, kicking her heels. I turned and looked out of the window. I hoped Bel wasn't going to make me pay for the taxi; she had a habit of doing that. I only had an emergency tenner in my jacket pocket. To Hampton Court in a black cab would be at least £35, if not more. My stomach gave another flip of hunger.

We hit one red light, then another; the meter crept up.

'Are you hungry?' I asked her. 'D'you want to stop some-where on the way and have dinner?'

'Oh, Giacomo always has food,' said Bel. 'Maybe even a barbecue.'

My *up* was fast dissolving; not going down as such, but more thinning out onto a kind of plateau. I felt edgy and light-headed, both sleepy and awake. Another song came on the radio and Bel carried on singing, although I wasn't sure she knew what it was. As she shifted about on the seat, I heard the clunk of her hip flask. I watched her, toneless and joyful, her fine-boned face striped amber by the emerging street lights as we drew nearer to Constantine's wharf.

Pause. Freeze. Bel and I are climbing out of the taxi, her arm around my shoulder, her sleeve brushing against my skin. Here is the wharf, with the chain of boats at their moorings and their elegant, childish names lettered on their sides. Just past the late-June sunset, there's enough light about to give the scene a kind of magical clarity. Bel is wearing white boots with little spike heels; I am wearing jeans and a T-shirt underneath my jacket; the smudges of my stage makeup. We are holding hands like children as we huddle at the driver's window. Me and Bel; Bel and me.

It's a frame I am almost fond of freezing.

Bel pushed a bundle of notes into the driver's hand.

'You look a lot like that Kate Winslet,' he informed her. 'Need a receipt?'

'No thanks, my good man,' she said.

She was still holding my hand as we walked away towards the dark-blue *Morgan le Fay*. The sun slipped down over the horizon, spangling the river with a spillage of fine gold rays. It was very quiet. There was no sound of a party. But it was still early.

'Bel,' I said. 'I actually don't feel that great.'

'Oh, don't be silly! We'll dose you with medicinal cocktails and you'll be right as rain in no time. It's theatre; it'll do that to you. The buzz wears off. I understand completely. Just give it an hour or two. Besides, I just paid an arm and a leg for the taxi.'

She propelled me closer, and I thought about how there would have been a time, three or four months ago, when I'd have given an arm and a leg myself, to go to a party on a boat with Bel. Now I hung back.

She took a low bow, ushering me ahead. 'After you, sweet pea. Leading lady. You really were fabulous, by the way. I felt rather in awe of you.'

I decided that the sooner I went to this party, the sooner I could leave it. That sometimes worked, with Bel – if you showed willing to go with her somewhere, no matter how late it was, she often didn't mind if you left not long after arriving. I walked across the gangplank, the Thames a muddy scrawl below, and onto the deck. The door to the wheelhouse stood partially open. Flowers, some alive and some dead, stood in terracotta pots at the prow of the boat.

'Oh!' said Bel, behind me. 'I left something in the cab.'
I turned back but she waved at me: stay there.

'Go right inside, angel. You're shivering. Go down and say hello to Giacomo. I'll be back in two seconds.'

She flapped away, her kimono a goldfish flash against the grey of the quay. She was a famous leaver of objects; usually I checked to see if she'd deposited the contents of her pockets on the seats of restaurants and taxis, but this time I hadn't looked. I put my hand against the door and pushed it; it swung open, and I stepped into the wheelhouse, where Zubin had slept in a chair while the party churned below with greenish revelry.

'Hello?' I said. 'Giacomo?'

There was no sign of life. A lamp with an orange shade burned in the corner, otherwise it was dark inside. I hesitated, wondering if I should go any further. I was beginning to feel loose-limbed with hunger. I couldn't hear Bel. Descending the steps, I saw no one about. Perhaps Giacomo had gone to the shops. I sat down on the banquette, suddenly too tired to stay on my feet. Why was I so far from home? It would take me over an hour to get back. I longed for my bed. And where was Bel?

For answer, the door to the wheelhouse above me clicked shut.

'Bel?' I called, going back up the stairs.

I went to the door and twisted the handle. It was locked.

'Bel, what are you doing?'

'We are going to have a chat, you and me,' she said, in what was almost, but not quite, her normal voice. 'Do you remember when we went swimming in the ponds, and I said that if you ever betrayed me I'd drown you?'

I remembered: green-gold water and her hands on my shoulders. Her laugh as she pushed me under.

'Well, I considered this for quite a while, and I realised, honey, that you're far too good at swimming. Like the sea snake that you are.'

'Bel, what's the matter? Can you please open the door?'

I twisted the handle again, rattled it, pulled at it. Nothing.

'I can't do that. I'd like you to sit and consider your actions, in silence. And while you do that, I'm going to tell you a story. A fairy tale, in fact. Once upon a time, there was a young girl. She was kind and beautiful and good, with the loveliest golden hair, and everyone who met her loved her at first sight. Now, one day she met another girl, who was lost. She was not so loved, and not so beautiful, but Goldenhair took the Lost Girl under her wing, and the two became friends.'

Her voice kept growing and fading; she was obviously pacing up and down, making showy hand gestures for the benefit of no one. It was a planned speech; I could hear that. She'd written a script. That scared me. If her speech was planned . . . what else had she planned to go with it? While she was talking, I reached into my pocket for my phone. I needed to text Darian: *Help. Come quickly.*

But I didn't have my phone. I couldn't remember whether I'd left it at home, or at school. It didn't matter; what mattered was that it wasn't there.

The orange lamp hummed.

Bel went on, 'Now it happened that one day a special troupe of actors came passing through the town, and they were putting on a magnificent performance – a Pageant of Purple Flowers – and they needed one little girl to come and play the part of the Grand Sorceress. Who did they choose? Why, the girl with the golden hair. No one could have been more suited to the part. And oh, her friend pretended to be terribly pleased for her. But inside she schemed fiendishly, thinking of all the tricks she might be able to play so that she could have the part of the Sorceress herself. Because the lost little girl was not a true friend. Not the slightest bit.'

There was a pause. It was the end of Act One, and she was waiting for the audience to applaud her.

'I must continue,' said Bel. 'The day of the Pageant approached, and all the while the Lost Girl kept pretending, helping our golden-haired heroine with her lines, her steps, her outfits . . . even her hair. But while our heroine's back was turned, she stole by the dim light of dusk to the ceremonial rooms where our heroine's family lived.'

A pause.

She was breathless now, as though she were carrying something, or moving things about.

'Shall I go on? The Lost Girl crept on tippy-toes until she came to Goldenhair's father, the Lord of Moving Light. A mighty and all-powerful fellow he was. He loved his daughter very much, but he loved something more than his daughter, and that was Show Business. It was important to him that the Pageant should be a success. The Lost Girl knew this, and she worked on him and worked on him as though he were a piece of embroidery, until he almost believed that it was his own idea.'

Silence now.

I wondered if she'd gone. Was she planning to abandon me here, on the boat, until somebody heard me screaming or Giacomo returned? I looked through each porthole in turn. There was no sign of her. But I was sure that she was still there. Then came a slithery sound, a sheet of paper appeared under the door. From the print, I could see that it was an email chain.

'Any guesses, Nora, as to the identity of the villainess?'

'Bel,' I said. 'This is madness.'

'Just read the goddamn thing.'

They were emails between Anton Ingram and Gabriel Glass. How she'd got hold of her father's emails I hadn't a clue – but then, it seemed that Bel was capable of so much more than I'd ever imagined. The emails were dated from late the previous night. Anton would have sent the first when he'd got home after our drink in Soho.

Have an idea, which I'd love to run past you. It seems
that Nora – you met her in Cannes, and liked v much
– is not only a serious budding actress but knows every
word of Clementine. Worth looking into? As you know,
I've reservations about Annabel, as passionate as I know
she is about this opportunity. Let's speak as early as you
like in the a.m.

'I don't know how I gave him that impression . . .' I said.
'Honestly, Bel! Everything I did was to help *you*.'

'Read on,' said Bel.

Gabriel's response was short and interested.

Then came another from Anton.

Suggest we approach Nora and see if we can take things
further. I got the impression that she'd be very up for the
challenge. Bel won't be pleased, but I'm prepared to
handle things this end.

'Apparently,' said Bel, 'Daddy thinks you're the next best
most talented thing since white . . . sliced . . . *baguette*. I
don't know what you said to convince him last night, Nora,
but I assume you used all your feminine wiles. You're a bit
of an expert at feminine wiles, aren't you?'

'That's not true,' I said.

'Oh, methinks the lady doth protest. I know what you
did to the Art Man.'

'Look,' I said. 'Your dad did ask me if I thought you were up to it. And I said *yes*. I said yes in a million ways. I *promise* you I did.'

I remembered the previous evening: low-lit club, beautiful people, green-shaded lamp. Another scene in the Drama of Nora, played to perfection. Or so I'd thought. But here I was, on the wrong side of a locked door, and there was a girl in a red kimono with potentially psychopathic tendencies (should I not have seen this, all along?) on the other side, and she was the one with the key.

'I must just tell you the end of the story,' said Bel, still in that worryingly even tone. 'Goldenhair's father thought nothing of casting his own daughter aside. With open arms, he embraced the Lost Girl, who had betrayed her only friend.'

Her voice got gradually fainter. I began to think she'd gone.

'But they'd both forgotten one small thing,' said Bel. 'His daughter was very, very adept at revenge.'

A little later, I heard the sound of somebody striking a match.

9

Denial came first.

Yellowy flames sprang up like weeds, feasting on the kerosene that Annabel Ingram must have poured onto the deck, and still part of me couldn't believe that it was happening. *No*, I kept thinking. She wouldn't. She couldn't possibly. But Bel – gone in a whirl of silk and hurtling boots – would, and could, and did.

With a crackle and a growl those flames – those angry flames – grew bigger, owning the spaces, claiming the boards, reaching for the door with hungry hands. I was forced to accept it: they were real, and they weren't going anywhere. This was no film set. It wasn't a conjuring trick. I shrank back towards the stairs as they climbed the walls of the wheelhouse, and while darkness fell outside, the ill-starred *Morgan le Fay* lit up with light of its own.

Denial gave way to anger as the smoke thickened. In English and French, I cursed her – and I cursed myself too, for being so unutterably stupid. I'd thought that I was more intelligent than other people. But in my greed – in my blind desire for the part of Clementine – I had ignored every warning, every indication that Bel was not an ordinary, predictable person.

Could I really have believed that if Anton and Gabriel cast me in *Jacaranda* that Bel would have somehow just accepted it? *Idiot, idiot, idiot Nora*, I chanted, while a veil of heat shrouded the boat and anger became fear. To mess with Annabel Ingram was literally to play with fire, and here was the result.

Back down the stairs I ran, into the now-tidy inner reaches of *Morgan le Fay*, where the greenlight party had once raged with fire-like intensity. I looked for a phone, but knew in any case that there wouldn't be time for anyone to reach me. I looked for another door, but there wasn't one. The small, rectangular windows in the sitting room and the other cabins were locked. Every one.

I had nowhere to go.

Now was the moment for panic, and yet somehow it still didn't seem real. Months of charades and costume parties and makeup and make-believe had diluted my sense of what was, and was not, pretend. But a splutter of singed wood and an almighty groan told me that the wheelhouse overhead was well and truly aflame. Already, fingers of smoke were trailing below deck. Heat bloomed like the malevolent wishes of Morgan le Fay herself.

Darian warned you, I thought. *Azia did too. Anton had no idea what his daughter was capable of. You did. Triple imbecile, Nora; this is nobody's fault but yours.*

I wished I could have seen Evie to say goodbye. It wasn't fair that my father and then I should leave her without saying goodbye. Would she be all right? Who would check on her? My head was hazy with smoke; my thoughts untied themselves like shoelaces, became looser, less complete. Like a trapped rat I wandered from the banquette to the kitchen counter and back again, sometimes frantic, other times almost calm. A strange picture came to me of Sarah Cousins, laughing like a witch as she ignited a gigantic Bunsen burner.

Then, with a dull blink, the electric lights went out and everything went dark.

They say that scenes from your life flash before your eyes, and I can confirm that this is more or less true. But they did not flash, precisely. They *played*, an old-fashioned film reel unravelling, full of clicks and hisses. Footage of my life spilled into the dark around me: walking down a cobbled Paris street; standing on the deck of a ferry; turning over my rainbow onto the kindergarten table; hopping around a toadstool under the poison-gaze of Rita Ellory; drawing Vanessa in Life Class with both hands; kissing Jonah Trace in a forgotten corner of a London park; playing a fairy in St Michael's hospital; sitting in Bel's conservatory while the rain fell, reading *Jacaranda*.

I felt my body chime with channelled energy; I felt points open up from head to toe; a humming seemed to come from somewhere inside me. I lost myself inside that dark open space. There was no tightrope now. There was just water. Not the ponds. Not the pool. These were the chilled waters of the Channel. A faint trail of churned surf was all that was left of the ferry that must have passed on. I floated, adrift. There were the flowers. Red, orange, turquoise, yellow, green, violet, blue . . . I had never seen anything so sinister and so exquisite. They formed a chain around me in the darkness, shimmered, blinked, faded.

A faint humming seemed to be coming from somewhere. My hands tingled with energy; my breathing was steady and slow. I was ageless, and almost shapeless, a Norian shadow-form, no more. I went on and on through that warm and watery darkness until I came to the shore, and then, after a time, a small white house, a cottage with a window either side of a red door, and I knew at once where it was. It was our old cottage in Normandy. I opened the door and went inside.

And there he was.

He was sitting at his desk, angled three-quarters away from me. He turned as I came in, put down his pen and his reading glasses. For the first time in ten years, I saw his face. He saw me.

Felix Tobias regarded me in silence. It seemed that this silent scrutiny went on for the longest time. And then he said, very simply:

'*Qui êtes-vous?*'

* * *

I opened my eyes. Overhead was the roar of fire, harsher and harder than ever, the bitter smell of chemicals and burning wood. And suddenly it came to me – and it should have come sooner – I couldn't allow this to happen. I couldn't allow Bel to do this. I couldn't leave Evie.

And I didn't want to die on Giacomo's boat.

There was no point in going back upstairs. That left only the windows. I tried them all, one more time – the one over the banquette, the main cabin, the two smaller ones. All were locked tight. Could I smash one? I grabbed first a torch and then a doorstop, and tried, and tried . . . Bel, so much more in touch with her physical side, would surely have had no trouble. The windows were tough, tougher than me. It was hopeless, and I felt like a fool. Even so, I tried each window again, once more wrestling with the catches, pounding at the glass.

Then I realised I'd forgotten the window in the bathroom. It was round, narrower than my chest. Too small to fit through. But it was worth a try. I climbed onto the black-painted toilet seat while the headless doll dangled from the light cord and the skeleton leered behind the cistern. It was almost too dark to see what I was doing. The window was firmly shut, and at first I thought it was locked as well. But it wasn't. It was just stiff. Every minute the heat and the threat of the creeping smoke redoubled, and I understood the absolute urgency of getting out *now*, and the urgency lent me speed as I wrenched the window open. Crumpling myself up, not caring if I broke things – mine or otherwise – I folded my body into the metal frame, feeling the scrape of something sharp, a vicious twinge of pain, and then the hot night air moulded itself briefly to my skin before I slithered with a splash into the river.

Swimming ten metres, I turned, treading water, to witness Bel's handiwork. *Morgan le Fay* was hunched low in the water, tilting, smothered in a halo of flame. It was eerily silent on the wharf; whether the other boats were unoccupied or their owners were simply away, I didn't know. I had cut my wrist badly on something, and my lungs felt heavy and congested.

But I was alive.

I swam to the side and pulled myself onto the quay.

The second night of *A Doll's House* – the night that Bel set fire to *Morgan le Fay*, with me in it – was the 25th of June. It's August now. I've been sitting here, writing this, for almost four weeks. I'm not sure, but I think I've managed to get the Chronicles of Nora into some kind of coherent shape. I have followed the trail of my memory, and although I haven't always liked where it's taken me, I feel I've learned a lot as I've tried to set things down truthfully.

I should explain why I am here in Scotland. It stemmed from a misunderstanding on Evie's part. I've always said how tuned in I am to Evie; well, it seems that my mother is also tuned in to me, because she said afterwards that she was on the set of the short film that was shooting in Manchester when she was hit by a bolt of clearest, surest, absolutest *knowing* that there was something the matter with her daughter.

'After what happened with Dad,' she said, 'I just . . . knew.'

Back to London she drove, getting home early on the Saturday morning. She found me in the bathroom, naked, with a ragged cut snaking along my underarm like a map of the Thames.

She drew a conclusion. It was impossible to get her to undraw it.

'All these years, I've known you weren't happy,' said Evie, halfway down a tub of Pralines and Cream ice cream. The bleeding had stopped and she'd bandaged the cut well with her capable hands; in the morning, we'd get it looked at by a doctor. 'But why now, Nora? When everything's going so well for you? Was it the pressure of the play? A boy? Something to do with that girl? I thought there was something wrong when you came back from Cannes, but I didn't think . . . oh, Nora, and your beautiful skin. What the hell did you *use*? It doesn't look like a razor.'

I said nothing, which was safest and best. I had my reasons for silence. I had no intention of telling my mother about the fire and the failed attempt on my life by my so-called friend. Although I was a little sorry that my mother thought I'd hurt myself on purpose, it was easier to let her believe that this was true.

'I want to go somewhere quiet,' I said, 'and just . . . think. Or not think. Just be. Totally alone, for a while.'

As I'd predicted she would, Evie said: 'Petra's house.'

And I said that would be just the place.

So here I've been, all summer, in self-imposed near-solitude, with the rat-dog and the rain for company. Evie's come a few times, to see me and then to visit Nana. Sometimes I go with her – it's always good to see Nana, who seems much better. I don't hear from anyone apart from Megan, who checks in on me from time to time. I don't know if we'll remain friends, now the play is over, but the fact that I seem to be Honest Nora around Megan is something I find both attractive and scary. I don't read the papers; I've no idea what is happening in the news. It's important to switch off, in order to heal, says Petra. The last thing I read in a newspaper was the little square that appeared two days after the fire – *Thames Houseboat Goes Up in Flames*. There was no mention of cause. No mention of casualties.

I said that I needed to think, and I have been thinking. And while I've been writing, I've been thinking more. I've thought about every lie I've ever told – the ones recounted here, and others too. I can count them like beads on an abacus. Still I am not able to decide whether I was born a liar, or whether I grew into it, shrugging Falsehood over my shoulders like a mink coat. But let's say that it doesn't matter *why* I have told so many lies. Even though I believed, and still believe, that I was to some extent wronged by these people – Toby, Rita, Jonah, Bel . . . I don't know if I can honestly say that my actions were entirely justified. Could I have done things another way?

What I've also been thinking about is this: I will never feel good about myself if I continue to live in this way. In many ways, lying – and scheming and planning and getting people to behave in exactly the ways I anticipate, like my own personal chess pieces – has been fun. I won't deny it.

But when I had that vision of my father, as I stood there on the burning boat, and he *did not know who I was* . . . that was no fun at all.

'*Qui êtes-vous?*' he said. *Who are you?*

To my father, I was unrecognisable.

He'd been gone such a long time – twisted into stories I told without even hearing them any longer – that I forgot something important.

Felix Tobias valued truth.

And if he'd known half the things I'd done, he'd have been horribly, heartbrokenly disappointed. As indeed would Evie. I love few people on this earth, but I do love my parents. I would like Evie to know me (and I would like to know her, because I realise that she is stronger than I give her credit for, even if she asks questions that I do not ask, and wants things that I do not want). I would like her to be proud of me. I would like to think my dad would be proud of me. Unlike Evie, I don't believe in a Rive Gauche café in the afterlife, where one day Nana will unfold her knitting in the company of Felix and her long-dead dogs.

But if that café does exist, I'd want to be there too.

I have been thinking also – I am reminded every time I go past the octagonal studio – about what really happened on the cold February night when we contacted the dead. In opening up the Chakra Flowers of Doom, guided by Petra and her poorly-educated signposts, did I really manage to reach Felix Tobias? For all that Evie was totally convinced, I never was. Everything I said he said was a lie, for a start. But the flowers, and the dreams that followed, had a resonance and potency and other-worldliness that felt so . . . uncanny. And then there were those words, written by my unknowing hand:

O angry flame. Attention, Aliénor.

I puzzled for a long, long time, about those words. They felt like a strand of some unravelling tapestry that I hadn't quite followed back to its source. It wasn't until I sat down the other day with Petra and Bill for a fireside game of Scrabble, which I had no doubt I'd win with ease, that I finally noticed something interesting. I'd drawn an *A*, and also *G*, *M*, *N*, *O*, *R* and *Y*.

I made *angry* first. Then I made *Nora*.

I pushed them around, making different shapes with them, experimenting.

And then I saw it.

O angry flame is an anagram of *Morgan le Fay*.

Now Felix Tobias loved an anagram, it's true. It's possible that he was trying to warn me. (Beware the boat. Not bad advice, all told.) But I love anagrams too. Maybe I was just trying to warn myself. It's the kind of complexity that Nimble-minded Nora is more than capable of carrying out. Or maybe it was neither me nor my father, but just the memory of him that I carried in me, somewhere. Or maybe – just maybe – I am too quick to see anagrams in everything.

One thing I'm sure about: I will never try anything like it again.

Today, before I settled down to write, I went for a walk. I love the peninsula at first light, on the rare days when it looks like there won't be rain. This morning was one of those. I had breakfast alone – rye bread, honey, banana; Phyllis Lane's habits die hard – and, of my own accord, found Oscar, who was delighted to join me.

Just as I was about to leave, I heard footsteps upstairs. The girl in the room next door, who'd been in recovery, was up and about. It occurred to me to invite her to come with me. She wasn't often awake at this hour, but like I said, we were on almost friendly terms and I thought she might fancy the exercise.

Instead of walking down to the loch, we took the path above the house that leads through the woods and then out onto open land that stretches for mile after mile of sheep-studded green. Oscar roamed freely, delving into ditches and rabbit holes and skittering about. My arm, I realised, was much better. I held it out experimentally. There would always be a scar, a bad one, but that was no bad thing. It would be a useful reminder, for a long time to come, about the dangers of flying too close to the sun.

The girl from the room next door caught me looking at it and said, 'You're healing, honey.'

'So are you,' I replied.

It was true. She'd come to Aunt Petra's house not long after I arrived, with dressings on one side of her head and all down her neck and shoulder. They still needed to be changed every couple of days, and though the skin underneath was the colour of an ugly sunset – coral and burnt-orange and irritated pink – it was new-minted, and would improve, if slowly. Her hair existed only on one side, like an eccentric, blonde-bubble wig.

Bel was, typically, quite proud of her burns.

'After all, they're a bit like badges of heroism,' she had already pointed out, several times.

She claimed that she didn't start the fire. Oh, she locked me in and left me. This she admitted. But the fire – no, not she; the revenge she'd had in mind was leaving me alone on Giacomo's boat, to think about what I'd done.

'You don't seriously believe that I'd do something like that?' she asked more than once, her face a mask of bandaged indignation.

'You're saying you *didn't* pour lighter fluid onto the deck and light a match?'

This last from Darian, only a few days after the fire as he sat next to her four-poster bed while I stood, a little cautiously, in the doorway. From downstairs floated the smell of chicken soup; Anton was busy cooking.

'Christ, of course not. I *do* remember a smell of fuel,' she said, wrinkling her nose as though she could smell it now.

'Maybe it was a spark from someone's barbecue. I mean, Darian, that's the story we're *all* going to stick to, remember. A barbecue. Nowhere near the river. Nowhere near the boat.'

'You maintain you had nothing to do with the fire. You just locked Nora in for fun,' Darian repeated.

'Cross my heart and hope to die,' said Bel. 'It was probably someone on a passing boat, chucking away a lit cigarette.'

She looked towards the doorway, holding out her hand for me. Slowly, I approached.

'When I turned back and saw the fire, my heart could have *stopped beating*,' she said.

Darian rolled his eyes and muttered 'bullshit' under his breath. It's funny: he was so angry – on my behalf, on Giacomo's – that it made me, by default, calmer and more reasonable than I might have been otherwise.

'Giacomo will put two and two together eventually, if he ever sees you,' he said.

'I'll make sure he doesn't,' said Bel.

She winked, on the good side of her face. Her burns looked worse than they were, but it was still hard to look at her. It was as though she'd spent too long in a special-effects booth. I found it incredible that she never once, to my knowledge, mourned the loss of her beauty. It would take a very long time for her skin to recover. If it ever did. Perhaps she was in denial. But perhaps she was just braver than I'd ever imagined she could be. After all, it takes more than a pretty face to be an actress.

Bel looked sad for a moment. 'I loved that boat too, you know,' she said.

Downstairs, while she slept, Darian and I dosed ourselves with chocolate, barely speaking.

'Is she beyond help?' he said at last.

'What do you mean?'

'She's lying. I *know* she's lying. But she believes what she's saying,' said Darian.

'She's just . . . Bel,' I said.

I didn't believe her, either. I wanted to, but I couldn't.

One thing, however, was irrefutably true. Bel came back to the boat for me. Not long after I pulled myself onto the quayside, I heard the thud of her boots. A banshee-wail of my name, louder than I'd ever heard it before. Huddled in the shadow of a barge two or three boats down from *Morgan le Fay*, I was just out of her line of sight. Before I could say or do anything to draw her attention, she ran past, hair and kimono flying like streamers, and onto the burning deck.

I'd never seen anything braver.

Now I got to my feet and ran after her, calling her name. Through a garden of fire, she made for the wheelhouse door. I watched as she fended off a wall of flame with her sleeve. It happened very fast. Her sleeve seemed to melt in a red-gold wave; her cry turned into a higher-pitched scream of rage and pain.

You will have to believe me when I say that I did not hesitate as I scrambled over the gangplank. In moments like these, there isn't time to think about the accountancy of friendship – of who did what, or who deserved what. As I got to her, she was already falling backwards; I caught her, and dragged her to shore. In a heap, we collapsed.

'Nora,' she gasped. 'I am so very sorry.'

It was the only time she ever said it.

I battered her with my jacket. We'd done this in a first-aid course at school. I had a memory of Megan, bent over a life-size plastic torso, demonstrating her skills to the rest of us. I would be as capable as Megan was, for once. I willed the flames to go out. And they did. But I could see that Bel was badly burned on one side of her face and body. Somehow I got her out of the charred kimono. I threw it into the river.

'Give me your phone,' I said. 'We need to call an ambulance.'

'No,' she said. 'We have to get out of here.'

I don't remember the next part well. She leaned on my shoulder as we walked. A woman in a car stopped for us and drove us to the nearest A and E, asking no questions. By the time Bel was seen by the triage nurse, we'd agreed on our story. That was the story we told everyone, Anton included. Only Darian knew the truth.

'She tried to save me,' I reminded Darian, before I left to go home.

'She tried to kill you first,' he reminded me, in turn.

* * *

Flip forward a final time, to the here-and-now.

When we came to the top of the hill above Petra's house, Bel ran ahead of me in a skip-hop gait, chasing after Oscar, of whom she has grown fond. It has been odd to see her in civilian clothes – non-costume-clothes, I mean. No silvery kimonos now. No papery dresses. This morning she was wearing grey tracksuit trousers, a white T-shirt. Old-Norian camouflage wear. Sometimes, indeed, we do swap clothes, since we keep forgetting to use the laundry room. It has also been odd not to talk of anything to do with schoolwork, even though her A-level results are just around the corner, and promise to be – even with the blemish of the missed exam – very good. But she didn't come here to talk. Like I did, she came here to heal. ('I wanna see trees,' she'd said, on the phone. 'Can't I come and join your retreat? Daddy says I can.') Even after everything we had done to each other – or was it because of it? – Bel and I found that we wanted to be together.

We don't talk about *Jacaranda* any more, either. Principal photography is unlikely to begin this autumn, after all. A major backer dropped out, which stalled production, and they lost their window for Dennis Havelock, who would have played the lead role of Matthew. Now, it's probable that they'll shoot in the spring.

One afternoon before I left for Scotland, while Bel was playing with the cat in the garden, as much like Alice in Wonderland as ever, Anton said to me: 'The part's still yours, if you want it.'

I massaged the underside of my arm, where the cut still hurt.

'It's kind of you,' I began.

'Kindness has nothing to do with it. As you know, Annabel won't be in any position to act in anything for a long while, in any case. I've spoken to Gabriel. You're a promising young actress, Nora.'

I thanked him. But I wouldn't be able to do it.

'I have A-levels next year. My mum agrees.'

'As you wish.'

He was silent for a while. Then he said: 'It's funny. Annabel always wanted to look like her mother – and, in so many ways, she does. She sounds like Phyllis; she has so many of her little tricks and mannerisms. Even with those terrible burns, she still reminds me of Phyllis. But I think Bel's beginning to realise that there is so much more to performance than bearing a resemblance to someone else. If she really wants acting to be a part of her future, I hope that she'll be able to embrace who she really is, and not just the person she wants to remember.' He sighed. I wondered if he realised that he, also, had to let Phyllis go, and if he knew what he'd need to do in order to make it happen. 'It wasn't a barbecue, Nora, was it?'

'I'm sorry?' I said.

'It wasn't a barbecue.'

'It was,' I said. 'I wasn't there, but . . . it was an end-of-year house party. These things happen easily . . .'

Bel was rolling on the grass, holding the cat above her and singing. Anton watched her. I tried to imagine what he was thinking.

'I was worried, you know, that she'd found out that Gabe and I had you in mind for Clementine. And that was why . . . But, of course, she didn't know that,' he said, more to himself than to me. His phone began to ring. '*Jacaranda* was never the right project for Annabel,' he said as he left to take the call. 'I was wrong to encourage it.'

I believe that Anton and Gabriel have now cast Hannah Corbett, who – coincidentally – played Nora in *A Doll's House* at the National Theatre. I think she will be exceptional as Clementine. She's just right for the part. I will be right for other parts, some other time. And so will Bel. Right now, we're planning to write something together. Another fairy-tale play, probably. We like *Snow White and Rose Red*. *Sleeping Beauty* too. Bel is going to take a year out before she goes to drama school. They've deferred her place. I've been thinking about applying myself. Perhaps to the same institution; perhaps not.

This is the last frame. Pause. Freeze. Bel – half-head of hair dancing in the clear-day wind – is midway down the hill, with Oscar at her heels. She looks like the greatest friend I ever had. Maybe she is. Maybe I am the greatest friend she ever had too. The burn mark on the right side of her face matches my birthmark on the left side of mine.

Unfreeze the frame. She looks up at me, shrieking something I can't hear. She turns and runs back towards the woods. The Gareloch is a dark twinkle in the distance. Bel waves, summoning me.

I follow.

ACKNOWLEDGEMENTS

I would like to thank my agent, Louise Lamont, for believing wholeheartedly in Nora and Bel from the beginning; for offering insightful comments at every stage of the process; and for encouraging me to write the best book I could. I would also like to thank my editor, Chloe Sackur, who held my hand through many a redraft with patience, warmth and grace. *Little Liar* is a better book for the involvement of you both.

To the team at Andersen Press: thank you all very much for your faith in *Little Liar*. Special thanks to Kate Grove, whose inspired cover design captures all the playful mischief I could have dreamed of; thanks also to Harriet Dunlea, Paul Black, Sarah Kimmelman, Charlie Sheppard and, of course, Klaus Flugge – you're a lovely group of people to work with.

No book is created in a vacuum, but *Little Liar* did begin in a place of total isolation: a residency at Cove Park on the beautiful Rosneath peninsula in July 2015. While six months pregnant, I spent three weeks living in a small white 'cube', with no internet and no phone, and nothing to do but read, write and wait for the grocery delivery van.

The first draft of *Little Liar* was written there. I owe a huge debt of gratitude to Polly Clark and everyone at Cove Park for looking after me so well, and to the Sophie Warne Fellowship and Birkbeck for enabling me to go.

Thanks to Harriet Amos and Libby Farthing, who talked to me about school matters; Susan Luciani and Ruth Ivo, who talked to me about boats; Sara Crystal, who advised on hair dye; Mélanie Bugnet, who checked my French; and Calum Gray, whose knowledge of the movie business could fill a hundred books, and who spent hours talking me through the finer details of film finance. Thanks also to Sue Cook for the eagle-eyed copyedit. Any errors in any capacity are mine.

Imogen Russell Williams: once again, thank you for sharing your invaluable support and bookish knowledge so generously; long may our lunches continue, ideally with Bobby 'What are you being so tiny for?' Star in tow. Kellie Nelmes: thank you for everything.

I want to thank my family, especially my parents, Stanley and Jennifer Johnson, who have always made me believe that I could be a writer (and who bear no resemblance to any of the parents in this book); my brother Max, and my grandmother Lois Sieff. *Little Liar* is in part a love song to the theatre, and you are responsible for that great love, Grandma.

Lastly, to my son, Jonathan, and my husband, Calum: I love you both.